The Cowboy's Game

Clean & Wholesome Cowboy Romance

Jenna Hendricks

Contents

Books by Jenna Hendricks (Clean & Wholesome Romance)

<u>Triple J Ranch</u> –

Book 0 - Finding Love in Montana (Join my newsletter to get this book for free)

Book 1 - Second Chance Ranch

Book 2 – Cowboy Ranch

Book 3 – Runaway Cowgirl Bride

Book 4 – Faith of a Cowboy

Book 5 – Cowboy Blessings

Book 6 – The Cowboy's Game

<u>Big Sky Christmas</u> –

Book 1 – Her Montana Christmas Cowboy

Book 2 – Her Christmas Rodeo Cowboy

Book 3 – Her Mistletoe Cowboy

Book 4 – Her Sleigh Ride Christmas Cowboy

<u>Crooked Arrow Ranch</u> –

Book 0 - Wounded Hearts Ranch (join my newsletter to get this free)

Book 1 – A Broken Heart Mended

Book 2 – Hope's Healing Love

Book 3 - Love's Healing Balm

Book 4 – A Crooked Arrow Christmas

Book 5 – Tripping Over Christmas

<u>Saguaro Bookshop Mysteries</u> –

Book 1 – Saguaro, Snowflakes, and Murder

<u>Standalone Novels</u> –

Christmas Crazy in July

Rebel Hearts Anthology

See these titles and more: https://JennaHendricks.com

Prologue

Roman Manning couldn't believe the events of the past few months. Not only was he a new uncle to a brand-new baby girl, but now he was an uncle to a four-year-old girl. The cutest little girl that none of them knew existed until just a few months ago. What a wonderful Christmas present this was.

Seeing baby Noel on FaceTime wasn't anywhere near as exciting as finally holding her in person. And seeing Daisy on FaceTime was nothing to trying to keep up with her at the Christmas fair. Roman had no idea what made him think he could take her to the kiddie Christmas fair booths and not have a problem keeping up with her.

The girl had more energy than a two-hundred-and-fifty-pound linebacker chasing a quarterback. Something he would know plenty about, seeing as how that was exactly what he'd done for the past three seasons at college—get chased by giant linebackers. One more year to go and he'd have his degree and come home.

Roman missed his family and their ranch. And now that they had two little girls in the family, he missed it even more. By the time he finished college, John would be married, and he'd be the only one left to get married. Chloe was already planning her wedding to her fiancé Brandon for the spring.

He wanted to be married and have kids, eventually. It was his dream to have his own ranch and populate it with at least a dozen kids, some of whom would be adopted. He'd never want his wife to have to go through so many births, or to have such a huge age gap between the oldest and youngest as his family did.

Roman was lucky. Even though he and Matthew were twelve years apart in age, Matthew always took time for him. Probably because the oldest Manning had only recently met the woman of his dreams and married. They'd probably be announcing they were pregnant soon, and he would be ecstatic for them. Although, he hoped they had some boys in this family soon. No way would he let girls take over the Manning family.

Daisy ran from him, again. And he followed, yelling, "Daisy, wait up. Where in the world do you get all this energy?" With a chuckle, he grabbed her hand and slowed her down.

"Ducks! Look, Uncle Roman, ducks!" Daisy yanked on his hand as she pulled him to the little pond with rubber duckies floating around.

Chuckling, he pulled out two dollars and handed them to the game operator. "One..." When he looked into eyes as green as a Scottish fairie pool on a bright, sunny day, his heart stopped. The short, pretty game operator with strawberry blonde hair smiled at him, and he lost all ability to think or speak.

"One set of rings for your daughter?" The pretty girl smiled at Daisy before looking up into the tantalizing eyes of a tall and handsome cowboy that made her mouth water.

They both inhaled deeply and stood there staring at each other as a connection between them sparked and sizzled.

"Uncle Roman," Daisy whined, "come on, I wanna play." She yanked on his hand, jarring him out of his dream.

"Hm?" He unwillingly turned to the adorable child yanking his hand. When he noticed the frustration on her face and the downturn of her mouth, he smiled. "Of course. It's your game."

Now that he was thinking again, he turned to the game operator and put his hand out for the rings he'd paid for.

Pink tinged the pretty girl's cheeks, and she averted her gaze from the cowboy with the latte-colored eyes and looked at the little blonde girl bouncing on her toes, waiting impatiently for her turn to play the duck ring-toss game.

Chapter 1

1 ½ Years Later

"**R**oman, are you still looking for that girl with the green eyes?" John asked, the right side of lips turning up in a smirk.

Roman ignored the dig from his brother. John knew exactly what Roman was doing. When Roman had met the woman with the fascinating green eyes at the duck ring-toss a year and a half ago with John's daughter, Daisy, he knew he'd met the woman for him. The only problem: she'd left town the next day and he hadn't seen her since.

He could have sworn he'd caught sight of her last summer in Wyoming at their county fair, but since he didn't know her name, he wasn't sure. In his mind she was known as the *green-eyed beauty*. But he couldn't exactly ask all of the game operators he came across if they knew the green-eyed beauty with strawberry blonde hair. That would make him sound like a wacko, or possibly a stalker. Which he wasn't, right? But he did ask if there were any petite blondes with green eyes who worked the duck ring-toss games. However, not all of the carnivals had that particular kiddie game.

If he hadn't been so tongue-tied, he would have asked her what her name was and if he could take her out for coffee. Instead, he'd paid for Daisy to play her game. While he was staring at the beautiful woman with just the right amount of curves, his little niece hit a duck with her ring and won a giant duck.

When Daisy began screaming and jumping up and down, the game operator turned her gaze from him to the little girl. She got down a giant yellow duck and handed it to Daisy, who immediately dropped the heavy beast.

Roman had to bend over to pick it up off the ground and clean off the dust. By the time he had the monstrosity all sorted, the green-eyed beauty was busy with multiple players. It seemed having a little four-year-old win the big prize was the best marketing a kiddie game could get. She was busy every time he tried to go by her booth and see her.

The next morning, he was up early and hoped to catch her before she left, but the carnival had packed up overnight and driven away before he could get there. All that was left was a flyer and piles upon piles of trash bags waiting for the dump truck beeping in the background.

"You really should give it up. She's probably not even a part of any carnival anymore. You heard what the last guy said, most of these game operators work a few events and then quit. They move on to something else." John waved a hand at the chaos of the carnival outside of Kalispell, Montana. "This isn't something that most people do for very long. It's not like they offer 401ks and bonus plans." He chuckled.

"Ha, ha. Very funny. Not." Roman rolled his eyes heavenward and sighed. "But you might be right. It's been a long time since I first saw her. For all I know, she's married now with a kid on the way."

"Sorry, bro." John put a hand on Roman's shoulder and guided him to the nearest food truck. "Why don't we try some elephant ears?"

"Sierra, how many times are you going to search for your dad's name? He's probably changed it by now." Annabelle restocked the small ducks under the counter as Sierra pulled her phone out to do another internet search.

They were at a small-town carnival just outside of Helena, Montana.

"Annie, I'm not giving up. He's here, I know it." Sierra put a hand over her lower abdomen. "I can feel it in my gut." Then she turned pleading eyes on her friend and bunkmate. "I just need a break."

"Well..." Annie stood and looked around to ensure no one was waiting to play the duck ring-toss. The carnival was about to close, and most families had already left for the night. Only the older kids who enjoyed riding the zipper, tilt-a-whirl, or roller coaster were still around them. None of whom looked to be interested in tossing rings to win a giant fluffy duck. "It seems that Bartholomew Baker doesn't have social media. I highly doubt he's going to all of sudden open a Friender account."

Sierra's hands dropped to her sides, and she blew her bangs out of her eyes. She really needed a haircut on her next day off. "I know, but I keep hoping that some sort of news article, or someone else's social media account, will have something about him."

"Maybe he left the Midwest and went south? Did you ever consider that?" Annabelle cut short what she was about to say when a younger teen came strolling up, smirking.

He handed his ticket to Annie. "I got this, easy-peasy." Then turned a cheese-eating grin over his shoulder at two other boys his same age.

Annie shrugged; without a word, she handed him four red rings.

When she stepped back out of his way, he leaned forward, stuck his tongue out of the corner of his mouth, and tossed. A whoosh and a plunk sounded his loss. He tried again, this time standing tall, and aimed for a farther duck. He nicked the head of the duck, but the ring still missed and fell into the water.

Frustration tinted his words. "How do little kids win this thing?" He leaned over lower and tossed again, but his ring went to the other side of the booth, totally missing the ducks and the water.

"Quack, quack." One of the boys in his entourage put his fists under his arms and danced around more like a chicken than a duck. "Quack, quack. You're gonna miss me again."

"Knock it off, Dusty. If this is so easy, you try it." The original boy held out his final ring for the kid, but he grimaced and shook his head. "Fine, then shut your piehole."

The kid with the ring ran a hand over his forehead, wiping the sweat away. Even at nine at night it was a hot one. He focused and moved the ring back and forth as he aimed for the duck bobbing in the center of the makeshift pond. He released his ring and it sailed through the air. When it dropped onto the beak of the duck for only a second, the boys began to whoop and holler, but then the ring fell into the water with a small splash.

"Aw, come on. You saw it." Dusty threw his hand out in the air and pointed to the duck. "The ring was on the duck before the wind blew it off."

Annie shook her head. "Sorry boys, but it has to go around the head and stay on the neck of the duck." She pointed to a sign above her that stated the rules and even showed a few pictures of how it should and shouldn't look.

The original boy who had purchased the rings slapped his thigh. "Ah, come on. Let's go ride the tilt-a-whirl and see who pukes first."

The boys walked away laughing and patted their friend on his back.

"See who pukes first? This is what our youth has come to?" Sierra shook her head. "I fear for our future."

Later that night as they all worked to pack up and head out to their next destination—a small town not far from Bozeman—Sierra got a funny feeling in the pit of her stomach. Almost like a premonition. She wasn't the carnie palm reader or anything like that, but she did sometimes get a *feeling* when something big was coming. And if this intuition was anything to go off of, whatever was coming would be a whopper.

"Will we finally get a day or two off in the next town?" Sierra asked the carnival manager, Red.

He grinned. "Yup, we get two days for setup and two for take-down in our next town. So you'll have time to go and search fer ya pa again."

Red knew why she had joined the carnival and why she on occasion left them, only to come back a few months later dejected and hopeless. It was always Annie who helped to cheer her up. And Red was always happy to have a pretty girl who worked hard to operate the games. It was the pretty girls who got the most players to lose their money on their games. Games that weren't exactly set up fairly.

"Great, I think it's been almost two years since I checked out Bozeman or any of the surrounding towns.

Maybe this time I'll find something to work with." Sierra put her phone back in her pocket and helped Annie.

"And maybe this time I'll find a cute cowboy to ask me out who *isn't* all hands." Annie rolled her eyes, loaded up her hand truck with the final items from their booth, and took it to the truck used to haul their game.

<h1 style="text-align:center">Chapter 2</h1>

"**A**re you done yet?" Luke teased Roman, who was struggling to cinch the saddle on his horse.

"Give it a rest, Luke." Roman didn't look up, but kept on working. His mind wasn't in the work lately. He'd spent all summer heading out to carnivals within a day's drive looking for those green eyes that kept haunting his dreams. One of these days he was going to have to give up and admit that she was either a fantasy, or she'd moved on and would never be back to Montana.

"Come on, we gotta go check the lines and move the herd to field four." Luke got on his horse and left Roman to catch up.

"Why didn't I just agree to work with Matthew this week?" Roman shook his head, put his boot in the stirrup, and launched himself on top of his gelding, Rock Star. The horse stood just over fifteen hands high and held himself with pride and strength. Roman had missed his horse whenever he was gone for college, but each time he came home, Rock Star remembered him. And it seemed he'd missed Roman while he was gone.

The first time he'd see his horse, it would rear up on its hind legs and whinny a greeting. When Roman would come closer, the horse would nudge his shoulder and head with his nose. Then Roman would pull out an apple or a carrot and all would be right between man and beast. They'd go for a long ride and the horse would soar across the open fields almost as though he was about to take flight. It was how they always greeted one another after Roman was gone for a long period of time.

It was during those solo rides where Roman felt the most at home and could think. He always took off for long rides when something nagged at him.

Now that he was home, he still brought Rock Star treats. But now it was only as a way to thank the horse for his undying devotion to Roman, and for being his best friend.

The horse must have known something was wrong with Roman, as he whinnied and swished his tail so hard that Roman felt it as he was getting on the horse. "I know, I know. We need another long ride. But first, it's time to work." He patted his horse's neck and settled on his saddle before catching up to his brother.

As they rode through their land, the two brothers chatted about nothing of consequence. Until Luke noticed Roman looking off into the distance. "You've got it bad. It's been what, a year and a half? And you only spoke a few words to the girl. How is it you can't get past her?"

Roman sighed and looked back at his brother. "It's her emerald-green eyes. They call to me like a siren's song in my dreams. Just as I'm about to let her go, she calls again."

Luke chuckled. "Sounds like love at first sight." He narrowed his gaze at his brother. "Tell me about the dreams. How does she call to you?"

"You'll think I'm nuts." Rock Star whinnied his agreement, and Roman clicked his tongue to get his mount moving faster.

When Luke caught up, he asked again. "Seriously, I want to know. And I won't think you're nuts. Scout's honor."

Roman snorted. "You were never a scout. None of us were."

"True." The older brother considered for a moment. "Alright, how about brother's honor?"

Rock Star came to a halt, and Roman glared at his brother. "If you can keep this between us. And I mean us." He motioned between the two. "That means no telling your wife anything."

Luke nodded. "You have my word."

He sighed, and then Roman began his tale. "It's like I said: she calls to me like a siren's song in my dreams. It's almost always the same thing. She's in a pool of water surrounded by the most vibrant flowers I've ever seen. There's even a waterfall there."

"A waterfall and a pool full of flowers? This is definitely a dream." Luke chuckled.

"Hey, no lip from the peanut gallery." Roman glared at his brother. "Or I won't finish my tale."

Luke released his horse's rein and held up his hands. "Fine, fine. I'll stay quiet. Keep going, loverboy."

"You just had to get in one more dig, didn't you?" Roman tapped his horse's sides with his boots and clicked his tongue to get Rock Star moving again.

"Oh, come on, Roman. You know all we ever do is joke and tease. Why would this be any different?" Luke grabbed the reins, pulled his horse's head up from the grass he was grazing on, and urged him forward.

"This isn't a joking matter. It's serious. Every time I'm ready to let her go, it seems God, or someone, puts her back in my thoughts. I don't understand why God would keep her at the forefront of my mind for so long if she wasn't ever coming back." Roman had prayed and prayed for months about this girl. But God never seemed to answer him. Instead, the dreams continued.

With a whistle and a nod, Luke urged his brother to continue on with the story.

"So, she's in that paradise swimming around. She's smiling and her green eyes are sparkling. Then she motions to me, and when I get closer, all of a sudden it becomes dark. Clouds move in and I hear thunder in the distance. The pool goes from a pretty emerald green to a black, inky mess. Then I see a fin coming at her from out of nowhere. She's still looking at me, trying to get me to come closer."

Roman stopped his story and shivered. After taking a deep breath, he continued on, shocked Luke had stayed quiet. "I point and shout for her to look back. To get out, or get to safety. I yell out *shark*, but she doesn't see it. Instead she flaps a tail behind her and just keeps smiling. Then it dawns on me that she's a mermaid."

Luke stopped his horse and held up a hand. "Wait, she's a mermaid? With a tail and all? Do you think the fin you saw in the water was hers?"

Roman shook his head. "No, it was too far away when I first saw it. Then it starts to come closer. Just as I get to the edge of the water, she turns and screams. Then I awake with a start."

"Does it always play out like that?"

"Pretty much. Sometimes colors are different, or the storm changes. But basically, it's always the same. I get close, but can never help her. Then my dream ends."

"How often do you get these dreams?" Luke rubbed his chin with his gloved hand and waited for Roman's response.

Roman began their forward movement again. He looked up at the sun-filled sky. There wasn't a cloud in sight that morning, and it was looking to be another warm, late-summer day. Fall was just around the corner, and so was another fall festival. He prayed she'd be there this time. If she wasn't, he was going to do whatever it took to put the girl with the green eyes behind him for good. Even if it meant getting professional counseling.

"Roman?"

"Huh? Oh, yeah. I think I get them anywhere from two to four times a month. It just seems to come on when I decide to put her out of my mind." Roman shook his head. "Like I said, it's a strange dream. She only comes to me when I'm trying to move on. If I keep looking for her, I still dream about her, but it's totally different. More of a fun dream."

Luke raised his eyebrows suggestively. "Fun, huh? The kind of fun you can't talk about?"

"Oh, dude. Don't go there. Not all of us have racy dreams." Roman wasn't sure if he should laugh or be offended for the green-eyed beauty. The dreams were nothing like that. It was usually something like going on a carnival ride, horseback riding, or the occasional carnie game. He had never even kissed the girl in his dreams.

"Fine, fine. Keep the juicy details to yourself." Luke paused. "Just tell me one thing."

"Shoot."

"Does she kiss good?"

That was the final straw. Without a word, Roman kicked his heels into Rock Star and they took off at a fast pace. One that Roman knew Luke wouldn't be able to keep up with. If Luke was going to be a jerk, he would leave him in his dust.

Sunday after church, the entire family gathered for Sunday supper. They tried to get everyone together at least once a month, more if possible. However, now that there were children in the family, it wasn't always easy to gather everyone in one place. But this was the first Sunday in August, and they always met the first Sunday for supper.

"I think we need to make a trip next Saturday to Bozeman and check in on the homeless ladies." Elizabeth passed the plate of potatoes to her husband, Logan. "The last time we were there, one of the women seemed like she might be ready to come back with us."

"Are you talking about Amanda?" Claire passed the slices of roast beef to her husband, Matthew.

"Yes. I think she misses Amy and wants to come and see how she's doing."

"I'm actually surprised Amy has stayed with us for so long. I thought for sure she'd take off and maybe even go back to Big Bart's gang." John took a bite of the tender roast beef and held up his thumb. "Fantastic, Ma, as usual."

"Thank you, sweetie. I'm glad you're enjoying my meal." Judith Manning smiled at her son and everyone else at the table. "I'm so grateful to have you all here today. And I'm grateful for the ladies who help me out on the ranch."

Whenever they took a woman off the street, she came home with the Mannings and helped out around the ranch.

"I think Amy stays because of Regina. The older woman has taken Amy under her wing and is like a mother to her. I bet they'll stay together." Elizabeth took a drink of her sweet tea.

Callie looked at her sister-in-law and bit her lower lip. "I hope so. When Amy first arrived, she was a handful and I worried I might find her somewhere she shouldn't be." She arched a brow at Roman.

He held his hands up. "Whoa, I would never invite any of them anywhere they didn't belong."

"I never said you'd invite them in." Callie cleared her throat. "It's just the way she ogled you and kept following you around, I was afraid she'd climb in through your window one night."

Luke patted his brother on the back. "Nah, Roman's only got eyes for one girl." He winked at his brother before shoving a homemade roll into his mouth.

Roman shook his head. "I keep my windows and doors locked at night. I learned that early on in college."

Everyone at the table chuckled as they all remembered the story Roman shared after his first game in college as the starting quarterback. They won, and a female fan was so enamored with him that she broke into his room that night. Not to attack him, but to take his jersey. After that, he never went to bed without double-checking that his door and window were locked. The habit came home with him, even though it wasn't as much of a deal at home as it was at college.

Chapter 3

"I thought we were going to be right outside of Bozeman on this event?" Sierra complained as they drove past Bozeman and finally stopped in Livingston, Montana. The small town was beautiful. It sat alongside a river that also boasted several small lagoons and creeks weaving their way through the town limits.

Annie's eyes widened as they watched the sunset on the Yellowstone River. The sky was full of fluffy white clouds turning all shades of orange, and a small edge of blue and purple in the distance added to the ambiance of the sleepy little town. "I'm glad we came here. Look at this place, it's beautiful. And that downtown, it's almost a place that time forgot."

Sierra sighed. "I know, it is beautiful, but it's also pretty far from Bozeman. I'll need to rent a car to head into that city."

"Nah." Annie waved a hand. "Once we're all set up, I bet Red lets you take the truck. And I'll go with you. We can come up with some excuse, like we need something that can only be picked up in Bozeman."

Sierra laughed. "Yeah, like they don't have a Wal-Mart or a Target. Doesn't matter that they have a tiny mall and several small boutiques."

With arms wide, Annie smiled. "Yes, because we all know that only Wal-Mart carries the makeup we need to look our best."

"Fine, let's hurry up and get set up. I want to head out first thing in the morning to see if there's any sign of Pa in Bozeman. Then we can look around here once the carnival opens."

Annie nodded. "I bet we could even ask some of the people who come in to play the games if they know Bartholomew Baker. Small towns like this, everyone knows everyone."

"True enough." Sierra tilted her head and searched the faces of the people walking down the street. Couples strolled hand in hand while children ran around them, staying out of the street. The moment they eyed the carnival trucks and ride vehicles coming into town, everyone stopped in their tracks and gaped. The kids who seemed to have endless energy stopped as though they'd run out, their eyes sparkling and their mouths opened wide. When hands shot into the air, pointing, all Sierra could hear were the sounds of excited screeches and screams of, "Carnival!"

It never ceased to amaze Sierra how townies loved to watch them drive in. For the locals, they brought laughter, amazement, and even adventure. For the carnies, it only brought work and a little bit of coin to line their pockets. No one ever made it rich working in a carnival. It was long hours, lots of mean people, sticky-fingered kids, and the occasional drunk to avoid. Not to mention how few days they had off.

When Sierra first thought about joining the carnival, it was to have a means to travel around safely while looking for her dad. Little did she know she'd rarely have time to go through each town asking about him. At first, it was fun and exciting. Then as the days blurred into weeks and months that she couldn't even remember, she started taking time away once she had a little bit of money pocketed.

The Greyhound schedules were bookmarked on her phone's browser, as well as a map of Montana and any other state they traveled through. Wyoming was the last state she had heard her dad mentioned, but she quickly learned he'd left that state long ago after getting out of prison. Then she found out he had moved around from state to state in the upper Midwest for a few years. The last person who said they knew her dad claimed he saw Bartholomew in Montana, somewhere near Glacier National Park.

Sierra had left the carnival when she heard that tip and spent every last bit of money she had searching Kalispell and Whitefish. She was so broke, she had to call Annie and ask her to buy her a ticket to wherever they were heading next. Then she spent the next seven months working hard to make more money to take more trips around the state.

It never panned out. She never heard much other than that he had gotten into some sort of trouble and left. But no one who did know her dad had seen or heard from him in years. She was about to give up and move on, but she had no clue what to do when she left the carnival.

Sierra turned back to her friend and traveling companion. "Do you think this would be a good place to settle down?"

Annie looked at the people and the town. She narrowed her eyes and pursed her lips. "I guess if you wanted to settle down and get married, this would be a good place. Looks like a nice town to grow up in." She pointed out the window. "Look, they even have a skate park here." She grinned at her friend.

They shared a skateboard and scooter, and whenever they found a skate park they would sneak out in the middle of the night and try it out. Most of the time no one bothered them, but on occasion a security guard or cop would chase them away.

"Are you thinking what I'm thinking?" Sierra waggled her brows.

"You know it!" She high-fived her friend.

When Sierra's alarm went off at two in the morning, both girls grinned before donning black pants, black shirts, and fastening black headlamps to their foreheads.

They crept out of the travel trailer they shared with two other single girls and covered their mouths as they tried to stifle their giggles.

"And just where do you two think you're going?" A big, beefy man stood in front of their path with his arms crossed.

"Now Daisy, you be good for your grammy, you hear?" River Manning kissed the head of the little blonde girl who was almost six years old. The Mannings had planned a big birthday party for her next month.

"Yes, Momma." Daisy smiled up at her stepmom and hugged her waist.

"That's my little princess." John tickled his daughter before grabbing her and picking her up.

Daisy squealed with delight and kissed her pa's cheek. "Are we going to ride Pickles today?"

"If you can talk your aunt Leah into taking you riding, then yes, you can." John kissed his daughter again and set her down.

"Why can't I ride with you, Pa?" The girl's lower lip protruded, and as usual it stabbed at the special place in John's heart for his little girl.

"Tomorrow after supper I'll take you riding. Today I'm heading into Bozeman with your momma to help some ladies."

Daisy nodded. "Momma told me you were helping street women with food. That's nice of you. Can I come and help?"

He chuckled. "When you get a little older, then you can help. Right now it's too dangerous for a five-year-old."

She put her tiny fists on her hips and narrowed her eyes at her pa. "I'm almost six now. I'm older."

Both River and John chuckled. "Sweetie, what I meant to say was when you grow up. And"—he pointed a finger and lifted a brow—"you aren't six yet. Not until the end of next month."

Her lower lip made another appearance, almost as if she knew exactly what it did to John. And she probably did know.

"Now, now. Come here." John picked her up again and held her tight. "I promise, after Sunday supper just you and I can go out for a ride."

She wrapped her little arms around his neck. "You promise?"

He nodded. "I do."

"Okay, I'll be good." She grinned, and he set her back down on her feet and kissed the top of her head.

The entire group who was heading out to Bozeman for the day filed out of the house and jumped into three trucks.

Roman patted John's shoulder once they were heading down the road. "I still can't get used to you having the oldest kid of everyone in our family."

John looked at his brother in the rearview mirror. "Neither can I."

"So"—Roman turned his gaze to River, who sat in the front passenger seat of John's truck—"when are you going to announce your pregnancy?"

It was just the three of them in the truck, with Roman in the back of the quad cab.

Both sets of eyes looked at him.

"And just what makes you so sure I'm pregnant?" River turned in her seat to glare at her brother-in-law. "Surely you aren't suggesting I'm fat?" She and John had married earlier in the spring.

Roman grinned and put his hands in the air in surrender. He would have kept teasing her, but he'd learned long ago to knock it off once a woman thought you were calling her fat. "You keep putting your hands protectively on your stomach. After all of the pregnancies in my family lately, I've learned to pick up on the signs."

Elizabeth had a baby girl who would turn two in November. Claire had just had her first baby, a boy. And Chloe came home two weeks earlier to announce her pregnancy. That baby was due in February. The one thing Roman had noticed was that all of his sisters instinctively put their hands on their bellies, even before they began showing. And their husbands also put protective touches on their wife's belly.

River looked to John, who laughed. She backhanded his shoulder.

"Hey, I'm driving here. You can manhandle me all you want once we're back home in our room." John grinned at his wife.

Her cheeks turned pink, and Roman smothered a laugh of his own. The two of them were always heading out to their room to be alone. It was no wonder she was pregnant already. They were worse than Mr. Johnson's ol' bull.

"So, when are you due?" Roman wasn't going to let it go. He knew what he saw. Not that she had the telltale baby bump or anything like that. Not yet, anyways.

River sighed. "I might as well tell you. But do me a favor?"

"Sure thing."

"Keep this to yourself until we're ready to announce it?"

"When will that be?" Roman hoped he didn't have to keep it in for long. He hated secrets; he was horrible at keeping them.

Instead of River answering, John said, "We want to wait until after the first trimester. So probably later this month we'll announce that we're due February 25th."

Roman's eyes widened. "That's right after Chloe's due date."

John took his wife's hand and squeezed it. "Yes, and we're ecstatic."

"I hope Chloe and I both have boys. It would make it easier for the boys to share a birthday. Girls don't tend to want to share their special days with their cousins." River squeezed her husband's hand in response.

Roman scratched his chin. "I don't know. Elizabeth and Chloe shared their birthday every year. I don't remember there ever being a problem."

"That's because they're twins. They weren't cousins," John added.

River chuckled. "And since they'll live far enough away that they won't always be together, I think it would be better to have birthday parties together for the boys every year."

"What if you have a girl and Chloe has a boy? Or vice versa?" Roman just had to get in the other option.

"You're a stinker, you know that?" River harrumphed.

With a chuckle, Roman acquiesced. "Alright, you're gonna each have a boy." He thought about it some more. "Unless she has twins. I think the odds are higher for her to have twins."

John laughed. "I'd be very happy with twins."

River shook her head. "I should have driven into town and joined Harper and Sophia in their SUV instead."

"Nah, you wouldn't have had so much fun with them. All they talk about anymore is finding a husband now that all of us are married." John grinned at his wife.

Roman cleared his throat. "Not all of us are married yet."

"Dude"—John laughed—"you're way too young for the nurse or our gym owner."

"Oh, I don't know about that." He closed his fist partway and rubbed his nails against his chest. "I caught both Harper and Sophia checking me out just last week when I was in town getting supplies."

"Yeah, I heard about that." River snort-laughed. "You had toilet paper stuck to the bottom of your shoe."

John laughed so hard, he veered the truck to the edge of the road and almost went off into the dirt.

"Hey, now. John, you better pay attention," Roman barked. "Don't forget, your new wife is carrying child number two for you."

Both John and River quieted down.

"Sorry, babe. I didn't mean to lose control." He grinned but kept his eyes on the road and his hands at the ten and two positions on the steering wheel. "But, come on. When Harper told us that story, well, I still laugh about it."

"Honey, I'll laugh for the both of us." River started chuckling again. "I think the Diner Divas just about fell off their stools when the gossip hit them."

"Ha, ha. Very funny. Just laugh over my embarrassment why don't 'cha?" Roman crossed his arms and looked out the window as they passed one of the local ranches and he looked at their cattle.

"Hey, when did the Millers get Highland cows?" With a frown, Roman sat up straight and turned his head to get a better look at the cows with long hair and horns chomping at the grass along the Millers' fence line.

"What?" John looked back at his brother in the rearview mirror and frowned.

"Yeah, we just passed a small herd of furry cows with horns. They look just like our Scottish Highland cows." Roman and his family had started a new line of business in the last year: cow cuddling. They had bred Highland cows with their own Angus cows, and the horns that were very large on the Highland cows were bred out, while the long hair that made the Highland cows look distinctive still came through on the Angus cow body.

"Of course, they had to copy us." John shook his head.

"Well, you know that cow cuddling has become all the rage lately. You saw the line at the last rodeo when you brought in a few to test the waters." It was River who suggested they set up a stall at the rodeos and carnivals when they came to town. She had heard about cow cuddling, but thought it was funny. At least, until she tried it. Then she was hooked.

Caleb Manning had been considering bringing in some Highland cows for quite a while. Their meat was healthier than regular steer, and it had a different flavor that people were starting to seek out. Even the Mannings enjoyed chili and meatloaf with Highland ground beef. And their steaks marbled up so nicely that it grilled to perfection with his famous barbecue sauce.

"I take it they want in on the cow-cuddling business?" Roman asked.

"Could be that, but those cows have horns. My bet is the market for Highland beef is growing and he wants in on the ground floor." John kept driving toward Bozeman.

"Let's just hope the Johnsons' ol' curmudgeonly cow doesn't get over into the Miller lands and find himself some new Highland girlfriends." Roman snorted.

Chapter 4

"I'm hungry." With a hand on her gurgling stomach, Sierra looked around for a fast-food joint.

Annie agreed and looked at her phone for a place to get a quick bite to eat. "I'm sick of burgers. I want something different. Maybe a salad?"

"Mmm, a salad with chopped chicken sounds great." Sierra turned where Annie directed and they found a Hardee's.

"What do you say we try again tonight? Midnight skating?" Annie's eyebrows practically reached the top of her forehead.

They had been caught by security the first night in town. It wasn't the first time, but hopefully, they'd get their chance that night to have some fun. It wasn't like they were planning to rob a bank or anything, they just left camp and skated a park after it closed for the night. Nothing major. When Red found out, you'd think they were out rabble-rousing, or something. It was only their chance to have some fun without others around. It's not like they were hurting anyone, or breaking any laws.

Well, okay, maybe they were breaking local ordinances by skating in a park that had already closed for the night, but let's get real, who did that hurt? No one, except their testimony.

A slow grin crossed Sierra's face. "You know it."

After they ate, they walked outside and Annie started telling a joke. "What do you call a frog who wants to be a cowboy?"

Sierra slapped a hand to her head. "Oh, not that old one. Come on, Annie, can't you get some new material?"

"What?" Annie raised her hands and her shoulders and looked so innocent. "I happen to think Hopalong Cassidy is a great name for a frog."

"Okay." With a shake of her head and a little chuckle, Sierra moved along.

In the distance, a couple of good-looking cowboys caught Annie's attention. "Yummy, dessert." She nodded in their direction.

Sierra rolled her eyes. "You're cowboy crazy."

"So, what's wrong with knowing what I want?" Annie shrugged, but kept her gaze on the two cowboys who finally looked their way.

One of the cowboys was holding hands with a pretty woman, but the other stared at them with his mouth agape and pointed in their direction.

When Sierra noticed the cowboy staring and pointing, she hurried up toward the truck. He was surrounded by homeless people, but he didn't appear to be homeless himself. She wasn't sure what he was up to, but she didn't like the looks of that group he was with. "Come on, I'm getting a funny feeling in the pit of my stomach. Let's get out of here."

"Why?"

"Because, Annie, those guys are hanging out with a bad crowd. We don't need any more bad cowboys following us around." Sierra had been thinking about the time in Helena when a group of drunk men wouldn't leave them alone. At least not until Stella, Red's wife, brought out her rolling pin and threatened them.

She still couldn't believe the short, stout woman was so fierce. Stella pounded that wooden pin in her hand and gave them the evil eye so strongly that they all ran away, and as far as Sierra knew, they didn't come back.

"True, Stella's not here to scare them away." Annie chuckled. Her adoptive mom was a hoot. She always laughed whenever Stella brought out her pin. It meant she was in a foul mood and heaven help anyone who got in her way once she had it in her hands. Annie had even seen her hit a man on the back with it once. He deserved it. The louse had hold of one of the other girls in the carnival and wouldn't let her go. After Stella brandished her weapon, most men fled, but not that fool. At least not until Stella hit him. All it ever took was one hit and the men would run.

The fact that this guy seemed familiar stopped her in her tracks. Sierra took another look and decided he must be one of those bozos she'd met along the road.

However, she knew he wasn't one of the few crazies Stella had beaned. She'd remember each of them. But there was a glimmer of recollection. The fact that she couldn't remember if he was a good guy or a bad one told her to run. Better to be safe than sorry.

Roman couldn't believe his eyes. Across the street was the siren in his dreams. Only without the mermaid tail. "John, look." He pointed across the street and stared.

"Who?" John looked across the street and saw two girls hightailing it to a truck with a carnival logo on it. "Do you think they might know your green-eyed dreamboat?"

Roman shook his head. "No, I mean that's her. That's the girl of my dreams."

River looked at the two girls and eyed them both. "Which one? The brown-haired girl or the strawberry blonde?"

The truck zoomed past, and Roman noted the name of the carnival company—Dreamytime Carnival, Inc. "That was her. The strawberry blonde." He laughed. "She's real. And she's close by." He pulled his phone out and looked up the company name. "I've got their schedule."

"So now instead of your siren calling to you in a dream, she's calling to you in real life?" John arched a brow. "Are you sure that's her?"

Roman dropped his hands to his sides and frowned at his brother. "Really? I've been looking for a very particular girl who works at a carnival. I see one driving a carnival truck and you doubt me?"

"No, I don't doubt you. I just wonder if after our talk the other day, you aren't just looking for a girl, any girl, who is even close to what you've been dreaming about. That's all." With a wince, John looked down the street where the truck had gone, but it was already out of sight. "Where are they now? Do they have a carnival here in town?"

A slow grin crossed Roman's face. "No, but they are going to open up tomorrow in Livingston."

John nodded. "How long will they be there?"

"Three days. But guess where they go in a month?" A glimmer in Roman's eyes told his team it was close.

River guessed, "Bozeman?"

He shook his head and smirked.

"No, it can't be," John said.

"The entire first week of September they're in Beacon Creek, Montana for the fall festival and rodeo." He crossed his arms and smiled as though he'd just won the lottery.

"Oh, are you going to wait for her to show up in town? Or will you drive out to Livingston tomorrow after church?" River bit her lower lip. Livingston was close enough he could do it in a day, but he'd not get home until well after midnight if he did it.

"I'll talk to Pa and see what he thinks. I'd rather drive out on Monday and get there in the early afternoon, then be home at a decent time that night." Roman pulled his backpack off his shoulders and looked inside. They had brought out the last of their brown bags of goodies for the homeless.

Elizabeth was just behind them talking to Amanda, trying to get her to go home with them. "Amanda, Amy and Regina both would love to see you. They're very happy living on our ranch."

Amanda looked around and noticed Big Bart watching them carefully. He glared at her and ran a finger across his neck. She shook her head. "No, ma'am. I can't go. My place is here." She grabbed the brown bag in Elizabeth's hands and walked away.

Elizabeth tried to go after her, but Logan took her arm. "Let her go. When she's ready she'll join us."

"I know." A giant sigh left Lizzie as she deflated. "I just wish I could take all of the women today. I hate that they're so controlled by Big Bart."

Logan wrapped an arm around his wife's shoulders. "Lizzie, just be grateful that he stays away from us when we come."

"I still don't understand why he doesn't intervene any-more." Lizzie eyed the tall blond man. "Ever since Rocko went to jail the second time for trying to abduct Leah, he's kept his distance."

"But not far enough for my liking," Logan snarled. "One of these days, whoever is controlling him will let his leash loose, and I hope we aren't anywhere near him when that happens."

Roman snickered. "Leash loose. He's a dog alright. A big, nasty one who loves to attack those smaller than him."

"You got that right," Sophia added. "We're all out of bags. How about you guys?"

"Same here," Logan said.

Harper walked up to the group. "Any takers?"

Elizabeth shook her head. "No, Amanda's still too afraid of Bart to leave."

Chapter 5

Immediately after breakfast on Monday morning, Roman was in his truck heading to Livingston, Montana and their carnival. He couldn't believe his luck. Or was it God? He had been praying a lot about the green-eyed beauty lately and trying to give her up. Maybe God had finally decided now was the time? He prayed all the way to Livingston that the girl would be there and he could meet her—finally.

After he parked, he headed toward the kiddie games area. This carnival wasn't as big as the last time he had seen it in Beacon Creek, probably because they weren't on the rodeo grounds for this event. He knew that Livingston had a huge rodeo over the Fourth of July weekend each summer, and a carnival sometimes accompanied the rodeo. But he wasn't sure if they had a carnival here this year. Not that it mattered. All that mattered was that his green-eyed mermaid was here.

Roman weaved in and out of families and adults all walking around the carnival grounds. He was actually surprised to see so many people there; it was only early afternoon. Why weren't the adults working? Since it was summer, the kids wouldn't be in school yet. It wasn't a holiday. So this many people surprised him.

Although, after the difficulties of the past few years, he realized he shouldn't be surprised to see so many people out and about at a public event. People needed to be outside, and even if they didn't know those around them, they still needed community. This was probably a good sign for their upcoming harvest festival and rodeo. He'd have to tell his dad about this crowd and ensure they brought all of their cuddlin' cows into town for the event.

A smile spread across his face when he came upon the first of the kiddie games. It was a fishin' game. The little kids had a rod with a ring attached to the end of their line. They had to hook a fish. It was the type of game where all kids were a winner. The prize was a tiny stuffed fish, or gnome. The gnome prize didn't really make any sense since gnomes weren't water creatures. Maybe if they had a choice between a tiny fish or a mermaid, that would have made more sense. Or a turtle?

Ugh, he had to get mermaids off his mind.

He shook his head and walked past as a little girl about the same age as Daisy hooked a fish. When the game operator peeked inside the plastic fish, she pulled out a golden coin. "You won the special prize." The game operator pointed above her head where Roman had missed a selection of various stuffed water creatures, including a mermaid. A chuckle escaped his mouth as he walked on.

Then he walked past a water gun game featuring an under-the-sea theme with yes, mermaids. Were these games at his carnival a year and a half ago when he first saw her? If so, his dreams made more sense.

When he saw her, his heart skipped more than a few beats. Sun shone on her strawberry blonde locks. Her white teeth sparkled in the rays surrounding her, and he felt lighter than he had in almost two years. Roman's arms fell limp at his sides and his head tilted to the right just a little bit. And he felt a smile crossing his face from ear to ear. She was here. He had finally found his mermaid.

As of yet, she hadn't noticed him. Her duck-ring booth was busy with kids trying to win a giant duck like Daisy had. So far, none of them were winners. This was a winner-take-all sort of game. You either won the big prize or nothing at all. A lot like life.

Slowly, so as not to garner any attention, he edged his way to her booth. He wanted to drink her in as she smiled at the little kids and commiserated with their parents when the kids lost. She was exactly how he remembered her, though her hair was styled a little bit differently. When he first saw her it was all down around her shoulders, which made sense since it was December and cold. But today, with the heat, she had it up in a long ponytail with a pink doodad holding it in place.

Roman's heart quickened and he felt perspiration form on his forehead, but it hadn't started to drip yet. He told himself it was the heat of the sun, not his nerves. But he knew better. While the sun was shining, he had his Stetson on and a cold neckerchief. He shouldn't be feeling the heat yet, especially since it was only eighty degrees. Today wasn't supposed to be too hot. And add in the light breeze off the river running close by, and it was a rather nice late summer afternoon. The sort where he would enjoy sitting on a porch swing with his sweetheart sipping iced tea and watching the dogs run around. Or kids playing in the front yard.

Whoa, where did that thought come from? He must have been spending too much time with his nieces and new nephew. Roman was way too young to get married and have kids right now. It was something he wanted, but not yet. He had just graduated college and barely made it home a few months ago.

A small voice in the back of his head whispered, *If that was the case, then why were you so interested in finding this woman?*

Oh, Nelly. He was in big trouble.

"Oh, I'm so sorry. Better luck next time." Sierra turned sad eyes on the little red-headed boy who didn't win a giant duck. She wished they could at least give away tiny rubber duckies to all who played, but this wasn't one of those games that offered a prize to all.

When she lifted her head, she jumped. Standing right in front of her was the cowboy from Saturday. The one who had made an appearance in her dreams the past two nights. Each morning when she woke, she remembered his mocha-latte eyes looking into her soul, much like he was doing right then.

And it hit her. She finally remembered him. "Where's your niece?"

He startled. "You remember me?"

She smiled and relaxed. At first, she wasn't sure if he was the cowboy she had thought about for weeks after seeing him with his adorable little niece. She had won one of only three ducks they gave out that day. It was rare someone won, let alone a tiny wisp of a girl like her. It was usually the eight- or nine-year-old kids who won. That girl couldn't have been more than four or five. Two or three winners per day was the norm. However, today she had yet to have any winners. They needed one if they wanted to attract more players.

She remembered his strong shoulders and handsome face. If her memory served, he was in need of a haircut last time she saw him. Today, his hair was trimmed and his face clean-shaven. What stood out the most last time, and was the same this time, was his scent. He smelled of a ranch—horse, hay, and surprisingly spearmint. Sierra wondered if he chewed gum a lot or if he had just taken a mint before coming up to her booth.

When he took a closer step, she picked up slight hints of spice and orange. It must have been his aftershave. Whatever it was, she liked it—a lot. Her heartbeat picked up steam, and she began to hear the rushing of her blood pumping through her system. Then her cheeks warmed and she turned her gaze away. It wouldn't do to let him see her blush.

"Hi." The man waved and gave her a goofy grin.

Sierra's shoulders relaxed and she returned his smile. "I'm Sierra."

He looked surprised for a moment, then stuck his hand out. "I'm Roman. It's nice to officially meet you."

"Miss, we want to play. Can you give us some rings?" a mom interrupted her before she could say anything else.

"Of course." She turned toward the little family and smiled at the little girl. "Do you know how to play this game?"

The brown curls surrounding the little girl's head bobbed as she nodded.

Once the mom gave her the money, Sierra handed her four rings and moved closer to Roman to get out the girl's way. It was for no other reason. She certainly wasn't using it as an excuse to get closer to the cowboy.

Roman interrupted her thoughts. "I was surprised to see you in Bozeman the other day."

She bit her lower lip. "And I was surprised to see you, too." She narrowed her eyes. "Do you normally hang out with that sort of person?" While the people around him didn't carry signs screaming *homeless*, it was pretty obvious those people at least spent most of their time on the streets.

Roman chuckled. "Actually, I do. You see, my sister started a ministry..."

Before he could finish his sentence, the little girl jumped up and down screaming and stole Sierra's attention away.

"You won! Great job." Sierra reached up and grabbed one of the ducks hanging above her and handed the giant stuffed bird to the mom, whose arms were outstretched.

"Wow, Mia. Look at that. Your dad is going to be so surprised. Let's go find him and your brother. I bet they didn't win anything as big as your duck." The mother and child walked away laughing and chatting animatedly about what she'd won.

"I love it when little girls win the big prizes. It shows that girls can do anything they set their minds to." Sierra watched as more and more kids came to her booth. It was going to be busy for at least another thirty minutes, maybe even longer.

Roman stepped back when the booth became packed with families all vying to win their own giant duck. She lost track of him while she took money, made change, and rooted for the kids playing the game. When her booth finally emptied, she looked around but didn't see him anywhere.

Sierra sighed. She had hoped he'd wait around to talk to her again. It was almost time for her break. Annie would be there soon, and she could take her lunch break. A few more kids came and went without winning, as she kept her eye out for the handsome cowboy with brown hair and chocolate-latte eyes.

The more she thought of his eyes, the more she wanted to get a coffee with her lunch—something she didn't normally do, especially since it was so hot. Maybe today she'd get an iced mocha. She deserved a treat once in a while.

By the time her break started, he still wasn't around. "Okay, I guess I'm gonna head out. Be back later," she called to Annie before taking off her apron and stowing it under the booth.

When she walked out of the back of her booth, she jumped and put a hand over her heart. "Don't do that. You scared me."

The cowboy standing next to her took his hat off and put it over his heart. "I'm sorry, Sierra. I didn't mean to startle you."

Sierra sucked in her lips. "It's fine. I'm taking my lunch break now." She considered her idea for a moment and then went for it. "Care to join me?"

His eyes widened and he smiled so big, she could see his white teeth. "Yes, ma'am. I'd love to." He got in step next to her as she took off to her favorite lunch truck.

The chicken-and-rice bowl set inside of a hollowed-out pineapple was the perfect meal to get her through until dinner. "Do you like pineapple?"

"Who doesn't?" Roman answered.

When they got up to the window, she ordered two meals and was about to pay when Roman put his credit card up to the window before she could get her cash out of her pocket. "Thanks, but you don't have to buy. I can get it."

"I was brought up to always pay for a lady's meal." Roman took his card back after the cashier swiped it.

"At least let me pay for mine?" Sierra wasn't sure if he was going to expect something in return. She didn't get a bad vibe off of him, but one never knew with strangers.

He shook his head. "My momma and pa would be upset with me if I let you pay for the first date."

Her eyes widened. "Date?"

"Yes, you did ask me to join you for lunch, right?" He grinned. The sort of smile that said he knew exactly what she was up to.

Sierra narrowed her eyes. "I wouldn't call this a date since I asked if you wanted to join me. I didn't ask if you wanted to go out, and you certainly didn't ask me out."

He nodded. "So, carnival food doesn't make for a date?"

She narrowed her eyes and shook her head.

"Okay, then how about a date when your carnival comes to my town?" Roman slid his thumbs through his belt loops and nodded once.

Sierra scanned her memory, trying to remember where they had met. It was winter. They normally went south for the winter, but two Christmases ago they stayed in Montana because Red had to have cataract surgery on his eyes and he couldn't travel until after he was released from his doctor's care.

"In about a month you'll be in Beacon Creek for a week. We have a harvest festival that lasts all week long, and the last three days there's a rodeo." Roman waited for her to remember.

"Oh, now I remember. It was your Christmas festival that we met at." She put a finger to her chin. "Your town must love festivals if you also have a large one in September."

Roman chuckled. "Yes, we actually have several throughout the year. But that year was the first time we had a carnival at our Christmas festival. We don't normally do that."

"I remember, it was a last-minute booking." She reconsidered. "Well, last minute for a carnival. I think your town booked us about six weeks out. We don't normally stay in Montana for the winter. We usually head down to New Mexico, Arizona, and Texas. Carnivals generally don't do well in snow."

"True, but I think you'll find that Montanans don't have a problem with playing outdoors when it's cold and snowing."

She laughed. "I remember. I was freezing cold under that tent, but plenty of kids wanted to play the games. It was as though they had no idea it was snowing and only twenty-five degrees outside."

"We sold plenty of ride tickets as well. My sister-in-law was on the planning committee and she said they made almost as much money from your carnival that year as they do during the harvest festival carnival."

Sierra finally understood why his town tried to get them to come back last Christmas. Red and Stella were adamant about spending their winter where it was warm enough you didn't eat your own breath. So they declined the offer and went south as normal.

"So, will you have an evening off while you're in Beacon Creek? I'd love to take you out for a real dinner. Not carnival food." Roman winked.

"You're a cheeky cowboy, aren't you?" Sierra tilted her head and considered his offer.

"I might be. But I was raised to be a gentleman." He took his hat off and asked if he could pray over their meal once they were seated.

Sierra considered his request and wondered if it was just for show or if he truly meant it. She'd seen her fair share of guys pray for meals only to go out drinking later and get sloppy drunk. She may not have been all that close with God these days, but she did know He didn't like it when His children did that. She smiled and felt a sense of peace overcome her as he prayed for their food and her safety.

After he prayed, they took a few bites before speaking again.

"This is really good." Roman pointed to his pineapple chicken. "Are you sure we can't count this as a date?"

She had to give him credit for not giving up. "I tell you what. If you take me out for a steak dinner, off carnie grounds"—she held up her index finger—"but still somewhere public, I'll call this our first date."

"Deal." He put his spork down and held out a hand to shake on it.

For the rest of their meal they talked about the different food booths in a carnival.

"Have you ever tried the fried twinkies?" He scrunched his nose and waited for her response.

Sierra laughed. "I've had every sort of carnie food you can think of. Although, I'm not a fan of fried food." She pursed her lips and tilted her head. "Well, that's not entirely true."

"Oh, really? What fried food do you like?" He took another bite of his meal and chewed.

"Fried pickles. That's one of those foods that is just classic. It doesn't matter if you're eating off a carnie food truck or in one of those fancy restaurants, they're always good with the right seasoning."

"Oh, yeah. The spicy ranch seasoning is my favorite." His head whipped around, looking at the different trucks.

"If you're wondering if we've got fried pickles, we do." She pointed to the pineapple truck. "It's behind that one."

When her lunch ended, Sierra couldn't remember a time when she was so full, or so happy. One of her unwritten rules was to never date a customer, but this cowboy was too cute and sweet. She'd give him a chance. When he asked for her number, she gave it to him, expecting that he wouldn't call her until the end of the month, if ever.

Chapter 6

*W**here are you this week?*

Roman and Sierra texted several times that first week. Now she was heading out to the next stop on her schedule, but they weren't due to arrive for another day.

Roman sat on his horse watching the three little circles on his screen that denoted a text from Sierra was in process.

We just entered Idaho. Not sure what town it was that we passed. It was one of those where if you blink, you miss it. You know what I mean?

He chuckled, attracting the attention of his oldest brother, Matthew.

"Who are you texting? That pretty girl?" Matthew grinned.

Ever since Roman arrived home a week ago from Livingston with a smile on his face, all of his brothers were giving him a hard time.

Roman ignored his brother's teasing tone and sent back a response. *If you just passed Ashton or St. Anthony, then you should be really close to your first stop.*

The carnival was scheduled to open the day after tomorrow in Idaho Falls. They'd be there for two days, and then pack up and head over to Twin Falls for three days.

They continued texting while Matthew sat atop his horse and watched with laughter while his little brother flirted with a carnie. He had already promised he was going to have to meet this girl before Roman could go out with her. His dad had a similar message when word reached him about the upcoming date.

"Hey, loverboy. We got work to do. Tell your little chickadee you'll chat later." Matthew threw a rope at Roman, who let it hit him and then drop to the ground.

Sorry, I gotta go. Matthew's being a pain. Almost as big of one as that crusty ol' Johnson bull I have to round up. He sent his text and hopped off his horse.

Roman looked out to the bull holding court with his lovely ladies. "I think we should dub him Romeo."

"Just don't let ol' Mr. Johnson hear you call his bull *Romeo*. I think he named him Diablo back in the day." Matthew tightened his hat on his head and pulled another rope from his saddle.

The bull was old, probably seventeen or eighteen by now, and it shouldn't still have a libido as strong as a teenage boy, but it did. Several times a year the Mannings had to find the spawn of Satan and take him back to his own pastures. Then they'd have to fix the fence line he'd broken down. Mr. Johnson always paid them back for supplies, but even Caleb Manning was getting tired of this bull.

"You know, now that we have Daisy out here riding almost daily, John has begun talking about ensuring Romeo stays out of our fields." Roman picked up the rope his brother threw at him earlier and began winding it up. They'd both have to work hard to lasso the devil and then tie the rope to the saddle horn of their horses.

"I was thinking on how we could do that." Matthew looked to his brother, and when they were both in position, he nodded. Then his rope was circling up above his head. When Roman called out, they both took turns roping the bull.

Of course, Diablo wasn't going down without a fight. Usually he wasn't too difficult to herd back into his own lands, but today he was in no mood to do as he was told.

"Why don't we just sell Mr. Johnson our cows that Romeo here can't do without?" Roman had asked this before, but no one ever answered him.

Diablo tried to make a run for it, but Matthew's horse knew what he was about. All of the Manning horses were probably sick and tired of this bull. Matthew and his horse held on to the rope while Roman and Rock Star pulled on their rope to get Diablo, or Romeo—whatever the daggum bull's name was—to get a move on.

Once they were all moving back to the Johnson lands, Matthew answered, "We tried that once. It seems Romeo only wants what he can't have. Pa sold the Johnsons three cows in the past, but ol' Diablo reared his ugly head and paved on through the fence line once he realized he could have those cows whenever he wanted."

"And I take it Mr. Johnson has tried putting the bull in his fields on the opposite side of his land?" Roman asked.

"Yup, and he steamrolls through any fence in his way. Doesn't matter how many there are." Matthew clicked his tongue and got his horse to move a little faster.

The sooner they got this part over with, the better.

Once they were back on Johnson land, they led him through three open fences, released the rope from each of their saddle horns, and hightailed it back through to their side. The one good thing was that it took Diablo a while to make his way through each fence.

"What about we put a gate up here and just open it up and let a few of Romeo's favorite girls hang out in the fenced-in area, then each day change up the girls? Have we tried that yet?" Roman would try anything to keep the bull from breaking down more fence lines. It seemed the bull had seasons where he was more amorous than other times of year. If they found a way to cater to the bull's needs, then maybe they could keep from replacing so much fence line each year.

"Pa and Mr. Johnson did discuss that, but honestly, we all thought Diablo would be done by now. He's supposed to be too old to sire any more calves." Matthew closed the last gate of the Johnson farm before they entered their own land and dismounted to begin work on fixing the fence.

"Uh, Matthew, I don't think those little ladies over there get impregnated by Romeo. I think he just enjoys their company." Roman snickered.

Matthew chuckled. "That might be more likely than someone feeding Diablo bull Viagra."

Roman laughed so hard he spit. "Bull Viagra. That's hilarious. Who suggested that?"

Matthew gave his youngest brother a sheepish look. "Mark."

"Pft. Well, there's your answer right there. You never should have believed the family jokester."

It took them an hour to fix the fence. When they were done, Diablo was huffing and puffing as though he was going to blow the last two fences down in order to get to their new fence.

"If that bull"—Roman pointed at Diablo—"brings down the fences, I'm just gonna wait until he's done with our herd. Then I'll come back out here and fix the line again." He shook his head and mounted his horse to head back in for lunch.

"You sure have been texting that cowboy a lot lately." Annie bit her cheek to keep from laughing.

Sierra looked up from her cellphone. "What's wrong with that?"

Annie snorted. "Look, it's probably none of my business..."

"You're darn tootin' it's none of your business." Pink tinged Sierra's cheeks.

With hands up, Annie stepped back. "Whoa, now. I'm not saying it's a bad thing. It's just, well, you've never wanted to chat with cowboys before. In fact, the last time I gave my number to a guy I met in a small town, you scoffed at me. You even went so far as to sit me down and tell me the perils of giving out my number to strangers." She arched a brow.

After she put her phone away, Sierra threw her hands in the air and sat down. "I know, I know." She scratched her cheek. "There's just something about him. I can't put my finger on it."

"I can." Annie tried to cover her laugh with her hand.

Sierra scowled at her friend. "I know he's cute. But there's more to it." She stood up and walked to the back of their little booth. It was the middle of a Thursday and they'd be taking down the booth that night and heading out to their next stop.

"Okay, enlighten me."

Sierra stopped her pacing and looked out at the almost empty blacktop surrounding their little booth. The day was slow, but it usually was during the week. That night they should see a lot more people. She turned back to her friend. "He has an honest face."

Brows furrowed, Annie opened her mouth and then shut it before she finally spoke. "What does that mean?"

"You know, he seems like a man that can be trusted. And in our line of work"—Sierra gave her friend a pointed look—"we don't meet too many honest men. Especially honest and cute cowboys."

"Plenty of cute cowboys." Annie giggled. "But you're right, most of them are anything *but* honest." She shuddered.

Sierra's eyes softened. "Are you thinking about that guy last week who followed you around after closing?"

Annie looked down. "I should have known he was up to no good."

During one of their evening shifts, a cute cowboy came sniffing around Annie. He flirted something awful, and Annie drank it up. She always did have a soft spot for blond cowboys. And this one had curly blond hair under a brown Stetson. He was tall and lean, and smelled like Old Spice. That was Annie's Achilles heel. She'd once told Sierra it was a scent that reminded her of her childhood, when she was with her parents. Before they dropped her off at the carnival and left her for good.

"I told you, never give your number to a cowboy who wears Old Spice. Every single one of them has been trouble." Sierra tsk'd.

A woman and her young daughter walked up to the booth, and all talk about the cowboys halted. "I heard you mentioning Old Spice and cowboys." The mother smiled at her daughter. "My husband used to wear Old Spice. He was a good man. Not all cowboys are bad, you just have to be more discerning."

The lady handed them two dollars for one play, and Sierra gave four rings to the little girl.

"Used to wear?" Annie asked.

A sad expression crossed the woman's face. "He had an accident."

Sierra covered her heart and tears welled up in her eyes. "I'm so sorry, I didn't mean to insinuate that all cowboys were bad." She looked to Annie. "It's just that my friend here has had some really bad luck lately."

The woman held up her hand. "No need to apologize. There are a lot of bad men out there, including cowboys. But just remember that not all men who wear Old Spice are bad."

"Momma"—the little girl pulled on her mom's sleeve—"I almost got one. Can I play again?"

"Here, on me." Sierra handed the girl four more rings and pulled out cash from her cellphone case. While she was paying for the play, the little girl yelled.

Annie chuckled. "Looks like we got ourselves a winner. Great job, little lady." She handed the girl her prize.

Within minutes, their booth was busy and all talk about cowboys was put aside for a later time.

Chapter 7

Daisy was all dressed up in her finest riding gear. She had on little-girl Wranglers, a pink long-sleeved blouse with purple and light-green flowers, as well as her new pair of heather-green cowgirl boots. Ever since she'd gotten her first pair of pink boots, the little girl had only wanted "pretty cowgirl boots," as she called them. So Leah would scan the catalogs as they came in looking for new boots for the sweet cowgirl. Daisy never went without at least two pairs of pretty cowgirl boots.

She ran into the kitchen that morning for breakfast with a giant smile on her face. "Momma, can we visit Scotty after I ride Pickles?" Scotty was Daisy's favorite Scottish Highland bull. He had some pretty large horns, but for some reason he didn't scare Daisy. River, on the other hand, shivered whenever Scotty came near.

"You need to ask your pa about that. I think Scotty is, uh, working today." Pink tinged River's cheeks. She still wasn't used to talking about breeding animals, and she certainly had no desire to explain it to her little girl who wasn't even six years old yet.

"What does she need to ask her pa?" John asked as he walked over to his wife and kissed her cheek. He gave his daughter a hug and tickled her sides.

Daisy giggled and squirmed. "Pa, I wanna go see Scotty today."

"Oh, my little princess. He's out back working this week. How about we go and visit Peaches? I think she misses your cuddles." He touched the tip of his daughter's nose and then went to get a cup of coffee.

Since the success of their new cow-cuddling program, the Triple J Ranch was on a mission to raise up more cows for various cuddling programs across the region. They even had a contract with the Crooked Arrow Ranch near Frenchtown to supply them with a dozen yearlings next year.

The more Caleb, John, and Roman looked into it, the more demand they found for cows that could easily be bred and used for various rehabilitation programs. They even spoke to a ranch owner in Wyoming who was planning to start a drug rehab program on his ranch and wanted to buy a few yearlings once they had enough to sell.

This next month, Scotty would be working hard and spending "quality time" with two dozen of the Triple J's finest Angus females. Roman was spearheading the program now that he was back from college, with the help of John when he had the time.

Roman entered the kitchen and joined their conversation. "I think Peaches would love a visit from you, Daisy-girl." He picked up his niece and blew raspberries against her neck.

She squealed and squirmed. And when Roman sat her back down, she smiled up to her uncle. "Uncle Roman, will you take me to see Peaches?"

River looked aghast at her stepdaughter. "What? I thought you wanted me to take you for cow cuddling?"

Daisy twisted her mouth and wrung her hands in her lap. "I'm sorry, Momma. You can come, too."

River and John both laughed.

"It's fine, baby. If you want Uncle Roman to take you to the cows, that's fine with me." River pretended to swipe a tear from her cheeks and sniffed.

Daisy jumped in her lap and hugged her momma. "I'm sorry. I want you to come, too. Please?" She kissed her momma's cheek and waited for her reply.

"Well, if you insist." With a smile and a laugh, River hugged her little girl before letting her go to eat breakfast.

"Y'all are just too cute together." Roman shook his head. "What time do you think you'll want to see the yearlings? I need to ride out and check on Scotty before I can join you."

"They're still close to the barn, right?" River asked.

"Yup, they're in the small pen just to the left of the barn. I'm keeping them close so we can have at least one person cuddle with them daily. I want to get them used to it before we bring them to the festival." Roman rubbed the back of his neck. "I'm actually not sure how much attention we should let them have. I hear we can expect a huge turnout, but I don't want to overwhelm the cows."

"You have a large enough pen that you can switch them out every hour, right?" River had helped with the research on cow cuddling and how to raise them. And of course, how much human interaction they should be allowed. They were cows and shouldn't be forced to cuddle with anyone. They should be allowed to walk away if they didn't like a person, or just didn't want to be touched.

The only problem with that was space was needed. When they had four cows at the summer festival, it was still a new concept to the area so not too many people came up and paid the twenty dollars for fifteen minutes with a cow. The cows were really great with the attention they received, and even seemed to enjoy it. Only one cowboy was rebuffed by the cows, and it didn't really surprise any of the Mannings. That cowboy was known to be a rapscallion. Cows, it turns out, have really great senses. They know better than most humans who is inherently good, and who isn't.

Roman nodded. "Yes, we have a spot on the edge of the carnival grounds and a large enclosed area, as well as a tent with spots for four cows to cuddle at a time. But we only have a dozen cows who are old enough to work."

"I'll come every day and cuddle Peaches." Daisy grinned and held a piece of bacon in her hand as she looked at each of the adults.

"That's great, honey." John put a hand on her shoulder. "But what about the rest of our cows?"

Daisy chewed on her bacon and nodded. Once she finished eating her bite, for she knew better than to talk with her mouth full anymore, she offered to cuddle them all today.

"What will you talk about with the cows?" Roman asked. He knew that a lot of people carried on conversations with the cows in addition to hugging them and just being near the warm-blooded creatures.

Daisy focused on her plate and her bottom lip protruded. Even Uncle Roman fell for the pout every single time. But this time, it wasn't so much of a pout as it was her thinking face. "I think I'll tell them all about school." Daisy was all set to start first grade after the fall festival ended. The town always waited for that event to finish before sending their kids back to school. And then the school year ended right before the summer festival began.

"Are you excited to start again?" River knew that Daisy had been leery to start kindergarten, but the little girl loved it after only one day.

Everyone expected the very social little girl would enjoy first grade even more. Especially since it lasted longer than kindergarten did and she'd get to play with more kids.

An enthusiastic head nod preceded her words. "I have lots of friends to meet."

"That's my girl." John mussed up his little girl's head and chuckled. "I bet you'll eventually be the rodeo queen."

She puckered her lips. "No, I think I want to barrel race like my momma Donna did."

River put a hand to her chest, covering the coffee cup and silly saying on her t-shirt, and bit her lower lip. She attempted to blink away tears. Ever since Daisy was born, River had told her stories about her biological mother, Donna, and how she was not only a rodeo queen, but also a champion barrel racer. Donna and River had been best friends and foster sisters until she died after giving birth to Daisy. This was the first time Daisy had said she wanted to be like her mom.

Roman knew the story of Donna and he had seen a lot of pictures of the young woman. She was beautiful. He knew without a shadow of a doubt that Daisy would be just as beautiful, if not more so, than her birth mother. However, he wasn't sure how River felt about Daisy wanting to follow in her birth mother's footsteps. He silently watched as the little family absorbed Daisy's words.

"Daisy, you can do whatever you set your mind to. If you want to be a champion barrel racer, then you will be." River nodded once and reached for her coffee mug.

The mood in the room was heavy. "Or you can be a champion cow cuddler, if you want." Roman grinned at Daisy.

The little girl scrunched her button nose. "Champion cow cuddler? That's not a thing. Don't pull my leg, Uncle Roman."

"Hey, only I can pull my little girl's leg." John squared his shoulders, crossed his arms over his chest, and stared down his little brother.

River giggled, followed by Daisy.

Roman held his hands up and sighed. "Alright, alright. I'll be the champion cow cuddler." He gave a serious look to Daisy. "Someone in this family needs to do it."

Two hours later, after Daisy had finished her morning ride on Pickles, she and River walked over to the other side of the barn where the young Highland/Angus crossbreeds were kept.

When the Mannings had first looked into cow cuddling, they learned that most any cow could be cuddled. However, horns weren't very welcoming. So they needed a breed of cattle that didn't traditionally grow them. Angus were great at that, and they would offer Angus cattle for cuddling. But in their research, they discovered the soft, hairy fur of the Highland cows were more sought after. And crossbreeding an Angus cow with a Highland bull worked quite well to breed out the horns, while still getting a hairy cow. Hence the addition of the hairy Highland cows—or coos, as the Scottish pronounced the word—to their herd.

Roman looked up from the young cow he was grooming when he heard footsteps. "Daisy, River, nice to see you both." He pointed to the cow next to him. "Peaches here needs to be groomed if you want to grab a brush and help out?"

The exuberant little girl clapped her hands and ran to the side of the new barn and picked up two brushes. She handed one to River before heading over to her favorite yearling.

"Remember, Daisy, you have to be calm around the cows," River admonished.

"Yes, Momma." Daisy stopped in her tracks and took a deep breath. "Calm."

Roman smiled and went back to grooming Cream, Peaches' sister.

"I'll visit with Butterscotch." River tried to hide her smile, but Butterscotch was her favorite of the yearlings. This little cross of Highland bull and Angus cow had some attitude. Plus, she loved to cuddle. River set down her brush and started out with a long hug.

Butterscotch ran her nose along River's head and snorted, sending the brownish wispies that had made their way out of River's ponytail flying behind her back.

River giggled and began talking to the cow. "You love hugs, I know it."

The little cow mooed her agreement.

Roman watched as River spoke to the yearling, and he turned his head to see Daisy talking to her cow as she ran the brush down the mottled brown-and-beige coat. A sense of accomplishment filled his soul. When John had told him about the idea, he'd jumped at the chance to help with this new project.

Roman enjoyed herding the cattle, feeding their stock, and all of the other chores. Except, well, he was tired of fixing fences, but that was another issue all together. When the idea of raising Scottish Highland cows came up, he was all in. When John brought up the concept of cow cuddling, he scoffed at first. Then that night he looked it up online. The next day, he told his pa he wanted in on the new venture.

"Son, you still have one year left of college. Focus on your game and studies. When you get home next summer, you can work with John on the project." His dad had always supported the various ideas each Manning boy brought to the table. Caleb never jumped in without research. If you brought him a viable plan and proof it was working elsewhere, then he'd give it a try.

That was exactly what Matthew had done with raising all organic and grass-fed cattle. Caleb let Matthew lead the way, and they were one of the most successful ranches in the area because of it.

When Roman came home earlier this summer, John said he wanted to go back to college and finish his degree online. Everyone was supportive of that decision, which meant that Roman would be leading the new program with the Highland cattle.

The only problem was that they needed more land if they were going to see the Highland cattle business and cow cuddling achieve its full potential. They had the land on the Triple J for a few more years, as he built up his stock, but eventually he would need his own ranch if he took this all the way.

"Uncle Roman?" Daisy's sweet voice brought him out of his reverie.

"Hmm? Yes, Daisy?"

"Can I ride Peaches when we're done?"

River chuckled but didn't say a word.

Roman schooled his face, but inside he was laughing at the sweetness of his little niece. She seemed to want to ride any animal on the ranch. Well, she had yet to ask about riding the chickens, which was probably a good thing.

"I don't think cows like to be ridden," John answered for his brother when he walked into the new barn. This past year he had overseen the construction of a new barn to house the Highland cows. He had created an area that was perfect for guests to come and pet, groom, or just plain hug the cows.

"But Paaaaa." Daisy's complaint ended with her little lip protruding.

John put his hands on his hips and looked at his daughter. She continued to pout, and he sighed. "How about we go see about riding some sheep this spring? Maybe you can even enter the rodeo for mutton bustin'."

Roman had never been happier to see his brother. He stood up from where he sat with Cream and joined John next to Daisy. "Brother, I'm glad you came in when you did." He chuckled and made his escape.

Daisy always seemed to get her way with him. John was learning to say no to his little girl, but Roman had yet to figure out how to stand up to that perfect pout.

He really hoped he'd only have boys when he eventually married. They were so much easier to deal with.

As Roman left the barn, he heard Daisy's excited scream and chatter about finally being able to join the kids when they did the mutton bustin'. Although, if Roman were being honest with himself, he thought she should have done it at the last rodeo when she asked. He was only five when he competed in his first rodeo. All of the Manning brothers were only five when they began mutton bustin'.

Chapter 8

Today was the day. They were headed into Beacon Creek, and tonight after she finished her setup, she'd be going out for that steak dinner with Roman Manning. Sierra wasn't sure if those were butterflies in her stomach or if it was bees zipping around as a warning to her.

Annie still wasn't on board with Sierra dating a cowboy who had basically followed her to Livingston. It never went well when a cowboy trailed a carnie. And Sierra wasn't exactly the sort to mess around with cowboys and move on. Neither was Annie, but there were plenty of other women in the carnival who did just that. Annie hoped and prayed that Sierra wouldn't end up like them.

"Annie, have you ever seen me even kiss a cowboy?" She turned her head toward her friend and arched an imperious brow.

"No, but I do know how persistent these men can be." Not that Annie let cowboys push her around, for she didn't. But she had had her share of bad experiences. Thankfully, Stella always seemed to have a sixth sense about when her rolling pin was needed and she showed up before anything bad could happen. Well, anything bad to Annie. The immoral cowboys? The same couldn't always be said for their safety.

"Don't worry about me. Stella's taught me a thing or two about defending myself." Sierra snickered, remembering how the sweet woman also had a really mean streak when someone crossed her or those she loved.

Annie laughed outright. "You know, if she taught you the same techniques she's grilled into me all these years I've been with her, then I think you'll do just fine." She pursed her lips and held up one finger. "Just remember, call me if you need help burying the body. I've got a shovel just itchin' ta be used."

"Thanks, Annie." Sierra chuckled. "But I don't think I'll be needin' to bury any bodies any time soon." At least, she hoped not.

"You go ahead and laugh, but trust me, if you use some of those moves Stella taught ya, you just might need some help." Annie waggled her index finger and glared at Sierra.

"I hope you aren't speaking from experience." Sierra pursed her lips, trying to keep from laughing. She knew better than anyone that Annie couldn't hurt a fly. Which was why Stella was always around, hefting her heavy rolling pin.

Annie waved a hand. "Nah, not me." She winked.

Before Sierra could ask what her friend meant, they pulled into the fairgrounds. The rodeo wasn't due to open until Friday night, but there were already a lot of horse trailers and people setting up pens, corrals, and cleaning the stands. While they had been in Beacon Creek for their Christmas festival, they had never been here for their fall harvest festival. The amount of people working to set up the entire area astounded her. "Look at all of this."

"Whoa, this is gonna be one of those biggens," Stella said when the girls hopped out of the truck.

"Did you know this was one of the larger events we'd do?" Sierra asked.

"Well, being here for a week was a clue, and Red said this one would make more than we made for the entirety of August, but I didn't realize it was *this* big." Stella whistled and walked away rubbing her hands together.

"Do you think there'll be more food trucks than what normally accompany us?" Sierra looked around, mouth agape, and began drooling when she thought about those elephant ears she'd had the last time she was here. That particular food truck didn't travel with them. When she asked Red about it, he told her it was a local one.

Annie mimicked Sierra as she twirled around, checking out the area. "Oh, yeah. We don't have nearly enough food trucks to handle the sort of crowd that will be here."

"I take it we're gonna be extremely busy this next week." Sierra smiled. They were paid for each carnival based on what the entire company made. When they hit a certain revenue point, each member of the team received bonus checks. This would most definitely be a bonus check kind of week. It would also mean a lot of work, but work well worth it. She could bank the extra money for her next excursion. Maybe she'd even stay in the state for the winter if she made enough over the next two months.

"You got that right." Red snuck up on the girls, and they both jumped.

"Don't do that!" Sierra complained. Then she reminded herself it was time to watch her back. This was going to be a scary place after all the families left and the drunks came out. If only the carnivals and rodeos wouldn't sell beer. But they always had a beer garden. And why did they call it a "garden?" It wasn't as though beer grew in an actual garden. And all that alcohol never made the place pretty. Well, maybe those drinking the beer thought there were flowers and plants all over the place. But she always steered clear of that area.

"Alright, if you want your date night tonight with loverboy"—Red waggled his brows—"then you need to stop gawkin' and get to workin'."

"Yes sir, Red, sir." Sierra gave a half-hearted solute and walked to the back of her truck, where they towed the booth for her game. She and Annie got to work setting it up. They had done this so many times that when they focused, they could have the entire booth up and ready to go in less than three hours.

Today, it took them a mite over three hours. Only because the two girls yacked up a storm about Roman and his mocha-latte eyes.

Annie rolled her eyes. "Oh, please. You sound like a girl in love. Please, tell me you've not gone and fallen in love with a cowboy. That's my job."

Sierra let the box of red rings drop to her feet. "I thought you knew me better than that. I don't have time for love."

"Then what are you doing with him?" Annie finished putting up the red, white, and blue bunting that wrapped around the top of their booth.

"I'm just letting off some steam. Tracking my dad these past few years has really taken its toll on my nerves." With a handful of rubber duckies, she began placing them in the cold-water pond they'd just finished filling in the center of their booth. Sierra looked up at her friend. "Wasn't it you who told me I needed to find something new to do for a while?"

Annie redid her ponytail and glared at Sierra. "I said you needed a hobby, not a boyfriend."

"You said a hobby, or something." Sierra shrugged. "I took that to mean it was time I tried something new. So here I am, trying something new."

With hammer in hand, Annie went to the corner of their booth and began putting up one end of their sign. After hammering in the three nails used to keep the one side secure, she pointed the weapon at Sierra. "Just don't come crying to me when he breaks your heart. I don't do the girly tear stuff."

"Oh, please." Sierra rolled her eyes. "You most certainly do like the girly tear stuff. Remember that time when you got your heart broken and you brought back a pint of Ben & Jerry's phish food? Then put a rom-com in the DVD player? I don't think I've seen that many romantic movies in one weekend, ever." She pointed at her friend.

Annie was smart enough to shrink into herself and put the hammer down. "Well, I may do the girly tear stuff, but you've never been into it."

"That's right, I haven't. Maybe it's time I took a turn." Sierra twirled around and giggled.

"Alright, enough chatter. How much do you have left on your booth?" Stella put her hands on her hips and glared at her girls. While she raised Annie, Sierra had become an adoptive daughter ever since the two girls began running the duck booth together almost three years earlier.

Sierra looked around. "Looks like Annie's almost done with the sign. Then we just need to do touch-up paint to the booth itself before organizing the prizes."

The prizes were always the last thing to go up. Sometimes they put them up the night before the carnival opened and sometimes not until the next morning before it started. This time, they were going to put them all up before finishing for the night. That way they didn't have to be to their booth until fifteen minutes before they opened in the morning. They didn't usually open until noon on day one, which gave them a lazy morning.

Since Sierra had a date that night, she'd get to sleep in and not have to worry about doing anything other than wiping down the countertops and ensuring everything was in its place after they pulled back the drapes that covered the entire booth overnight.

Stella swiped her hand in the air. "Go on, get going. I'll help Annie finish. You've got a date with a handsome man tonight." She grinned. "But before you leave, I want to make sure you haven't forgotten everything I taught you."

Sierra held up her hand. "I've got my pepper spray. And I *never* go home with the guy, even if he says it's so I can meet his family." She rolled her eyes. Like any guy would want to bring home a girl on a first date to meet his family.

Well, any sane guy.

Sierra's phone pinged and she pulled it out of her pants' pocket. She smiled when she saw the notification that it was from Roman. She opened the text and read it to herself.

Sierra, I can't believe UR finally here. Where should I pick you up?

Hey there. How @ meeting me at the main entrance 2 the carnival, right next 2 the giant orange slide?

Perfect. Will U still be ready at 6?

Yup. C U Then.

With a bounce in her step, Sierra practically ran to her trailer to clean up and get ready for her date. Her first date since she'd joined the carnival. It wasn't that she was against dating, it was more that she had been so laser-focused on searching for her dad that she'd never once accepted an offer from any of the men who had asked her. Not even the guys she suspected were nice. At least, not until she met Roman.

The fact that he kept crossing her path told her *someone* was trying to get her attention. Then when Roman said something about his sister's ministry, she started thinking about God again. It had been almost three years since she'd last attended a church service, mainly because they didn't have time for church when they were always on the road or operating a carnival on Sundays.

When Sierra first joined the carnival, she knew she wouldn't get to attend services, but she thought she could keep up with her Bible reading and that would be enough for God. While she wasn't sure what God thought, she quickly found that she didn't have time to read her Bible on a regular basis, either. She was always too tired to get up early. And she was too sleepy at night before bed. In the beginning she did try reading God's word before bed, but she always fell asleep after only a few verses, so she stopped altogether.

The fact that this man freely mentioned God, and told her each week about the church service he attended, made her wonder if the Creator of all wasn't trying to get her attention. And because of this thought, she had found time twice in the past week to read her Bible.

God was there, just waiting for her to come back to Him.

It wasn't as though she'd just decided one day to turn her back on Him; her movement away from her savior was a slow process. One she didn't even realize she had done until she met Roman. One of the first text conversations they had was about God.

Roman had asked her if she ever had time to attend church. When she said she didn't, he asked her point blank if she was a Christian. As a little girl, Sierra had accepted God as her Lord and personal savior. And while her grandma was alive, she attended every Sunday and most mid-week services as well. But after her grandma died and she was all alone, it was easy to stop going. No one around her attended church. Most Sundays they were working a carnival, so they couldn't go.

At first it did bug Sierra that she couldn't go to church, but she reasoned with herself that God would understand. She was searching for her dad, after all. Didn't her Father in Heaven want her to have family around?

It wasn't until recently that she realized she'd gone about this all wrong. There was always an early Sunday morning service wherever they were. She could have managed going, even on days they were open. Laziness took over, or was it complacency? Either way, she was going to have to take a good hard look at what she was doing.

She made it to the front of the carnival two minutes until six, thinking she'd get there first. But when she walked up to the booth and looked around, she saw a smiling cowboy with a Stetson watching her. He was already there, holding a bouquet of bright-pink Gerbera daisies.

She smiled shyly when he held them out for her. "You remembered."

"Of course I did. Most women like roses or wildflowers. It's not too often someone says their favorite flower is a Gerbera daisy." Roman felt a zing down to his toes when Sierra touched his hand to take the offered flowers.

"I just think they look like sunshine on a stick. Know what I mean?" She put the petals to her nose and inhaled.

Roman chuckled. "Sunshine on a stick? Is that because you work in a carnival?" He always thought Gerbera daisies were bright and made women smile. Shoot, even he couldn't help but smile when he looked at daisies. Any type of daisy.

Sierra pursed her lips and tilted her head to the side. "Yeah, I guess so." She chuckled. "Before, I would have said they made me smile. My grandma had various colors in her garden and, well, they remind me of her."

When Sierra's smile vanished and a ghost of sadness crossed her features, Roman stopped himself from asking more about her grandma. When she was ready, he reasoned, she would share more. Until then, they needed to head out for dinner.

The drive to Bozeman went too fast for Roman's liking. Since it was just the two of them in the truck, they conversed easily and Sierra told him a little bit about her family.

"When I was only five, my momma passed away from cancer." With her elbow on the door where it met the window, Sierra put her chin in her hand and looked at the landscape as they drove by.

Keeping his eyes on the road since they were driving through the curvy part, Roman felt her grief. "I'm so sorry for your loss. I can't imagine what it must be like to lose a parent."

"Thanks, but that was a long time ago. I barely remember her."

After a pregnant pause, he asked, "What about your pa?"

She shook her head. "He left me with my grandma a year later. I haven't heard from him in over twelve years."

Roman took in a deep breath. The fact that a father left his motherless daughter and never bothered to return infuriated him. He thought about Daisy and all of the difficulty John went through to get her and wondered what sort of man could let his daughter go like that. "I'm sorry. That must be just as tough as losing your momma."

"Actually, it's worse. I know he's out there, somewhere. But I can't seem to find him."

With a quick look at Sierra, Roman turned his eyes back on the road. "You've been looking for him?"

"Yup. It's why I joined the carnival to begin with." She chuckled.

"Wait, you joined the carnival to find your pa? Was he a carnie?"

"Not that I know of." She looked at Roman, and he could feel her eyes on him. "I joined to have a way of traveling around and meeting a lot of different people.

Over the years I've gotten bits of information on him, and the last anyone has heard he was in Montana."

"Really?" Roman blinked a few times. "What's his name? Maybe I've met him."

"As far as I know, he's never been in the Beacon Creek area." She put her hands in her lap and sighed.

"Well, I know a lot of cowboys all over the state. If he's moved around, he's most likely a ranch or farmhand. And there's a good chance I've either met him or heard his name."

She shrugged. "His name is Bartholomew Baker."

Roman searched his memory for a Mr. Baker. Try as he might, he couldn't think of anyone with that name. "Is that your last name? Baker?"

Sierra nodded. "Yup."

"Do you look like him?"

Her lips twisted and her eyes narrowed, as though she were searching her mind for a memory of her father. "Not really. He's blond but he's really tall." She laughed. "I got my lack of height from my momma. She was even shorter than my 5'3" frame. Most of my looks came from her. Or at least, that's what grandma said."

"Was she your momma's mom?" He had wanted to talk about her grandma, but he also remembered the sadness when she first mentioned her, so he waited for her to bring up the topic.

"Yes." Sierra smiled. "She was. And she told me all kinds of stories about my momma growing up. I even slept in my momma's childhood room. It helped me to feel closer to her growing up."

"And I take it there was nothing there to remind you of your pa?"

"He and my grandma never got along."

That was a story Roman wanted to hear more of, but they pulled into the steakhouse parking lot and he decided it was probably not the best time to ask questions about her missing father.

"Wait here," Roman said as he exited the truck and made his way around to her door.

His momma had raised him to open doors for ladies and help them out of trucks, especially when they wore dresses and heels, like what Sierra had worn that night. She was beautiful in her pink-and-white polka dot sundress and white, heeled sandals. He liked her strappy shoes even though he had no idea what they were called. He didn't see too many women in sandals. Most wore pretty boots with their dresses. Even at the dances most wore boots and dresses.

"Thank you." Sierra smiled up at him and put her hand in his when he opened her door for her. Then she stepped out and he held her hand as they walked into the restaurant.

"Do you like chocolate?" Roman asked after they had been seated and handed their menus.

She peeked over the top of her menu and grinned. "What woman doesn't?"

Roman chuckled. "Perfect. This is why I came here instead of going to a restaurant in town."

When the waitress came by to take their orders, they ordered steak, but Roman also ordered the chocolate crème brûlée they were famous for.

When the puffy dessert was brought to their table along with long spoons, two plates, and two scoops of vanilla bean ice cream, Sierra turned a confused look to Roman. "I've heard of crème brûlée before, but I've never seen it."

The decadent dessert was in a large ramekin designed for two people to share. A fluffy chocolate cake-like topping was puffed up above the edge of the dish. And powdered sugar was sprinkled on top. A large scoop of ice cream was on each plate the waitress placed in front of them, along with chocolate sauce drizzled across the plate in a haphazard pattern. And a sprig of mint adorned the edge of the plate with a raspberry on top.

"I know, I always hate eating the dessert and messing up the beauty of the presentation. But trust me, the moment you take your first bite, you'll know that it was well worth messing up." Roman put his spoon in the top of the chocolate puff and watched as a bit of hot air escaped when he broke the seal.

"Oh, that's pretty." Sierra put her spoon in the dessert and brought out a bit of the cake topping and chocolate cream. Then added a little bit of vanilla bean ice cream to her spoon before putting it in her mouth.

Roman watched in awe as Sierra closed her eyes and moaned after taking her first taste of the decadent dessert. She slowly brought the spoon out of her mouth and her lashes fluttered open as she swallowed. His mouth watered watching her.

"That was the best dessert I've ever tasted. I see what you mean about it being worth destroying the presentation." She reached for another bite.

Roman's first bite still sat on the spoon in front of his face, forgotten as he watched the beautiful woman across the table from him.

When she noticed, she stared at him. "What? Do I have something on my face?"

He shook his head. "No, sorry. I was enjoying watching you eat the crème brûlée." He felt his face heat up, and he quickly added some vanilla ice cream to his spoon before taking a bite.

"Mmm, I never tire of getting this dessert." He took another bite and was careful to keep his eyes off her lips as she took more of the dessert. Roman had never wanted to kiss a woman as much as he wanted to kiss Sierra right then and there.

"I'm so glad you brought me here. The steak was fantastic, better than any I've had before. And trust me, I've had my fair share of great steak." Her spoon took another dip into the chocolate bliss. "But this is beyond chocolate. I don't think I've ever had anything even close to it before." She put the spoon filled with chocolate cream and ice cream in her mouth and moaned again.

Roman was going to go nuts if she didn't stop tempting him. He was about ready to jump across the table and pull her into his arms and kiss her until she said *his* kisses where the sweetest thing she'd ever had.

Man, he needed to stop watching those blasted rom-coms with his mother and sisters. They were getting to him.

When their dishes had been cleared away and Roman paid the check, it was time to leave. He couldn't remember when he'd had such a wonderful date. This was better than he had hoped. The only problem: she moved around so much.

"How long will you be in the area?" Roman asked as he opened the restaurant door for Sierra.

"We're here all week. Once the festival is over, we'll get a short break to pack up and rest before heading out to our next event. It isn't until a week from Friday, and it's only a day and a half drive, so Red said we can rest in Beacon Creek before heading out the Wednesday after your festival ends."

Sierra noticed a tall blond man across the street.

As had been her habit the past three years while searching for her father, any time a tall blond caught her attention, she turned to look. Anticipation filled her entire being. But the man across the street had a rugged look to him, and she got a foreboding vibe when he looked their way. It couldn't be him. Her dad, while he had neglected her, never had such a tough look. His eyes had been loving and soft. The man across the street glared at her and Roman.

She didn't like the way he watched them. "We should probably get going."

Roman looked to where she had been staring and stiffened. "Ignore him. But you're right, we should get moving. You've got a long day ahead of you tomorrow, and I promised I wouldn't keep you out late tonight." He opened her truck door and helped her inside.

After he closed the truck door, Roman looked across the street and returned the man's glare. Sierra watched as Roman walked around the front of the truck, not taking his eyes off the man.

Later that night, Sierra dreamed of her father falling off a cliff, lifting his hands out to her asking for her to save him. When she woke up with a start, she put her hand on her chest and looked around. She was safe, in her trailer. She wasn't on the edge of a cliff watching her father fall to his death.

Chapter 9

S ierra looked out at the crowd with a dreamy smile plastered across her face. Nothing had gotten under skin that day, not even when a group of teens tried to steal one of the ducks right off the booth. She laughed at them and said she'd tell their mommas if they did it.

They all looked at her and fear crossed their faces. The older of the group narrowed his eyes. "How do you know our mommas?"

She grinned. "Oh, I don't, but I'm sure Roman Manning does." She waved to him as he walked past.

He returned her grin and tipped his hat her way.

"Come on, it's not worth it," the older boy said as he stopped trying to get the giant duck off the wire holding it in place.

The thing they didn't realize was that the ducks on the outer edge were wired into place. At the end of the night, if needed they could be moved into the center of

85

the booth. That's where the ducks were up on "J" hooks, which made it easy to hand over prizes. The ones on the outer edge were there just to entice players.

Sierra smiled through the whole ordeal while Anna scowled and worried they'd have trouble. Once their booth was empty, Anna looked at her friend. "Okay, what gives? You've had this"—she motioned with her hand around Sierra's face—"goofy grin all day long. I take it your date went extremely well last night?"

"Better than I could have ever hoped." Sierra sighed and looked off into space.

"Uh, oh. That's not good." Annie tsk'd and shook her head.

Sierra frowned for the first time that day. "What do you mean? I thought a great date was what all women wanted?"

"Oh, it is." Annie nodded enthusiastically. "But what happens now?"

"Now?"

"Yeah. Now that you've had a fantastic date, you'll want to see Roman again, right?"

"Of course." Sierra had already made plans to spend her dinner break with Roman. Even though carnie food didn't make it a date, he said he'd bring a picnic basket full of dinner, which did make it a date.

"Okay, and when this week ends and we leave for the next stop?" Annie arched a brow.

It took Sierra a moment, then she deflated and her grin turned upside down. "I hadn't really thought that far."

"Exactly. I don't want you to get hurt. And if you're already all gaga-googoo over the cowboy, what's to say you don't fall in love by the end of the week? Then where will you be?" She put her hands on her hips and watched the emotions crossing her friend's face.

"Love? Do you really think I could fall in love in only a week?" Sierra always thought love took time, and wasn't something that could happen in days.

"Sweetie, how long have you known him now?"

"Oh." She realized she hadn't only known him for days, but for weeks. And if you counted the first time they saw each other, then it was over a year and a half ago. But she wasn't falling in love with the handsome man. Was she?

Annie sighed. "Just, well"—she scratched her cheek—"be careful. I've seen it before. Carnie girls fall head over heels for a local boy and they leave the carnival only to be back a few months later with their heart broken. I don't want you to fall for the guy thinking he would marry you only to find out it was a passing fancy of his."

Sierra shook her head. "I can't quit the team now—I still have to find my dad. Until then, I'm not going to settle down anywhere. Or with anyone."

"You tell yourself that now, but wait." Annie took two dollars from a cowboy standing there with his little girl. "If that cowboy of yours asks you to stay, you'll do it."

"No, I won't." Sierra looked at the little girl playing the game and recognized her. It took her a minute, but when the girl stuck her lower lip out after not winning, it hit her. "Daisy? Is that you?" She walked closer to the girl in a pink-and-white checked blouse with blue jeans and pink cowboy boots.

"You remember me? I won a duck at this game two Christmases ago." Daisy beamed with pride.

The cowboy with her smiled. "You must be Sierra. Roman told me all about you. I'm John, Daisy's dad." He put his hand out.

She took it and gave it a hearty shake. "Nice to meet you, John." She looked to the little girl. "And it's very good to see you again. I'm surprised you didn't win to-day."

Daisy's little lip protruded once more. "Pa, I wanna play again."

John chuckled and pulled out another two dollars. "Alright, my little princess. Your wish is my command." He bowed to his daughter before giving the money to Sierra.

Sierra couldn't help but smile. It reminded her of her dad when she was very little. He had showered her with love and attention, which was why she had such a hard time with him just leaving her. For a long time, she thought he had died and no one knew how to reach her. But over the past few years she'd learned he was still alive, just traveling around.

Both of them watched as little Daisy tossed her red rings at the rubber duckies floating in the water. Part of what made the game so hard was the tiny current moving the ducks around the pond. Most people aimed for where the duck was at, but by the time the ring got there, the duck had moved just enough that they missed the head.

Daisy, however, seemed to have a grasp on how the game went. For on her fourth and final toss, she snagged a duck head and the ring went down the neck.

"Winner!" Sierra and Annie both yelled out as Daisy jumped up and down yelling.

"I think we better warn all of the game operators this week. Your little girl is a ringer," Sierra joked as she pulled down a duck and handed it to the winner.

And as usual, the commotion brought over more players. A line quickly formed, and both operators turned their attention to the new players.

Roman had spent the morning and part of the afternoon at the space they had rented for the cow cuddling. He was finalizing the setup of the corrals and deciding how best to decorate the cuddling spaces. They had four spots set up with a tiny pen, water trough, and a place for someone to sit if they so chose. All under the protection of a large tent.

The patrons would get fifteen minutes in the corral with the cow of their choosing, and Roman wanted them to be comfortable. But he also needed to give the cows room to move around, or to walk back to the larger corral where they had privacy.

Their booth would open the next day, and he wanted it to be perfect. They already had people stopping by checking out what they were up to. He knew they should have started their setup earlier. It galled him to no end that his cow cuddling had missed opening day.

"Roman, your new girlfriend is nice. Daisy likes her, too," John said when he closed the corral door behind him. He had taken Daisy to River, and the two of them were going to hit up the kiddie rides.

Roman's head popped up from the cow he was cuddling. It wasn't that he needed to cuddle a cow, it was that he wanted to make sure the cows understood they'd be working in these corrals this week, so he was going to bring each of them into the corrals and spend a little time with each. Now that John was here, he would help.

"My girlfriend?" He quirked a brow.

"Yes, but you need to take it slow. Be sure you don't ask her to stay after the week is over." John chuckled. "I overheard her and her friend talking about you. Her friend was asking what she'd do about you now that she was falling for you." He slapped his brother's shoulder.

"What are you talking about?" Roman stood up and guided Peaches back to the main holding pen.

"Sierra, of course. I think she's falling in love with you already." He grinned at his younger brother, then helped to bring Cream out front.

Roman stopped in his tracks and took a deep breath. "John, we've been on one official date. Please don't try to get us married off before we even know each other." Even though Sierra said they could count that one day they had lunch together as a date if he took her out to a real dinner, not carnie food, when they got to town he

90

had decided he would honor her idea that carnival food did not make a date.

With another chuckle, John went into the main pen and found Butterscotch and brought her out. "Oh, I'm not the one pushing you two to get serious. It sounds like it already is." He waggled his brows.

Roman decided his brother was just razzin' him, and instead of playing his game he ignored him. "Take Butterscotch back—she's already spent time out front. Grab any of the others besides Peaches."

"You know"—John turned around and headed back to the big pen with Butterscotch—"it would be a better show if we had Scotty here for everyone to check out."

"No way. I'm not ready to have a bull on display. We still don't know enough about their temperament. The last thing we need is to have any of our bulls goring a kid." Even if a kid snuck into the pen on his own, Roman knew they'd be on the hook for any injuries. It was going to be tough enough keeping people out of the main pens with just the docile cows.

"True, but Scotty is so good with Daisy."

"And we're always around when Daisy visits him at home. There aren't kids running and screaming and all sorts of other animals around that he doesn't know. We can probably have a few older cows next year on display, but I don't want to take any chances."

John agreed. "You're probably right. But can you imagine the amount of traffic we'd get with a full-blooded Scottish Highland bull out for all to see? The people would love it."

"And that's exactly why I have these flyers with Scotty on the front." He pointed to a stack of light-blue trifold flyers highlighting their services. At one point, Roman did consider putting in their prices for a side of beef, in case anyone wanted to buy some, but he thought better of it. Maybe next year they could create the Highland Beef Food Truck, or something like that. He'd come up with a better name, but serving burgers and steaks from a Highland cow could really help get the word out about this healthier beef.

John picked up a copy and checked it out. He turned all the pages and read the content. "Dude, you've really thought this through, haven't you?" He looked at his younger brother, pride evident in his eyes.

Roman took a brush and began grooming Cream. "I have. I think this is where I want to focus. I've even been thinking I should get my own ranch and raise strictly Highland cows, and of course breed a few with Angus so I can have my own cow-cuddling services. Or maybe if I can get a ranch close enough, I take over the entire Triple J cuddling operation."

"You know, when we first started looking into this it was more for River and Daisy. But I do enjoy this part of ranching, too." John took a serious look at his brother. "How much have you saved for a ranch?"

"Why, you think you wanna partner up with me and start our own family ranch?" Roman joked, but as he said it he thought it might not be a bad idea. He and John were close in age, and had always been allies growing up. They were brothers and they had their fair share of fighting, but over the past seven or eight years their relationship had grown and they were friends as well as brothers. It might be nice to have John's help on a ranch of their own.

"I hadn't thought of that, but it is something to consider. Although, I wouldn't want to move out of the area. Do you know of any ranches that might be coming up for sale any time soon?" John wasn't one for cuddling, so he picked up a brush and started grooming Snickers. The Highland/Angus cow breed had caramel-brown fur mixed with peanut brown and a little bit of milk chocolate. He made Daisy think of a Snickers bar when he was born, hence the name.

"Honestly, I haven't even started looking. I'm still saving my money, what little I have after paying off student loans and my truck each month." Roman had made pretty good money off his family ranch, especially now that they had the new line of revenue from the new breeds. But his school loans were high and he wanted to get them paid off before doing anything else, so he'd been paying triple what his monthly payment was. He would have it all paid off in less than four years instead of the standard ten. He still had over two and a half years of payments to go if he continued at this rate.

One of his goals with this festival was to bring in more clients to make more money so he could pay his student loans off even faster. It was too early to tell if they'd make more from the festival or not. But if the interest from just the local ranchers who were setting up their booths was any indication, this year just might be better than he'd hoped.

"Well, let's get through this week and then we can talk. I have some money set aside for building a house. If River agrees, maybe we can all go in on a new ranch." John continued grooming Snickers, who mooed a few times. She really enjoyed being brushed. That was her favorite thing, but she was also good with most everyone when they came to cuddle her.

Roman only hoped that all of the cows they brought this week would be good with the cuddling.

Chapter 10

S ierra and Annie came early on day three to the Triple J Ranch cow-cuddling pen, just like Roman had suggested. When they had dinner together the night before—steak barbecue from one of the food trucks—Roman tried calling it date number four, but Sierra reminded him that carnie food wasn't a date. Even if it was the best steak she'd ever had from a food truck.

Roman chuckled. "You haven't had Triple J Ranch barbecue yet. Why don't you come by the pens tomorrow morning and I'll bring you a taste of what you've been missing? And you can even cuddle a cow."

She raised her brows. "You know how I feel about hugging animals." She held up her hands when he began to protest. "Now wait. I love cats and dogs. They should be hugged or cuddled, or whatever." She circled her hand in the air near her face. "But cows? Come on. Those are a bit big and dangerous, don't you think?"

He put his arm around her shoulders and sighed. "Oh, Sierra. You may think you've experienced a lot of what the world has to offer, but you haven't seen anything until you've felt the affection from a cow. Especially one bred from a Highland bull."

Sierra pursed her lips and narrowed her eyes. "Alright, I'll try your beef and hug your cow tomorrow morning. But Annie has to come, too. She'll never believe me when I tell her what I've done." She chuckled.

After he removed his arm from around her, he rubbed the back of his neck, considering her request. Then he nodded. "Alright, bring your friend along. You'll both be amazed. And neither of you will ever be happy with steak again." Roman grinned.

"You think pretty highly of your cattle, don't you?"

"Hey, it's not arrogance if it's the truth." The lights from the nearby pole glinted off his smile, and Sierra shook her head.

"We shall see, Mr. Big Shot. We shall see."

Annie rubbed her hands as she and Sierra walked up to the booth. "I heard you have the best steak in all of the country. Even better than a Texas barbecue."

"Well, good morning to you, too." Roman stood up after grooming one of the cows. "And yes, we do. But first, I'd like to introduce you to Peaches and Cream." He pointed to the two yearlings, one white as cream while the other looked as yellow as a fresh peach on a hot summer day, with a few dollops of cream on top.

"Oh, aren't they just the cutest." Sierra walked over to Peaches and knelt to pet her soft fur. "These are crossbreeds from the Scottish Highland cow you told me about?" She looked up as she continued to stroke the cow's fur.

Roman nodded. "Yes, and"—he turned to look at Annie—"don't worry, they won't bite. Just kneel down and run your hands along Cream's sides. Or, if you like"—he handed her a brush—"you can groom her. She actually prefers grooming."

"What about Peaches?" Sierra looked between the cow under her hand and Roman.

"You picked the cow that just loves to be cuddled." Roman chuckled.

Both girls took turns hugging and grooming the cows. Cream warmed up to Annie and even gave her shoulder a slight nudge and mooed her enjoyment of their time together.

Roman only wanted them to spend about ten minutes with the cows since they'd be working off and on all day. He didn't want them to become tired of people too soon. "How about we put the cows away and I share the sliders I brought?" He waggled his brows and pointed to an aluminum pan on chafing dishes.

"Sliders, huh? Afraid steak alone won't be tasty? You had to add biscuits and"—Sierra took a peek at what was under the lids—"cheese and a ton of barbecue sauce."

Roman's mouth watered. It had been a few hours since he had an early breakfast, and his stomach was more than ready for what it knew was going to be a superior mid-morning snack. "Just you wait and see."

After they had put the cows away and washed their hands, Roman served them each a full plate of his family's famous barbecue beef brisket sliders.

Sierra licked her lips when she smelled the spices and sweetness of the sauce. "Mmm." Before she even finished swallowing the small bite she'd taken, she bit off a larger amount and moaned again. Once she finished her entire slider, she said, "Alright, you win. This was the best beef I've ever had." She licked the dripping homemade barbecue sauce off her fingers. "Where can I buy this sauce?"

The cowboy looked between both girls, evidence all over their faces and hands that they had indeed enjoyed their Triple J Ranch barbecue sliders. "You can't."

Annie stopped with a finger in her mouth. Before she finished licking off the sauce, she said, "Share." Then she growled.

Roman laughed. "This sauce is homemade by my dad. We don't sell it."

Sierra's brows rose. "Seriously? But this is the best sauce—ever. I can't remember tasting something with the perfect mix of spices and sugar." She narrowed one eye. "What's the secret?"

He shook his head. "Sorry, I can't say. But I will let my pa know that you loved it."

"Seriously, dude, this is the best. And I've been all over the country and tried barbecue from Texas to Louisiana and up to St. Louis. Nothing is as good as this." She licked her last finger clean of the homemade sauce.

"I'm very glad to hear this." Caleb Manning walked up and put a hand on his son's shoulder. "Why don't you make sure your friends get a jar of it before they leave this week, Roman?"

"Sure thing, Pa. And I'd like to introduce you to Sierra Baker"—Roman waved between the girls—" and her friend Annie." He furrowed his brows. "You know, I don't think I ever caught your last name, Annie."

"That's because I don't have one." Annie shrugged.

"She generally goes by Annie No-Name." Sierra nudged her friend and grinned.

"Nice to meet you, ladies. I hope my son is being a gentleman?" Caleb tipped his hat at each woman, completely ignoring the strange response to Annie's name.

Roman kept quiet, but looked as though he wanted to ask more about her name. Maybe it was just a carnie thing? He wasn't sure, so he decided to ask Sierra about it later.

"Yes, he is," Sierra answered.

"Good. When do you ladies leave? I'd love to have you both out to our ranch for a proper barbecue when the festival is over." Caleb loved to entertain, and if single women caught the eyes of his single sons, then it was even better. Since Roman was the last of his unmarried children, they didn't have quite as many single visitors lately as they once did.

Sierra sucked her lips in between her teeth. "Ah, we work all day until the festival ends, and then we'll only have Tuesday night open." She looked to Roman, who watched her intently.

He hadn't had the chance yet, but Roman had been planning on asking Sierra if she would go out with him on her last night in town. He wanted a proper date, one that would count. Which meant dinner somewhere besides a food truck.

A barbecue at their ranch would be perfect. "Yes, I was going to see about taking you out that night, but I think having a barbecue—with the added bonus of dessert by our firepit—would be a perfect way to spend your last night in town."

"I'm game. Especially if this sauce is included." Annie wiped her hands on her napkin and licked her lips.

Sierra chuckled. "Well, if Annie's in, then so am I. What time should we be there?"

"How about five?" Roman looked to his father, who nodded. They wouldn't start eating at five, but that would give them some time to all sit around and chat while Matthew and their dad finished grilling the steaks, burgers, and ribs. With so many people in their family, and the addition of kids, they now had various offerings on the grill.

"Perfect, text me your address and we'll drive the truck out that night." Sierra cleaned her hands and waved as she walked back to her booth. They still had to prepare before the carnival opened in less than twenty minutes.

As they walked back, Annie looked over her shoulder and noticed Roman watching them. "He can be pretty intense, can't he?"

"Hm?" Sierra had been in her mind, thinking about Roman and how good he looked in his jeans, red-and-black checked snap-up shirt, and black Stetson. She had never been big on cowboy hats, but now she understood why the Stetson was so popular. The famous hat had its own aura, or personality. Like the cows did. That hat gave Roman a sense of mystery and awe when she looked at him.

"Roman. You know, your new boyfriend who's watching us walk away?" Annie giggled.

Sierra looked back over her shoulder and sent Roman a sweet smile before she looked down and back to where she was going. "Shh, be quiet. He'll hear you. And he's not my boyfriend—we just met."

"After texting each other for weeks and dreaming about him for almost two years." Annie took off before Sierra could hit her.

Sierra ran after her friend, and they were laughing when they made it to their booth.

Red stood there with his arms folded over his chest, glaring at them. "Where have you two been? It's just about time to open and you're not ready. You two are always ready." His lips were in a tight line and he let loose a heavy breath, almost like a bull getting ready to charge.

"Whoa, now. We were just checking out the cow cuddling before it opened for the day." Annie put her hands up and moved to get inside the booth so she could start the opening process.

Sierra smiled and patted Red on the shoulder. "Don't worry, we'll have it done before anyone shows up." She walked to the side, where she began pulling the curtain back across the front of the booth, showcasing the game and the oversized stuffed ducks hanging from the top.

"Hmph. You better." Red walked away grumbling under his breath.

"You know, he hates it when I date anyone. But I think he never expected you to fall for a cowboy." Annie nudged her friend as they put out the red rings along the side of the pond.

The handful of red rings Sierra held fell into the water. "Hey, watch it." She put her hands in and pulled them right back out. "Whoa, that's cold. It must have been really cold overnight."

Annie put her hand into the water and laughed. "Ah, it's not too bad. Wait for the winter carnival, then it'll get really cold overnight."

"I'm just glad we have a heater in our trailer and plenty of blankets." Sierra shivered and her hand dove for the last of the red rings.

They were the consummate team, and had their booth ready to go before the first patrons even walked by.

"So, that's the girl who's had you all tied up in knots lately?" Caleb teased his youngest son as they prepared their booth for the first of the customers that would come by that morning. "I was wondering when I'd get to meet her." He nodded. "I approve."

Since their booth opened yesterday, they'd had a non-stop line of customers from the moment the fair opened until after it closed. They even had to cut off the line the previous night because it was too long.

Ignoring his father, Roman asked about the stock. "Do you think we could bring some of the regular yearlings in for cuddling? That way we can give our cows a bit of a break. I hate to work them so long."

"I was thinking the same thing. None of us knew this was going to be so successful. I asked John to bring out six of the nicest Angus yearlings he could find. We could offer them in one stall and the Highland mix in the other three stalls." Caleb gathered up the trash from the early morning steak slider treats and walked to the trash can across from their booth.

When he went back to his son, Roman stood there looking over their cattle. "John wanted to bring Scotty out and just keep him in the large pen. Do you think having a full-blooded Scottish Highland bull would be good?"

Caleb rubbed his clean-shaven chin. "I think if we needed more attention, we could make it work. But as it is, we have a full pen and a line already starting. We don't need any more attention." He chuckled and pointed to the women lining up outside their booth.

Roman shook his head, amazed at the popularity of their booth.

Later that morning, with lines still too long for them to get to everyone, the fair coordinators came by.

"Luther, good to see you. What can we do for you?" Caleb had just come back to their booth with lunch for the team.

Roman, John, River, Daisy, and Matthew were there manning the booth and helping people understand how to cuddle or care for the cows.

"Caleb, looks like you're trying out quite a few different options from the food trucks." Luther was the head fair coordinator, a tall cowboy who wore a tan Stetson with a braided leather hat band. It didn't quite cover up the graying of his brown hair at the temples.

"Of course, we gotta eat. And the food here at the festival is always great." In Caleb's hands were three bags of food and one drink holder with four large drinks. When he set it all down, he pulled out cheese fries, burgers, and fried pickles for everyone.

Roman walked up, drying his hands off with a paper towel. "Thanks, Pa." He picked up a drink. "Luther, care to hug a calf?" He grinned at the older man.

Luther looked at the people lined up outside the booth, and then at the those grooming and hugging the cows. With a laugh, he shook his head. "I don't think that's my cup of sweet tea, but thanks, son."

"What can we do for ya, Luther?" Caleb put a hand on his old friend's shoulder. The two had gone to high school together in Beacon Creek and stayed friends ever since.

"Well, it's your lines." He pointed back to the line snaking its way out of their booth and blocking other booths. "We need you to find another way to help those waiting to cuddle a cow." He shook his head. "Honestly, when you first signed up for this space, I thought you were nuts. But now we're gonna have to find a better way to set you up next year."

Roman looked around at their area and tried to figure out how they were gonna move that line. They couldn't move people through any faster; there wasn't enough space for more hugging areas.

"Have you considered making appointments?" someone said from behind him.

The voice of an angel soothed his ears, and Roman smiled before he even turned around. "Sierra. That's a fantastic idea."

"You could even have them give you their phone numbers and you could text them when it gets close to their turn." The game operator had her hands in her back pockets and smiled at everyone when she walked up to the small group.

"Then we could only allow those with the next appointments to stand in line." Roman nodded. "That's a great idea. Thank you."

"So," Caleb asked the fair coordinator, "would that work for you?"

Luther grinned from ear to ear. "I love it. In fact, we can use that same idea for the other lines that get too long."

Caleb clapped his friend's back. "Glad we could be of help."

Sierra looked around the corner at the long line snaking past the guy selling homemade leather goods, past the booth that sold custom belt buckles, and even past the booth selling hats of all sorts, not just cowboy hats. There had to be more than they could take in for the rest of the day. "You might want to consider selling the spots on your sheet for the rest of the week as well. That way, you'll be certain to get them to come back to your booth."

Roman rubbed his chin. "Not a bad idea. We could sell them the spots. And if they don't show, maybe we give them a t-shirt if they come back later and we can't accommodate them?"

"Or you just sell the t-shirts and refund the cuddlers if you filled the spot with someone else?" Sierra shrugged.

"I guess working in the carnival for so long, you've come across all sorts of ways to deal with long lines." Luther considered the woman's suggestion and nodded to Caleb. "I like the girl's idea. Do you have t-shirts to sell?"

"No," Roman looked back at River and grinned. "But we have a few ladies in the family who can craft and recently started creating a design for the Triple J Ranch. I bet they'd be more than happy to make up a bunch each night."

"Oh, so you're gonna volunteer my wife and her crafting skills?" John walked up with a soda in one hand and a bag of food in another.

All of the Manning men planned to come out at various times during the day to help with the booth so that everyone could take breaks. Each day three would work the ranch first thing, and they would shift who worked the ranch the next morning. Then they all took turns working the booth at the carnival each day. However, Roman only worked the booth from morning till night. He did schedule breaks so he could spend some time with Sierra. And each of them took a turn sleeping in the trailer so someone would be able to be close to the cattle in case there was an issue.

The women also came by the carnival and helped out. Daisy was the only child old enough to work the booth. She loved showing the other kids how to cuddle a cow and where to pet them. The kids really got a kick out of an almost six-year-old, as Daisy constantly reminded everyone, teaching them about yearlings. Daisy was only allowed to work with the young cows. When they brought out the older ones, the adults helped with those.

"John, can you come over here?" River called out.

"Be right there," John called over his shoulder. When he turned back to the group, he smiled. "The wife's callin'. Catch ya later."

"She's got him wrapped around her little finger," Roman joked.

"Don't you mean Daisy's got him wrapped around her finger?" Caleb asked.

Sierra looked on, confused. "What are you talking about?"

Luther interjected, "John and River just married. Give them a break. All newlyweds are like that." He turned a devilish grin to Roman and then to Sierra and back at Roman. "I bet you'll understand soon."

Roman's mouth opened and closed like a fish.

Sierra's cheeks turned a pretty shade of pink, and she was about to turn and hightail it out of there when Roman put a hand on her arm.

"Sorry about Luther. He thinks he's the town matchmaker." A nervous laugh accompanied his burning cheeks.

"And on that note, I'm heading over to the booth to see how we can get your plan implemented and open up those booths our customers are blocking." Caleb walked away without a backward glance.

"So, about lunch?" Sierra bit her lower lip and looked toward the food truck area.

"How about we call this a date, even though it's carnival food?" He took her hand, and they walked toward the various scents mingling together to create a rumble in his stomach. "I'm gonna buy and we're gonna sit together, just the two of us, and talk about our day. That sounds like a date to me."

Sierra looked down at their intertwined hands as they walked away from the Triple J Ranch booth. "Okay, I think we can call it a date." She looked up and narrowed her eyes at Roman. "Just as long as your brothers don't come and join us this time."

He chuckled. The previous day, they had tried to have a quick lunch together until Mark and Matthew came over and sat down with them. The two older brothers stole the conversation and told Sierra all sorts of embarrassing stories about Roman as a boy. Stories that Sierra enjoyed hearing.

"You mean you don't want to hear again about how I fell out of a tree and sprained my ankle?"

She shook her head. "I'd rather hear about what you did in college. I never got a chance to go, and I'd like to hear about it."

After regaling Sierra with tall tales about playing college football and even playing in one of the big-bowl games, Roman's look turned serious. "How about attending the cowboy church with me on Sunday morning?"

Her brows furrowed. "Cowboy church?"

"Yeah, don't you see those when you're on the road?"

She shook her head. "No, not really. Most Sundays are spent restocking the prizes or cleaning up before we open. Saturdays are really busy and late, so we do most of the normal night work on Sunday morning."

"Hmm, how about I come over to your booth Saturday night and help you two clean up so you can attend service with me?" Roman hadn't had a chance yet to ask her if she believed in God, but it was very important to him. He really hadn't thought much about their relationship past this week. However, if he was going to pursue something with the pretty carnie, she'd have to be a Christian.

"Alright, that would be nice. You're taller than Annie or me, so you can easily restock the ducks above the water." She grinned at him and took a bite of her grilled steak and swiss sandwich.

"Alright, I'll come over after I've closed up my booth. Saturday night is my night to stay over with the cattle.

So maybe afterwards you and Annie could come over to my booth and we can play a board game?" He wanted to spend more time with her, but he also didn't want to tempt fate. Having Annie around would work as a sort of chaperone so they couldn't get into too much trouble. Maybe he'd even get one of his single friends to join them so they could play Spades or some other foursome card game.

Roman wasn't going to ask outright about her soul, but he was curious if she'd ever been to any of the cowboy churches. He knew from her response that the carnival didn't do a church service, but most large festivals that included a rodeo did have a cowboy church. "How long has it been since you attended any services?"

She put her sandwich down. "Growing up my grandma always took me to Sunday school and church services at the little white church down the road. We'd walk there every week until she couldn't. Then I drove us to church." Sierra looked off into the distance with a wistful smile as though she was remembering a simpler time. "But since I joined the carnival, I haven't had time." Her gaze went down to her sandwich and she picked it up.

"Sounds like your grandma was someone special," he practically whispered, wanting to keep this moment between them and not share it with anyone else around them.

After she swallowed her bite, Sierra turned glassy green eyes on him. Her eyes reminded him of sand glass he'd picked up once when he was in Florida for a weekend game. "She really was something special, and I miss her every day."

He took her hand and squeezed it. "I had a great-grandma who was really awesome. Grandma Holcombe lived with us her final years. She would make the best goulash." Roman chuckled, remembering the time he tried to make it and it turned out a mess of crunchy and soggy. He never did understand how he could mess up a simple dish like goulash, but he did. He did eventually master it. "Hey, how about I make us a batch of goulash for Saturday night? If you don't have dinner plans, you can come over to our trailer and I'll have it all ready to go. You can even bring some back for Annie, if you think she'll like it?"

"You wanna cook dinner for me?" Sierra pointed to herself and felt her heart begin to race. She'd never had a man cook for her before, let alone want to share a treasured family recipe.

A slow smile spread over his face, and he nodded. "Yeah, and we can call it a date, since it's not, you know, fair food." He laughed.

His deep, masculine laugh sent chills down her spine. If this cowboy wasn't careful, she'd fall for him. That thought brought her up short. What was she thinking? She couldn't fall for him. This was only a fall fling. Something to help her keep her mind off of the fact that she was never going to find her father.

But would it be so bad? Falling for a cowboy was never something Sierra had wanted. She always teased Annie about that. What would she do if she did fall hard for this gorgeous, generous man sitting across the picnic table from her? Would he want her to come back here when their fall carnival season was finished?

Chapter 11

Roman's hands were sweating. The way Sierra looked at him after he offered to make her dinner told him all he needed to know. The pretty woman with strawberry blonde hair that reminded him of a sweet summer day was into him. Of course she was; they had been chatting for a month and now they were—what? Dating? If she wasn't even the least bit attracted to him, she would have stopped texting him back at some point over the past month.

And this was a problem, a very big one with broken hearts written all over it.

The problem was that he was into her as well. And that thought scared the tar out of him. She'd only be here for a few more days and then she'd be off to the next town. Out of his life. When would she even be back? He was about to ask her if they had plans to come back to town, but decided he didn't want to ruin the afternoon.

He didn't have a chance, anyway. The moment Sierra looked at her watch, her eyes opened wide and she abruptly stood. "It's late. I've got to get going."

"How long have you been gone?" For Roman, it had only felt like ten minutes, although he knew it had been longer since they'd already finished eating and had been talking for a little bit.

With a wince, she said, "Almost an hour. It might not be too busy right now, but Annie hasn't had her lunch yet."

Being the gentleman he was raised to be, Roman stood and helped her clean their lunch away and then walked her back to her booth. Halfway to the duck game, he took her hand in his and a warmth spread up his arm as she squeezed his hand.

Sierra turned her head slightly, then looked up through her long, dark lashes. It made Roman's mouth go dry, and he wanted to run his thumb under her eyes and feel the silky strands of her eyelashes, then run his thumb down her cheeks to her lips... He had to turn away. His mind was getting away from him. This was not the place to kiss her, even though every fiber of his being screamed for him to do so.

"Thank you for walking me back to my booth. And for our lunch *date*. I've really enjoyed spending time with you, Roman." She winked.

He had to clear his throat in order to speak. The fact that she recognized their lunch as a date had him reeling. She had agreed earlier, but to hear her say it now told him that they were moving way past friends.

Roman squeezed her hand before letting go. "I've had a wonderful time with you too, Sierra."

And again, he had to hold himself back. If they were having a regular date, the kind where he picked her up from her house and then brought her back, he would kiss her goodbye. But he couldn't do it. Not here in the middle of the kiddie midway with families all around them. Little kids looking at her, and by proxy, him too.

One little boy pointed to Sierra. "Duck lady."

His mother laughed and told him not to point at people, it was rude. They moved on, and Roman chuckled as he mentally thanked God for the shift in mood.

"Will I see you later on?" she asked.

He nodded. "Yea, I'll come by on my next break and visit with you." His look lingered a beat too long, and Sierra blushed before she turned and headed into her booth. Roman waved at both Sierra and Annie before heading back to his own booth.

On Tuesday, they had a lunch date, again. If he was lucky, Roman would get to spend lunch with her every day. And maybe even a few more dinners, too. He tried to take her out to eat the night before, but her booth was so busy that he offered to bring both Sierra and Annie food so they could eat between players. He watched over their food as they took bites here and there of cold salads with wilted lettuce.

Roman wished he could have planned it—then he would have made them fresh salads instead of the pre-packaged chicken salads he'd found for them. Next year, he'd have to get Luther to find a fresh salad food truck. This prepackaged stuff was for the birds, literally. He even had to stare down a couple pigeons who had been eyeing Annie's salad when she turned her back on it.

Today, however, it was his turn to be extremely busy. Word was out about the cow cuddling, and people were stopping by their booth trying to get a spot in their reservations. Tuesday was all booked up, and Wednesday was just about full, too. Not to mention how many slots had already been filled up with reservations for the rest of the week. Then there were people who did try to line up in case someone didn't show for their slot.

Roman was smart about it, though. He told the people lining up that the line had to end at the edge of their booth. Those waiting around his booth probably wouldn't get a spot since they were completely booked for the day. And if they did, it would only be at the very last minute, and it wouldn't be for a full fifteen-minute session. If they were lucky, they'd get ten minutes. And of course the price was lowered to account for the shorter time.

None of that surprised Roman. What did was the fact that their t-shirts were selling like hotcakes. They couldn't keep them in stock. River was manning the cash register and little area they had where she was selling some of her other craft ideas, like fancy heart-shaped wreaths with various types of ribbon. He didn't understand why they were selling so fast, and for so much, but he wasn't complaining.

"You know, you're now going to have to work on these wreaths, t-shirts, and ornaments all year long so we have plenty of inventory for the various carnivals we're planning on hosting." The Triple J Ranch had always been sponsors of their local rodeos, but now that they had something to do at the carnivals, they had already decided the cow cuddling would expand next year. And with the success of the gift shop, they were going to have to figure out a way to expand that as well.

"Oh, don't I know it. I'm just glad I love crafting. As do Claire and Callie. Although, they don't seem to have as much free time at night as I do." River still put her little girl to bed early, and then had a couple of hours before she went to sleep at night.

Both Claire and Callie had jobs outside of the Triple J Ranch. Well, to be fair, Claire's job was technically on the ranch, but she ran her own horse-training facility which kept her very busy. She even traveled at times for work.

And Callie, well, she was the town's sheriff deputy-in-training, to take over for the sheriff. Probably within the next two years, since he had finally married Georgia and they wanted to do some traveling. Her schedule was wonky and she lived in town with his brother, Luke, who was supposed to help him that day at the fair.

But he figured the women would find more time to craft if it meant they could sell more at the fairs and carnivals. Beacon Creek may have been small, but they surely did have their fair share of events. Two rodeos a year, combined with carnivals. Not to mention the Christmas fair, and they would be busy working every night and weekend all through the year to build up stock.

The t-shirts looked to be the easiest things to make, so maybe he would lend his support on cold winter evenings when there wasn't anything else to do. Although, an idea was niggling at him.

He had heard several of their customers that day talking about a bed and breakfast they'd heard of that also offered cow cuddling to their guests. If he could get a place close enough to town, he could set up a B&B, too. The town never had enough rooms for guests who came for their events. And if he did something with the cow cuddling, then he'd probably be full most of the year.

When this week was over, he'd talk to John and see if his brother was serious about buying a ranch with him. For now he needed to get his head in the game, for a beautiful strawberry blonde woman with the prettiest green eyes he'd ever seen was heading his way.

She was wearing her usual jeans, Converse high-tops, and a burnt-sienna fall festival t-shirt with a bull in the foreground and a Ferris wheel in the background. That image was the theme for the festival this year, and the shirt hugged her in all the right places.

If Roman was smart he'd put a smock, or at the very least an oversized hoodie, over her to help cover up her perfect curves. With the way she looked, he was going to have a hard time keeping the drool from running all over his chin.

"Sierra, I'm glad you could come by." Roman took off his hat and swiped his forehead with his arm. It wasn't that it was hot, but he was busy. He'd probably done close to fifteen thousand steps already. If he had a Fitbit he'd know for sure. But he couldn't remember stopping since they opened three hours earlier.

She looked at the people and the line, then sucked her lower lip in between her teeth. "You look really busy. Should I go and pick up lunch and bring it back here for us?"

A huge sigh escaped, and Roman's shoulders sagged. "Would you mind? People just don't seem to understand that they can't block the other booths with a line that most likely won't get them in to visit with a cow today."

Sierra chuckled. "I kinda don't blame them. Cow cuddling is awesome. And I think your booth is the most popular one here this year."

Shocked, Roman asked, "Really? How do you know?"

Phone in hand, Sierra scrolled through her social media account. "Take a look at all of the posts for your booth." She handed her phone to Roman. "And check out the hashtag #cowcuddling. I think you'll be surprised to see that you're trending."

Roman furrowed his brow and handed the phone back to Sierra. "Does this mean I have to get a social media account now? I hate those things. They are such a time suck. And the vitriol people spew on their sites, it's almost criminal."

Sierra's soft laugh put a smile on his face. "Roman, you don't have to. But it might help if you did a page for the

Highland cows. Maybe have it be Scotty's page and then have him 'talk' about what it's like to be a Highland cow in Montana. He could share pics of the new cows and talk about the craziness of cow cuddling? It would be a safe way to promote your new business. And no one would expect you to talk politics."

He rubbed his neck. "I don't know. I hear once you start with something small, you can't stop."

She tilted her head from side to side. "That can be true, but I think you're gonna have a hard time just putting up a post a week. I seriously doubt you'll get sucked into social media chaos. Besides, everyone loves a cute animal video."

"True, I've seen enough of them to know they are the best part of social media." He narrowed his eyes. "Why don't you do the page for me?" Then he grinned.

If she stuck around, he'd definitely want to work with her on this project. But, no. She wasn't going to stick around. Sierra had a job that took her all over the country.

"If you don't stop looking at me like that, I just might quit my job and stay here." Sierra winked.

Roman licked his lips and his mouth went dry. When his heart began pounding against his chest, he knew he was in trouble. For darn his wild heart, he wanted her to stay. And not just to manage his social media for him. Roman wanted her to be his girlfriend. Not just someone he texted daily, but someone he could see, face to face, whenever he wanted.

This festival was going to be his downfall.

Chapter 12

Sierra's heart beat overtime, and the butterflies romping through her gut were driving her nuts. If Roman wasn't careful, she'd take him up on his joke of an offer and stay. With him. But she couldn't do that; her dad was out there somewhere, and she had to find him.

Just then, John walked up to the two of them, saving her from her fantasies of leaving the carnival and her search for her missing dad.

"Hey, why don't the two of you go to lunch? I'll take care of the lines, Roman." John patted his brother's back and smiled at Sierra.

She liked him and his new wife, River. They made such a cute family with Daisy. When she saw the three of them together, an ache formed in her chest. They reminded her of her family when she was young, before her mother developed cancer.

They were just like any other happy family. They went to their local carnival when it came to town. Although, they didn't have a rodeo. Sierra attended her first rodeo after joining the carnival. Talk about shocking. Watching grown men get thrown off a fifteen-hundred-pound bull was insane.

But watching the kids do their little mutton busting was priceless. That was the one event she loved the most. Those kids were so cute. Watching the kids stay on the sheep, and then their power pumps, it always made her laugh and cry at the same time. She even enjoyed watching the little kids fall of the backs of the sheep and jump up with their hands in the air. Secretly, she hoped to marry a cowboy just so she could have kids that did mutton bustin' at the local rodeo each year.

Sierra also wished she had been able to do that sort of stuff when she was little. Her dad never wanted to attend the rodeos when they came, but he did love the Ferris wheel. He said that was the first ride he ever went on with her mother. It held a special place in his heart. She didn't remember a lot, but that was the one thing that always stood out for her.

There were three very strong memories of her perfect childhood, before her mother got sick. They all had to do with the local carnival. *Huh*. She hadn't thought of it before, but maybe that was why she chose to join the carnival and travel around? Was it a way to keep her memories alive?

"You look like you're considering something pretty serious. Care to share?" Roman took her hand and led her toward their favorite food truck for the pineapple chicken.

"When we get seated, I'll share." A lightness enveloped Sierra, and she swung their hands as they walked.

"Okay, time to share." Roman handed her the plate of food and sat across from her on the white picnic table.

Sierra had carried the drinks, and she handed him his. Once she was seated, she thought about what she was going to say. "I've been thinking a lot about my dad and my mom lately."

"Any particular reason?" He just about moaned when he put his bite of pineapple chicken and rice in his mouth.

"Slow down. I know you love this stuff, but you don't have to inhale it." Sierra chuckled and took a small bite of her meal. It really was the best fair food, ever. She never tired of eating the juicy and sweet chicken with teriyaki sauce and rice. It didn't hurt that it was also one of the healthier options the fairs and carnivals offered.

Mouth full, Roman grinned and took a drink of his soda.

"I have only a few memories from when my life was picture perfect. Before my mom got sick." She put her spork down and wiped her mouth. "They're all of times spent at the carnival. My dad loved the Ferris wheel. It was his favorite ride. When we'd get to the carnival, that was the first thing he wanted to do. Then after that, it was always about what I wanted, or my mom." She smiled, and in her head she was only five years old, clinging to her dad's hand as they walked up to the larger wheel playing carnival music.

The fear that clung to her little five-year-old self seemed so minor, so unimportant. Sierra had tugged on her dad's hand, and she tried to pull back. He picked her up and held her. "Peanut, it's alright. Daddy's here, and I'm going to keep you and your momma safe. I'll always keep you safe."

She jerked out of the memory and frowned. "No, Papa, you didn't."

"What?" Roman's brow furrowed and he looked intently at her.

She waved to dismiss the memory. "It's nothing. Just an old memory. Probably better left in the past."

Roman reached his hand across the table and took hers. "It's something, Sierra. Please, share it with me."

With a deep sigh, she began, "My dad said he'd keep me safe. That he'd always keep me safe." The chuckle that escaped Sierra wasn't one of mirth—it was of disbelief. "I believed him. He was my Superman. When I was little, he did keep me safe. And I ended up loving the Ferris wheel."

He squeezed her hand when she stopped and looked out at the giant wheel overlooking the entire carnival.

"You know, I haven't been on a Ferris wheel once since he left me. But I came to work at a carnival that looked just like the one from my memory." She shook her head. "I must have some sort of issues, huh?"

"Actually"—Roman turned his head and looked at the giant wheel—"I think it's time we rode it. Together."

"What? Why?" Sierra pulled her hand back and set it in her lap.

"Because I think you need to move on. A part of you has held on to that memory this entire time. You've buried it deep. And until you can move past this loss, you won't be able to move on with your life."

"Ah, and that's the crux of my problem—moving on."

"Sierra, do you want to spend the rest of your life traveling around with the carnival? Looking for a man you may never find? Or do you want to find a way to enjoy your life? Do something that has meaning for you?" The intensity in Roman's gaze shocked her to her core.

Red and Stella had both tried to talk her into letting go of her long-absent father. They knew he had gotten himself into a lot of trouble. She shared that news with them over tears and a pint of Ben & Jerry's. And after that they would try and be supportive of her search, but as the years moved on, they did try to steer her to something new. Something that might bring her joy instead of sadness.

"You know, you aren't the first one to suggest I stop looking."

"You misunderstand me, Sierra. I'm not saying give up on your dad. I'm saying that you need to find your own life, and search a different way. I've got friends who could help you find your dad. If he had a driver's license, we can find him." Roman's hand was in the middle of the picnic table, waiting for her hand to join him.

"What would I do? I haven't gone to college, and I certainly don't have the money for college." She sighed.

Sierra knew that she had blown it spending every dime she could save on searching for her dad. A search that only echoed what her friends had told her. She needed to stop. If he wanted her to find him, he would have told her grandma how to find him. Or he would have shown up for her funeral.

A tear sliced down her cheek, and she looked at his hand. It was still waiting for her. Mind made up, she wiped the tear away and clasped his hand. "I don't know what I'd do if I left the carnival. Where would I live? I don't even have a car of my own. I drive the carnival truck when I can, and rent a car when I can't."

"Hm, I think the first step is to rid yourself of your fear." Roman stood and let go of her hand. When he walked around the picnic table, he picked up the remains of their lunch and threw it away. "Let's go get a ticket for that Ferris wheel."

Fear snaked through her being, just like when she was a little kid. "I don't know, Roman. This might be too much."

"No, I think it's perfect. You have to slay your demons in order to move on. And I'm not saying that you stop looking for your dad. Just that you start *living*."

"Because working at a carnival isn't living?" She pulled her hand away and glowered at him.

Roman shook his head. "That's not what I said." He pursed his lips and stared at her. "If working in a carnival for the rest of your life is what you want, then fine. Do it. But if you want more for yourself—if you want a home and a family one day—then you need to find a way to get it."

Sierra winced and looked down at her red Converse. "I know, you're right. I am the family type. I look at the kids with their parents when they come to my booth and I think that's exactly what I want. The white-picket fence, husband, two-point-five kids, and a dog." She turned around and put a hand to her head. "But how do I go about doing that?"

He pointed to the Ferris wheel not one hundred feet away from them. "First, you tackle your fears. Then you figure out what you want, besides hiding away in a carnival."

After she looked long and hard at the giant wheel, she turned her gaze back to Roman. "Will I know as soon as I get off that monstrosity?"

He shrugged. "Maybe. And maybe you'll need to take time to pray and ask God what He wants you to do." Roman turned soft eyes on her. "Have you asked your Heavenly Father for guidance?"

She shook her head. "No." Feeling guilty all of a sudden for moving so far from God, she shrugged. "I think he's forgotten about me."

"No, He hasn't forgotten about you, or any of his children. Sierra, He's here, waiting for you to come back to Him. There are multiple verses in the Bible that talk about God being with you. He will never leave you, nor forsake you. All you have to do is call to Him and accept His love and protection." Roman pulled her close to him and hugged her tight.

For the first time since her dad left her, she felt safe. Really and truly safe. Like there was someone there who would protect her. She wrapped her arms around his waist and held on for dear life.

"I think I'm ready to ride that Ferris wheel." She pulled her head back. "Maybe I should do it alone?"

He grinned at her. "If you wish. I'll be here waiting for you."

Sierra worried her lower lip. "You don't mind?"

"I'd love to ride the great wheel with you, but this is your fear to conquer. I'm here for you, if you need me. But it's God who's going to carry you through the rough times. I can help, but He's your rock." Roman brushed his lips across her forehead, and her heart kicked up so fast she almost fainted.

Sierra held on to Roman until she got her heartbeat back on track again. Then whispered, "Okay, I'm gonna do this."

The entire walk to the entrance, Sierra wondered if she was doing the right thing. It was Roman's idea; maybe he should ride with her. But he did have a point: she shouldn't rely on him to get her through anything. She was a strong, independent woman who didn't need a man to hold her hand. Only, she wanted him to hold her hand. She wanted him to tell her it was all going to be alright and that he would protect her, always.

But wasn't that exactly what her dad did? Then he left her. Maybe, just maybe, Roman had it right. She couldn't depend on anyone but herself. Although, he did say she could count on God.

Growing up with her grandma, she did just that. She read her Bible, went to church, and prayed regularly. She lived the life God said she should. Then it all went south when her grandma died. Turned out, she relied on her grandma to make sure she did what she needed to do.

"Ticket." The guy who manned the Ferris wheel didn't even look at her. If he had, he would have recognized her.

Sierra smirked and handed her ticket to Wayne and walked up to where Stella stood, loading people into the seats. "Stella? What are you doing here?"

"Sierra?" Shock covered the older woman's face, followed by a smile. "I see you've finally decided to tackle this beast?"

Nodding, Sierra sat down and Stella locked her in. "Yeah, a friend told me it was time."

"I think I like this friend of yours. Where is he?" Stella winked and pushed a button to move the ride vehicle forward.

Sierra laughed and shook her head. Of course, Stella knew exactly who it was that had talked her into riding the Ferris wheel and conquering her fear.

<h1 style="text-align:center">Chapter 13</h1>

Roman watched as Sierra smiled and looked out over the carnival. She was halfway up the wheel, and he couldn't take his eyes off her. He had walked to the front of the giant ride to get a better look at the woman who had stolen his heart.

A hand clamped on his shoulder, and he startled. "What?" He turned to see who'd grabbed him. "Red. Howdy."

Red pointed to Sierra. "Was that your doing?"

"Sorta. I think she was ready and just needed a nudge."

"I like you, Roman Manning. I've asked around, and it seems your family is one of the most respected ones in the entire state." Red eyed the young man. "Is this a fling for you? Or do you have real intentions toward my Sierra?"

He gulped. Roman had never had a father figure ask him what his intentions were. He remembered once when he was really young, a boy had come to pick up Chloe for a date and his father sat on the porch cleaning his rifle. When the boy walked up, his dad grilled him until Chloe rescued him. Of course, Roman thought it was funny. He never understood why Chloe got so upset with her father that weekend. But now, he finally got it.

Red didn't have a rifle and he wasn't threatening him, but the intensity in his look sent a shiver down his spine. Sierra was protected and loved. She had a father in Red. Did she know it? Was that why she had stayed with this particular carnival group for the past three years?

"Sir, I don't know Sierra well, but I do like what I know." Roman looked back at Sierra as she raised her arms above her head. She was on the very top of the wheel now. Even though she was so high up, Roman could feel her joy at riding the Ferris wheel, finally. And it sent a jolt through his entire being. He had helped her to loosen the grip that her fear held on her. A sense of pride washed through him, and he realized that he wanted to help her even more.

"Uh-huh. And what about when we leave town in a week?" The older man who ran the carnival crossed his arms over his chest and glared at Roman.

"We haven't actually thought that far in advance." He took his hat off and wiped at the sweat developing across his forehead. "If she was a local girl, I'd court her."

"And what if she stayed here in town now? How would you feel?"

"I'd be very happy to get to know her better."

A stern look crossed Red's face, and his mouth tightened.

Roman put his hands up. "Wait, I didn't mean anything untoward about that. I just meant that if she stayed here, I'd take her out on proper dates. She'd be invited to the family barbecues after church on Sundays. And we could take our time seeing where this could go. And it would all be proper." He lowered his head and looked right into the man's eyes.

"Humph." Red nodded. "Is there a way you could help her find a room to rent and a local job?"

This was moving fast. Why was Red asking him this? Did Sierra talk to him about staying here? Was that what John had overheard earlier in the week? "Ah, I don't know. Maybe?" Now Roman was starting to feel like it might be some sort of setup. Did Sierra plan this?

Red waved a hand. "Don't mention this to Sierra, but I know she's too good to keep on the road with us. She's smart and can do so much more. Same with our Annie."

"Have you spoken to them about this?" Roman looked back at Sierra, who was close to the end of her ride.

"Naw, it's just something Stella and I have been discussing lately. We love the girls, but we also know they could do so much better. We just don't know how to help them do better than this." Red waved a hand around.

It made sense. Red and Stella were Annie's guardians, and they had taken to Sierra as well. If his dad were here, he'd probably offer to help the girls, both of them. Roman could probably help them, but only if they wanted it. "How do you think they'd feel about you trying to offload them here?"

Red turned quickly. "I'm not trying to offload them." A guttural sound followed his words, bringing Roman up short.

"I'm sorry, that came out all wrong. It's just"—Roman ran a hand over his face—"this is strange, isn't it?"

"Yeah, I suppose it is." Red nodded. "I'm just worried about the girls. They're still young enough to go to college if they want, or to do anything else." The man deflated, and his arms hung at his sides. "I'd love to see them settle down with the right men and have families. Not that I expect you marry one of them. But if they could live somewhere with good people who could watch over them, I'd feel much better."

Sierra was exiting the ride when Roman turned to Red. "I'll ask my pa how we can help, but Sierra and Annie both have to want to leave the carnival. I'll not pressure them, or let you pressure them to leave."

Red nodded once. "Deal. Just, please keep this between us until you know if you can help or not."

"Fine." Roman hated keeping this from Sierra, but he really couldn't say anything anyways, could he? How would that conversation go?

Hey, you know your father figure, Red? Well, he wants you to leave him. And he's asked me to take you in.

Roman might not have much experience with women, but he knew that wouldn't go over well. It would do more harm than good. And since he didn't even know if he could do anything to help, he couldn't offer the girls a place, anyway.

They did have an extra cabin on their property. They had plenty of space for Sierra and Annie, but they would need jobs. It wasn't like Beacon Creek had a lot to offer newcomers. Most of the possible jobs were on farms and ranches during harvest and calving seasons. Most ranches and farms had already brought in their crops. They were now preparing for winter. Over the next month there would be a lot of canning; maybe the girls could help out his mother with their winter preparations. With the new babies, and more on the way, his sisters-in-law might not be enough help.

But that wouldn't pay a lot. They'd get their room and board covered, and maybe some pocket money. Nah, that wouldn't help much. He needed to speak with his dad.

Red walked away before Sierra reached him.

"Was that Red? What'd he have to say?" Sierra was breathless, and a spark of something he hadn't seen before entered her eyes.

"He was happy to see you on the wheel. Does he know about your fear?" Roman pulled her in for a hug. "I'm so proud of you for doing that on your own." He pulled back to look into her eyes. "But I would like to ride it sometime this week, with you." He winked. "Maybe even at night."

A pink hue tinged her cheeks, and she looked away from him. "I'd like that. And yes, he knows I hated the Ferris wheel. I never told him why." She bit her lower lip. "You're the first one I've told about my parents and the Ferris wheel."

Roman kissed the top of her head. "Thank you for sharing that with me. And thank you for letting me be a part of this today."

Something had changed inside of Sierra ever since she rode the Ferris wheel earlier that day. She and Roman walked hand in hand back to her booth. When they arrived, he kissed her cheek and said he'd stop by later on one of his breaks. Since then, she had a permanent smile. Not even the idiotic teens who always tried to mess with the booth bothered her.

Annie grinned at her. "So, does he kiss that good?"

"What?" Sierra looked at her friend.

"You've been on cloud nine ever since you got back from lunch with Roman. Spill it. Was the kiss everything we've ever seen in movies?" Annie leaned against a pole that held her booth up. They didn't have anyone at their booth for the first time in hours, so it was her first chance to ask about the lunch date.

Sierra giggled and pushed her friend away. "No, silly. Our first kiss wasn't in front of everyone at the carnival. Sheesh."

"Wait." Annie held up a hand. "The cowboy hasn't kissed you yet? What's wrong with him?"

"He's a perfect gentleman. Nothing's wrong. Most of our dates seem to be here, at the carnival." Sierra shrugged. "It's not like we've had any real time alone. At least not since our first date at that steakhouse in Bozeman."

"What a waste." Annie sighed. "If it were me, I'd pull him toward me the next time I saw him, not caring about spectators, and give those lips a workout." She waggled her brows.

"Ugh, please. Next thing you know, you're gonna wrap your arms around yourself and start kissing the air." Sierra covered her eyes and laughed.

"Oh, good idea." Annie did just that. Until a little boy yelled *gross* and ran away.

"Oops." Sierra looked to the kid's father and winced. "Sorry about that. She's not been housebroken yet." And pointed to Annie.

Annie's face had turned a bright red, and she sat down on the dirt floor and hid from the little audience.

A teenager, probably about sixteen or seventeen, yelled, "I'll kiss you." Then he and his friends made kissy noises and laughed as they walked away.

Sierra rubbed her hands over her face. "Sorry, Annie. But it looks like they're all gone if you want to come out."

"This is why you don't kiss at a carnival." Annie nodded to herself and wiped the dirt off her backside. "Okay, how about we focus on getting some kids to come and play the game and stop talking about boys?"

With a little giggle, Sierra agreed.

After her dinner, Sierra began searching the area for any signs of Roman. He had said he'd come by on one of his breaks, but she hadn't seen him. She would have gone to his booth, but she didn't want to seem needy. Plus, they were so busy, she didn't have time for anything other than grabbing food and bringing it back for her and Annie.

Once they got past the embarrassment of earlier, their booth was one of the hot ones. A little boy of about seven won a duck, and he ran all over the area telling everyone the game was super easy. Nothing worked better for advertising than a little boy with a big mouth. Since him, two others had won. They had five winners that day in total, and the day wasn't even over yet. It was also turning out to be one of their best days of the week. So far.

With this amount of traffic, they were bound to have a lot more winners before the week was out, and in turn, their booth was on target for an extra bonus.

About thirty minutes before closing, Roman asked his brother to take over the booth. He was going to see his girl.

"Dude, I'm surprised you didn't go over there during your dinner break. Aren't you and she eating all of your meals together lately?" John ribbed him, but Roman knew it was because he liked Sierra.

In fact, just that day all of his siblings who had stopped by to help mentioned how they liked Sierra.

River suggested they invite her over to eat with them one night this week.

"I'll ask her to come and join us for dinner when she can," Roman said as he picked up his jacket and walked toward the woman. He had planned on heading over to her booth for dinner, but when his father showed up that night, he decided to speak with his dad about the woman on his mind.

"Son, I'll talk to your mother and see what she suggests." Caleb looked as though he wanted to offer Sierra a place on the ranch, but Roman knew it was his mother who ran the household.

So, with a spring in his step, he hurried over to the duck game booth.

"Hey beautiful." Roman's deep voice was soft.

"Hiya, cowboy." Sierra smiled up through her lashes at the man who'd captured her heart.

"Have you heard about the lantern walk?" Roman wanted to pull her in for a hug but he was separated by the booth, and with the way Annie grinned at him, he knew better than to try and hug Sierra for all to see.

She shook her head. "No, what's a lantern walk?"

"Thursday night, down by the river, we all take lanterns that we made during the week and put lights inside. They used to be real candles, but now it's mostly the LED kind. Anyway, it's a chance to welcome the fall and do something under the stars." Roman looked deep into Sierra's eyes. "Do you think you could get away long enough to go on the walk with me?"

"Sounds romantic. Go ahead, Sierra. I'll make sure our booth is covered." Annie grinned at them both and waggled her eyes.

"Where do I get a lantern?" Sierra chewed on her bottom lip.

He put his thumbs in his belt loops to keep from reaching out to her. All Roman wanted to do was capture her lips with his own. Maybe if they could get away at the lantern walk, he could *finally* kiss the girl. "There's a few booths mingled throughout the carnival. Have you seen the craft tables with paper, mason jars, and leaves?"

"Oh, I have. I thought it was just a thing for parents to do with their kids." Annie kept interrupting their conversation, but Roman wasn't going to ask her to butt out. She probably felt a bit left out since he had taken so much of Sierra's time this week already.

"Yeah, I've seen them, too. I just didn't know what they were for." Sierra grinned.

"You can buy a kit there to make a lantern. If you like, we can do that tomorrow for our lunch?" Roman waited patiently for her response.

"Yeah, as long as it's not too busy. Maybe we can bring the kit back here to the booth." Sierra looked at Annie. "And bring one for Annie, too."

A slow smile spread across Roman's face. "Of course, that would be fun for all three of us to work on it together."

"Really? You want me to join you?" Annie's incredulous expression caused Roman to take a beat.

"Well, not on the lantern walk. That's more for couples. But yes, it would be fun for all of us to work on our lanterns together."

"Ah, so the walk is a chance for lovers to kiss under the stars. I get it." Annie laughed and pointed to Sierra. "What did I tell you?"

Sierra swiped her hand at Annie's finger. "Stop that. Didn't you see all of those kids making lanterns? It's a community thing." She turned to Roman. "Right?"

His eyes sparkled, and he nodded. "It starts out at twilight as a family event. Then, as it gets later, it's more an opportunity for couples to enjoy the beauty of the Montana night sky."

"Like I said, a chance for couples to smooch." Annie winked at Sierra.

Sierra put a hand over her face and shook her head. "Annie, come on. Don't start this again. Remember what happened last time?"

Pink tinged Annie's cheeks, and she turned toward a family with two little kids as they approached the booth. "Hiya, wanna try your hand at winning a duck?" She pointed to the area over the pond full of ducks.

"Sorry about her. She's got cowboy on her brain." Sierra chuckled.

He wasn't sure what that meant, but he smiled anyway. "No problem. I'll pick up three kits for us tomorrow and bring lunch, too. Text me what you and Annie want for lunch before noon and I'll bring it all over by one."

"You don't have to do that. We can get our own lunch."

"I know, but I want to. I don't know Annie very well, and since she's your best friend I want to get to know her better, too." Roman reached for her hand. "Besides, this way she won't be able to keep asking us about smooching." He winked, squeezed her hand, and walked away without a backward glance.

Roman felt Sierra's eyes on his back and heard her intake of breath before she laughed. He knew he'd gotten her, and she'd taken it like a champ. Sierra could fit in with him and his family. And if he and John got their ranch up and running, both girls would have places to work. Well, if they liked cow cuddling.

Sierra liked cow cuddling, and Annie seemed to like it that one day. But, well, he was probably getting ahead of himself. Now he would have to see if John was serious about their idea. And if they could find a ranch with a big enough house to run a small B&B.

Chapter 14

Roman didn't know what he was thinking by offering to bring over lunch for the three of them along with three lantern kits. When he told River and Claire what he'd planned for his long lunch that day, they both looked at each other and laughed. Did he say something funny? He wasn't sure.

"Roman, you're gonna need a cart to haul all that. Plus, you'll need scissors, glue, and..." River looked at Claire, who shrugged.

"Don't ask me. Matthew didn't want to do the walk this year, so I don't know what all you'll need." Claire grinned at him.

"River, aren't you doing the walk with Daisy and John?" Roman had heard them talking about it and thought for sure they were doing it.

She nodded. "We made our lanterns at home already." River pursed her lips. "How about you get those kits and take my extra scissors and one of the craft glue bottles I have?" She had brought supplies to their booth so she could work on crafts in between customers. "I doubt I'll have time to craft while you're out, anyways." She got up to go get the supplies.

"Thanks, I appreciate it." Roman paused. "Are any of the other members of the family doing the walk this year?"

"I don't think so. With the booth, I don't think anyone else really wanted to take the time. Since River, John, and Daisy are doing the walk, and now you and Sierra, the rest will need to either work at the ranch or cover the booth." Claire looked out to the crowd by their gift store. "I think we're gonna need all hands on deck this weekend." She got up from her chair and went to join Callie in the shop.

"I can't believe how much we've sold already. Do we have anything left for this weekend to sell?" Roman took the kit from River's outstretched hands.

She sighed. "We're all working hard to at least keep t-shirts in stock. But I doubt we'll have much to sell this weekend. I'll probably have three wreaths finished, and maybe a handful of ornaments. The next couple of days Callie is on duty so I don't know how much she's gonna get done. However, your sister told me this morning that she was able to get another vet to cover her shifts, so she might be able to help out more the next couple of days."

Elizabeth was the town veterinarian. She had taken over the local practice from Milton, who retired earlier this year. As far as Roman knew, she didn't have another vet on staff yet. She had put out a call for someone, but he hadn't heard that the position had been filled. "So, she got herself an intern?"

"No, she hired a single dad. He had his own practice in eastern Oregon, and when his wife died he decided he needed a fresh start. So he brought his two kids and moved here last week." River looked at him funny. "How long has it been since you spoke to your sister?"

That caused him to stop in his tracks. He'd seen her at the last family lunch, but he didn't talk to her. And he'd been so busy preparing for this event that he really hadn't spoken to her for at least two weeks. Well, not about anything important, like her veterinary practice. "Wow, I guess I need to spend some time with my big sister when the carnival is over."

River chuckled. "Well, I guess you have been a bit busy."

Once Roman had the supplies in the little red cart, he waved goodbye to the family members manning their booth and headed out to get the kits and then lunch. As he made his way through the throngs of people, he thought about his conversation with River. Lately, his life had revolved around cow cuddling, breeding, and Sierra. While he was in college he kept in better touch with his family and knew more about the goings on, even though he wasn't even in the same county as his family.

After Roman had everything in his little cart, he began slowly making his way to the duck booth.

"Roman!" a voice he recognized called out.

He turned his head and saw a tall, lanky guy only a year younger than he was. "Boone, good to see you, man."

"Where ya going with all that?" Boone pointed to the cart. He worked on the Triple J ranch for the Manning family. He and his two foster brothers had been on the ranch for the past couple of years, ever since his brothers had found the boys in a cave back behind their property. All three boys turned out to be hard workers, and after they worked off the money they owed from their life on the road, they decided to stay.

Roman grinned. "I'm heading over to Sierra's booth. Annie is going to join us in making lanterns for the walk tomorrow night."

"Walk? Are you doing something to raise money for charity?" The cowboy's forehead creased, and he got in step with Roman.

"No. Well, I guess. The money from the sale of the supplies goes to an organization that helps to keep the river front clean. Last year, they finally had enough money to make a nice walking bridge over the river by the park. But we're making lanterns for the lantern walk. It's how we celebrate fall every year."

Boone looked at the supplies in the cart. "Looks cool. Can anyone do it?"

"Sure can. You wanna go get yourself a lantern kit, lunch, and then meet us at the duck game?" Roman grinned. He just might have found the fourth for the game night he was planning for Saturday with the girls. He'd see how Annie and Boone got along today and then invite him to join them.

Thursday night came so fast that Sierra couldn't believe it. She wanted to go and change into a dress, or at least a sweater. Her fall festival t-shirt and hoodie didn't exactly scream *date night* wardrobe. It was more like, *I'm too lazy to change my clothes for you*. But, it was a work night. And Roman knew it. She would just have to make sure to look her best for when she went to dinner at their house on Tuesday.

Annie and she had put their lanterns up for display all day long. Both girls were very happy with their craft project. Sierra just wished Annie could have gone with them, but they couldn't get two people to cover their booth. So Sierra kept an eye out for Roman to come and get her.

"Be sure to tell me everything. And I mean *everything*." Annie glared at Sierra and pointed her index finger at her friend's mouth. "I fully expect to hear you finally got a kiss tonight, got it?"

Sierra chuckled. "Sorry, but I don't kiss and tell."

"I hope not."

The deep voice sent shivers down her spine. *Roman.*

She turned around, already feeling the heat go up her neck and all through her face. Out of the corner of her eye, she saw Annie smirk. Oh, she'd get her friend back alright. It might take a while, but Annie was not going to get away with this.

"Roman." Sierra picked up her lantern and smiled at the handsome cowboy. He hadn't dressed up, either. He was in his regular Wranglers, snap-button shirt, and Stetson. But he looked good. She was sure he was much better looking than she was.

He grinned.

Mortified, she knew he was thinking about what she'd said. She lifted her lantern. "I'm all ready to go." She looked at his hands. "Where's your lantern?"

"It's in the truck." He took her hand and waved with the other to Annie, who smiled from ear to ear as they walked away. "I think you're really gonna love tonight. The Montana sky over the river is beautiful. And then add in all of the lantern light as people walk along the river and over the bridge, and it's a sight to behold."

"So, you've done this before?" she asked.

"When I was younger my whole family would make lanterns and we'd do the walk together. I haven't been home for a fall festival since I went away to college. The bridge is new this year, so I can only imagine how that will look, but I do think it's going to add to the ambiance of the night."

"Sounds like this was a pretty fantastic place to grow up." Sierra looked out at the carnival.

Roman wished she could have had a childhood like his. "It's the perfect place to raise a family. Most kids grow up and want to go away, try the big city. But almost all of them come back, or end up on a ranch or farm somewhere else." He sighed. "There's nothing like camping out back and laying on your sleeping bag looking up at the sky. We have a telescope, and looking at the universe, I can see God's hand in all of it."

"Yeah, I always wondered how someone could look at the stars and not know that there's a Creator." Sierra pointed up. "Even with all of the lights around us here, I can still see Creation. With twilight on us, the different colors in the night sky, the clouds, the moon peeking out." She sighed. "It's too grand not to have been created by an almighty being."

"So, does this mean that you believe in God?" Roman looked at her with something in his eyes—expectation? Hope? She wasn't sure which.

"Yes, I have believed in Him for a long time now. But"—she winced—"I've not been close to him since joining the carnival."

The silence between them was peaceful, and Sierra heard all of the families talking, laughing, and even some teens yelling. She wondered if any of them would be doing the lantern walk, or if any of the young families had already done it.

"I heard you the other day, you know." She looked at him out of the corner of her eye.

"What did you hear?" He squeezed her hand.

"When we were talking about God still being here for me." She licked her lips. "I know you're right. I can feel him at times. Like tonight." She looked up and watched the colors of the night changing from the yellow of the sky before Roman came to get her to the current shades of orange. She also knew that by the time they reached the river park, there would be swatches of purple and blue overhead until it became a canvas of dark blues with bright twinkling lights.

"Does this mean you're gonna attend the cowboy church with me Sunday morning?" When he originally asked her, she really hadn't responded. She had accepted his offer to help close up on Saturday night and then join him for a late dinner and board games, but she hadn't really said she'd go to church with him.

Now she was seriously considering it.

"Yes, I think I want to attend services again." She bit her lower lip, wondering how it would feel to be in God's presence again after all this time.

"Good, I'll come and get you before the nine o'clock service. Just wear whatever you would for work since most of us will head straight to our booths once service is over."

When they reached the river park, Sierra looked up and realized church wasn't the only place she'd be in God's presence. She was always in his presence. The only difference was, she'd ignored him before. Now her eyes were open, and she was paying attention.

Roman had noticed that Sierra seemed to be off in her own world once he brought up church. He didn't want to break into her thoughts, but he was curious if she was thinking about God, or something else.

Ever since Red approached him the other day, he'd been praying about what to do about Sierra. And even

Annie. They had room for the girls, but he doubted they'd be happy living on the ranch if they didn't have jobs.

Last night when he got home, he spoke to his mom about them. Thankfully, his dad had already had that conversation with her. Judith Manning was one of the most hospitable women he'd ever met. She was always inviting people to join them for supper, or offering a bed when someone needed it.

So he was surprised when she asked what they would do for a living.

He had shrugged. "I don't know. I guess they could help out around here for now, and then see if there's anything in town."

Judith put a hand on her son's shoulder. "Roman, those girls work hard all year long. Do you really think they'll want to live on our charity?"

"Are you saying you don't want to help them out?" Roman couldn't believe what he was hearing from his mom. She had never turned anyone away—that he knew of.

"That's not what I said." She pursed her lips. "I asked if you thought they'd be able to live here without a job. I don't have that much for them to do after the canning's all done and put up. And that won't last but a couple of weeks."

"Ma, you said so yourself, they're hard workers. Surely we can help them find a job somewhere." He had thought a little about it. "The Johnsons next door probably need someone who can cook and clean, right? Maybe they can do that?"

His mom shook her head. "No, son. The Johnson boy is getting married. His wife will take care of the house."

"Well, I'm sure there's another ranch around here that could use help in the kitchen."

"Do the girls even know how to cook? It's not like they've had much opportunity for anything more than campfire grilling since being on the road."

"Oh." Roman realized he hadn't even asked what sort of skillset the girls had, other than working a carnival. "If they can find a job, would you be open to them living here?" Surely his mother couldn't object if they had jobs, right?

"I'd be happy to have them here, as long as they'll be happy."

Today, he had asked around about available jobs once the carnival left town. Roman couldn't find anything for two uneducated young women to do after the carnival and rodeo left town. Sure, come November there would be some part-time seasonal jobs, but until then, nothing.

Getting himself back to the present, he looked up to where Sierra's gaze was focused, and Roman smiled. "I love the Milky Way. And I don't just mean the candy bar." He chuckled.

Sierra giggled and smiled at his lame attempt at a joke. "Same here." She sighed. "There's nothing like looking at the universe from our place on Earth."

"Yeah, it really does show how little we are." Roman turned the LED light on in his lantern.

Sierra followed suit. Then she took his hand in hers and grinned at him. "Now, show me this walk you've been talking about the past two days."

And he did. They walked hand in hand under the stars with their lanterns in their other hands. Some parts of the river walk had lights, but not all of it did. Their little mason-jar lanterns provided just enough light to help them see where they were stepping.

All around them, people had decorated the outside of their jars with real leaves, pieces of tissue paper, and even a few had buttons glued on. One little kid had a Minnie Mouse glued to the side of her jar, and her brother, who looked to be about nine, had a T-Rex glued to the outside of his. That little family had just walked over the bridge and were heading back to their car.

Sierra had brought a few wildflowers from outside her trailer and used them to decorate her jar. And she even plucked one of the pink Gerbera daisies from the bouquet Roman had given her on their first official date.

"Is that from your bouquet?" Roman noticed what she had added after he left them yesterday to finish on their own.

"Yes. When I got back last night to my trailer, I thought the jar needed something extra. Your flowers were sitting in the middle of the tiny table in my trailer and I just knew it would be the perfect accessory." She lifted her mason-jar lantern and looked at the flower in the middle of one side of her jar. "And I was right."

"Yes, you were. It's perfect." Roman looked into her eyes after she lowered her jar. "Let's walk to the other side of the bridge."

With a shy smile, she agreed.

Roman stopped them in the middle of the bridge and took a deep breath. He took their lanterns and set them on the side of the bridge, illuminating the slow-moving creek beneath their feet. Then he pointed to the sky. "See the large W up there?"

"Yeah, that's Cassiopeia, right?" Sierra leaned against him and looked where he pointed.

Before Roman could get his voice to work, he had to take a few deep breaths. Having her lean against him in such a romantic venue as this was setting his blood on fire. He whispered in her ear, "Yes."

Sierra breathed in a shallow breath. "Don't do that."

"Do what?" He leaned in even closer, if that was possible, and trailed his lips from her ear to her cheek. Annie may have joked about them kissing tonight, but he was most definitely going to kiss his girl.

Breathlessly, Sierra whispered, "Don't kiss me if you don't mean it."

He pulled back and put his hands on her face. "Sierra, I mean it." He waited a couple of breaths before leaning in. Roman wanted to give her time to say no or pull back if she wasn't into this. When she continued to look at him with longing in her eyes, he moved forward slowly.

Sierra licked her lips, and her eyes darted toward his lips and back to his eyes.

Roman gently touched his lips to hers. They were soft and moved with his perfectly. He moved his hands from her face. One held the back of her neck while the other moved to her lower back. He pulled her in closer to his body and she wrapped her arms around him.

When his lips began moving faster, more intensely, she joined his fervor and they moved almost as though it was a choregraphed dance that the two of them had practiced many times, until perfection.

In that moment, Roman knew he had to ask her to stay. While he hadn't kissed a ton of women, he had kissed enough to know that this was special. The connection between them was like nothing he'd ever experienced before, and he didn't want to let it go.

When he finally pulled back, he rested his forehead against hers. "Wow."

"Yeah," was all Sierra could say.

They both stood there in the middle of the bridge, breathing heavily.

Roman's heart was beating out of control. This was his chance; he wanted her to stay. He was third and five, and he wanted to score that touchdown more than anything else. And he was the guy who got what he wanted. But he wouldn't bulldoze his way through if she put up a defense.

"Sierra, I don't want you to leave town. I think what we have going between us is something worth keeping, worth fighting for." Roman lifted his head and looked into her eyes. "Would you stay here, in Beacon Creek?"

She blinked a few times before her words came out. "And do what?"

"I don't know. But we know a lot of people in the area, and I'm sure we can help you get a job. And Annie, too. If she's interested in settling down."

"Um." Sierra's mouth opened and closed a few times, and her brows furrowed. "Where would we live? That trailer isn't ours—it belongs to the carnival."

"You could live with me," he blurted, not wanting her to find a reason to turn him down.

Sierra pulled back and shook her head. "I don't know what kind of girl you think I am, but I don't move in with guys." She took a few more steps back and said under her breath, "I should have known it was too good to be true."

Roman waved his hands in front of his face. "No, that's not what I meant." He blew out his breath. "I said it all wrong. Let me start over."

She was still keeping her distance, but she had stopped shaking her head.

When he realized how his proposition sounded, he was horrified. He would never have a woman live with him who wasn't his wife. Shoot, his family would disown him if he did that.

When his heart dropped into his stomach, he took a deep breath and slowly let it out. "What I meant to say was that we have several cabins on our property. You and Annie could live in one of them. Just the two of you."

"Oh, well. That's a different story." She winced. "What's the rent? I don't think we could afford a cabin without a job."

"Room and board would be free."

Sierra interrupted him. "No. Annie and I don't need handouts—we work for our living. And besides, she's basically Red and Stella's kid. I doubt she'll leave them."

"As for payment, my mom could use some help with the canning. By the time all of the winter preparations are done, I bet we would have jobs lined up for both of you."

She tilted her head and looked at him funny. "Why do you want Annie to join me so badly?"

Uh-oh. He had gone about this all wrong. Red had asked him to not let the girls know he wanted Annie gone for her own good. He had to come up with a plausible idea for wanting Annie to join Sierra here.

"Well, uh, I just thought..." He blew out a breath. "Don't you want your best friend to stay with you?"

"Oh." Sierra's eyes softened. "That's so sweet of you. But, I don't know. I mean..." She sighed. "You know that I need to find my dad, right?"

He nodded. "Yes, and I also know you haven't had any real leads on him in a while. You could stay here and we could all help you. You do know that my sister-in-law is a sheriff's deputy, right? She can easily look up your dad and track him down."

"I've tried that route. He seems to be off the grid. I doubt he even has a current driver's license."

Well, that would make it more difficult, but Roman knew his family would be able to help. Something in his gut told him that they could. "Why don't you stay with us and see what happens?"

"Can I think about it?" The earnest expression on Sierra's face hit him in his gut. Something about the way she looked at him and bit her lip told him she was tempted, but unsure.

"Alright, just let me know. The offer will stay open, even if you leave next week." He wanted to pull her back to him and kiss her again, do anything to tempt her to stay with him. But he wasn't going to force his desires on her. If she wanted to stay, he would move heaven and earth to help her. If she wanted to leave? Well, he'd deal with that when it happened.

Annie hadn't stopped asking Sierra all about her date the night before. The carnival had been open for three hours already and the girl hadn't stopped talking. Well, except for when they had players. But even then, she'd help the kids and then start grilling her all over again.

Sierra had tried to keep some details private, but Annie was having none of it. During a lull after lunch, Sierra turned to her best friend and sighed. "Alright, alright. Yes, he kissed me."

The high-pitched screech that came out of Annie's mouth was almost as annoying as the vise grip Annie put on her hands when she took them and began jumping up and down. "I knew it! He kisses really good, doesn't he?" She waggled her brows.

"Ugh, Annie. You gotta stop acting like a teenager. We're grown women now." Sierra couldn't help the chuckle that escaped. Annie was a hoot, which was part of the reason she had come to love her like a sister. The sister she had always wanted. "But yes, he does."

Annie wrapped her arms around Sierra and jumped up and down and screamed some more. When she pulled back with a huge smile all over her face, she said, "Come on, tell me all the juicy details."

Sierra pushed back. "No, I'm not going to do that." She looked around. "But I will tell you that he asked me to stay here."

"*No way!*" Annie slapped Sierra's arm.

"Yes way." A slow grin spread across Sierra's face. "And you wanna know what else he asked?"

Annie pulled her hands to her face and lifted her legs as though she were running in place. "Do tell!"

At that moment a woman and her young son walked up. "Hi, is this the duck game that little kids can win?"

Sierra winked at Annie, knowing how much the wait was gonna kill her friend. Then she turned to the mother and son. "Yes, it is. We get small kids your son's age winning every day."

"Great." The mother handed over her two dollars and smiled at her little boy. He couldn't have been older than six.

Sierra gave the boy four red rings, and when he said he knew how to play the game, she stepped back. She sent up a quick prayer for the boy to win, which caused her to pause. Prayers hadn't been something she did much of lately, and a prayer that a kid would win was something she didn't think she'd ever done before.

Was Roman becoming a good influence on her? He prayed before each of their meals, including the ones out in the open at the carnival. Something her grandmother would have done, too. Now that she thought of it, it was something she did in high school every day before each meal, even when she alone and her grandmother wasn't hovering, expecting a prayer.

How had she gotten so far away from God?

That was a question she would have to think on, and possibly pray about, when she had a moment to think. For now, the little boy's winning cries and jumping up and down had attracted two more families to their booth. Sierra knew that she and Annie would be busy for a while. Especially since it was Friday afternoon.

And she had been right. After that little boy won, she and Annie only had time for a quick bite to eat. They were busy the rest of the day. Even when Roman came by to visit, she couldn't talk long.

"Are we all still on for tomorrow night? I'm making goulash and will have several board games to choose from, or cards. Whichever you prefer." He looked between Annie and Sierra.

Sierra nodded. "Yes, we're looking forward to a home-cooked meal. Even if it won't be until after midnight."

The weekend hours were later; the fair itself didn't close down until midnight. Roman's cow cuddling ended at eight, but his gift shop stayed open until the fair officially closed each day. He had said he wanted to make sure his cows had plenty of rest. They had already brought in a total of twenty yearlings and four mother cows. They didn't have room to bring in more this year, and they knew they couldn't expect the cows to work so long, either. Next year, they would double the size of their space.

Roman chuckled. "You'll be starving—admit it. I know you both go and sneak snacks after you close each night." He looked around conspiratorially. "But don't worry, everyone else does it, too."

"You know it." Annie grinned and helped the next family who walked up to their booth.

Roman eyed another group coming up, and he waved to Annie and told Sierra he'd see her tomorrow.

Chapter 15

As he walked back to his booth, which was just as busy as when he'd left, he realized how truly blessed he was. The Mannings had become a very large family. With the exception of Chloe and her husband, Brandon, every single one of his family members had been there to help with the booth. Which was what gave him the ability to go and visit Sierra so much.

Sadly, Sierra only had Annie to cover for her when she took a break. What would happen to their booth if both girls stayed? Or worse yet, what if Annie left with the carnival? Who would work the booth with her at the next venue?

When his worried mug showed up at his family cow-cuddling booth, his father approached him. "Son, what's wrong?"

Roman's head jerked up. "Huh? Oh, I was just thinking about how blessed I am."

"And that has you worried?" Caleb scoffed. "Son, usually when someone realizes how blessed or lucky they are, they smile at the very least. They don't scowl."

He waved his hand between him and his father. "No, I'm truly happy and thankful for all I have. I was thinking about Sierra and Annie."

"Ah, I take it Sierra hasn't told you her decision yet?"

"No, and I had never considered what her leaving would do to Annie or the carnival. And what if Annie decided to accept our offer? What would happen to their booth at the next event?" A heaviness entered his heart, and Roman rubbed his chin.

Before now, he'd never thought about what decisions could do to other people. Sure, he was part of a team and decisions were made all the time by the teammates, and they thought about each other. But no one left the team unless they graduated. No one left his family, either. Even Chloe, who had moved away, was still part of his family. She came back to visit and they had regular family video chats. But most importantly, her leaving never left anyone in the lurch.

Would the carnival be in trouble without one of its booths? Or were there people just waiting in the wings to join them? Like his football team. When one person graduated, there was a new body to join the team. But that was a well-oiled process. One that didn't see people leaving unexpectedly. Even when Chloe moved away, it wasn't unexpected.

If Sierra and Annie, or even just Sierra, left the carnival, it would be unexpected. Although, Red did ask him to help the girls leave.

Caleb put a hand on his son's shoulder and steered them both toward the private area of their booth, where they kept the little trailer that only slept two—uncomfortably. "Son, I wouldn't worry about the carnival. I think they'll be just fine. People come and go all the time in these jobs."

"Yeah, I know. I guess." Roman sighed. "For the first time, I'm having to consider what leaving might do to someone else. I don't know. Adulting is hard."

Caleb chuckled. "Son, it's all part of life. People come and go all the time. Some without warning, and some with plenty of warning. It's how we handle their leaving that counts. I'm sure the carnival owners know how to replace game operators on the fly."

"Yeah, probably." Roman looked around to make sure they weren't being observed. "It's just that Red, the owner, he asked me to take Sierra and Annie."

Caleb's eyes widened. "He what?"

"He approached me the other day and asked if I could help the girls stay here and find work. Maybe even go to college. He didn't think the carnie life was for them." Roman shrugged.

"Ah, is Red Annie's dad?"

Roman took off his Stetson and scratched his head before putting his hat back on. "No, not really. It's complicated. But Annie did grow up under his care. Sierra

163

has been with them for about three years now, and I think Red looks at her as a sort of daughter as well."

"Then"—Caleb scratched his chin—"it sounds to me like Red already has a plan in place if he wanted the girls to stay here in Beacon Creek. So what's bugging you?"

"That's just it. Red wants them to stay here. Why here?" Unsure how to word what was going around his mind and heart, Roman shook his head. "I don't know. Something feels weird about it all."

Caleb put up a hand. "Stop. How do you feel about Sierra?"

Roman looked his father in the eyes. "Oh, I like her. And I want her to stay, but only if that's what she wants."

"Do you think this Red fellow might be trying to force her out?"

Roman shook his head and twisted his mouth. "No, I got the impression that Red cares about both girls. Maybe that's not it. When I pray about it all, I feel as though the Lord is warning me." He threw his hands in the air. "Oh, I don't know. Maybe I'm overthinking this."

Before answering his son, Caleb paused and considered the words just spoken. "No, I don't believe you're overthinking it all. The Lord is trying to tell you something. Why don't you go home early and spend time in prayer? I'll close up for you tonight."

"Thanks, Pa. You might be right. I've been so busy that my regular morning devotionals have been shorter than normal. Some time with God might be just what my spirit needs." Roman clapped a hand on his dad's shoulder and nodded before heading home.

On his drive home, Roman put on praise music. He began singing with the songs, and he prayed that God would lead him to make the right choices. Then, once he was home, he got ready for bed and spent the next two hours in his room reading God's Word and praying.

Of course, he went and double-checked that his windows were locked. Not that he expected anyone to try and sneak in to his bedroom, but it was his habit.

And as he prayed, a theme kept coming up: God said He would never leave us or forsake us. That was what Roman had told Sierra just the other day. As the evening progressed, another theme emerged: Fear not, for I am with you always.

What did fear have to do with anything? Roman didn't fear Sierra, did he? That thought caught him off guard. As he considered his feelings for the pretty girl, he knew he didn't fear her. If she stayed, he'd be ecstatic, not fearful.

And if she left, he'd be sad, but not fearful.

God, why are you telling me to fear not? Is something coming? Something I need to prepare for? Is this what you're trying to prepare me for?

Roman fell asleep as he continued to pray for guidance and strength. He knew God was preparing him for something that was still to come. It may not even have to do with Sierra. She wasn't the only thing going on in his life at the moment. There were other things, such as the new business venture. Maybe that was what he should be focused on.

Saturday came, and Roman woke with a smile on his face. He had slept good and hard. It paid to pray before bed. Even if he didn't get as many hours of sleep as he wanted, he woke refreshed and ready to go.

"Ma, I need a few things to make goulash tonight in the crock pot." He was looking around the pantry when his mother asked Roman what he was up to.

"Here," she offered, "let me get it all together for you." She looked for her crock pot and then up at her son. "How many will you want to feed?"

"Um, at least four hungry adults." Roman grinned. "Sierra, Annie, and Boone are coming over to the trailer for a late-night dinner and games after we finish for the night."

Judith Manning stood up holding her six-quart crock pot. "Oh, to be young again and able to stay up so late and then get up early for church the next morning."

Roman snorted. "Please, don't tell me that youth is wasted on the young, again. I've had enough of that."

"Did I hear you're gonna make Grandma Holcombe's goulash?" Caleb grinned as he walked into the kitchen and poured himself a cup of coffee.

"Yup, I am. It's not difficult. Just throw everything into the crock pot and turn it on, right?" With a box in his hands, Roman began putting ingredients into it.

"No. Well, yes. But first you have to brown the ground beef. Then you can just pour it all in the pot. And cook on low for six hours." Judith passed the crock pot to her son. "Oh, wait. You can't put the pasta in until about thirty minutes before you're ready to serve it."

"Why?"

"If you put the pasta in too early, it will get mushy."

"Ah, ok. Thanks, Ma." Roman kissed his mom on her cheek and pulled out two pounds of ground beef. After he browned it, he packed it up and headed out for the carnival. It was also a rodeo day, and he knew the place would be crazy busy. So he also packed a thermos of coffee and grabbed two of his mom's famous orange scones.

"Say, I thought Highland cows all had horns?" A bewildered cowboy and his family looked at the Highland/Angus-mix yearlings and furrowed his brows.

"They do. But we've crossbred Angus cows with our Highland bull. That keeps the long hair and gets rid of the horns." Roman wanted to add that the meat was pretty darn good, too. But with two little girls grinning at the cows they were cuddling, he decided not to talk about them as though they were food. Even though most of the cows they bred did end up on someone's dinner table.

The man and his wife talked to Roman while the girls did their cuddling and grooming. River, Daisy, and John were watching over the cuddlers while Claire took care of what they had left to sell in their gift boutique. Even though it was only three in the afternoon, they were just about cleaned out. He figured they'd be totally sold out within another hour.

"I love what you're doing here. Will you be going to other fairs and rodeos with your cow cuddling?" the wife asked.

"No, we're ranchers. This is just a side project my brother John and I started recently. We might one day, but for now we only plan to offer this service on our ranch or at the local fairs and rodeos. We do have several throughout the year. That's enough for us." Roman wanted to add that he was thinking about opening a B&B down the road, but since he hadn't spoken to John yet, he refrained.

The woman nodded. "I recently read an article about how good cow cuddling can be for wounded vets and others who have medical conditions. Have you heard anything about this?"

He nodded. Roman had heard about cow-cuddling programs opening up all over the country for wounded vets. "Yes, we are going to supply a special ranch over in Frenchtown with a few yearlings for their wounded warrior program. And we're also offering something similar at our ranch. It's not the same, but we have a few local vets returning home soon, and they'll come out and try it, according their doctor's orders."

"Do you have a doctor on staff? Or any other medical personnel?" the husband asked.

He hadn't thought that far in advance. It was all new, and mostly they just wanted to offer the service for fun. Roman hadn't planned on making it a full-blown medical program, not like what Jerod was doing at the Crooked Arrow Ranch. "We aren't really licensed as a medical treatment facility. We're just offering the program up as an option for those who want a little bit of comfort."

Although the local VA clinic had contacted him recently about helping a few of their vets, Roman knew that the Triple J wouldn't oversee any medical treatment. If the VA wanted their patients to spend time with cows, or even horses, they would have to oversee the medical treatment part of it all. Unless... Well, he did know a very capable nurse.

The rest of the day went by so fast, and he even had a few more people like that family, asking questions about using the cows for medical treatment for various issues. One family had a daughter with Down syndrome, and the girl walked away talking more than her family had heard in quite some time. Or at least, that's what the father said. Maybe there was something to this, from a medical perspective.

Roman was wondering about the various treatment options when Nurse Harper came by and observed one of her patients who had scheduled a slot after dinner that night.

"You know, I think you're gonna have to purchase more cows for this program. I'm planning on talking to Dr. Montgomery about adding your services to his treatment program for PTSD patients."

"Really? You think cow cuddling is that effective?" Roman scrunched his nose, not believing it. He knew that all sorts of people with emotional disorders had come through and walked away feeling much better. They had told him so. But making it a part of an official program? That seemed too strange, even for his aspirations.

"It's a scientific fact. One that I've witnessed this week on several patients," Harper said.

"I know you can't tell me who, but you've seen your patients come through here and get relief?" The sun was setting, and Roman looked out at the people leaving the tent where the cows were kept for the program. "What works better, a yearling or a full-grown cow?"

Harper pursed her lips and looked as though she were contemplating his question. "I think we need more data, but it appears that both sizes work. Why, do you think one is better than the other?"

He shook his head. "No, I don't really know. I have noticed that kids all want the yearlings. But that makes sense. The kids are small, and the calves fit nicely in their arms. At least much better than a three- or four-year old cow."

"Yes, that does make sense." The ponytail on Harper's head swooshed when she turned her head and grinned.

Roman looked to see what had his friend smiling. And he groaned. "Not now. Please, not now. We almost made it the entire week without incident." He shook his head and waved to Harper as he walked toward one of the biggest problems their town had to deal with.

The tall, blond-haired man who had been nothing but problems for the Manning family stood in front of their booth.

"Mr. Johnson, what can I do for you today?" Roman asked.

Well, the man may not have been an issue, but his bull sure was. To be fair, Mr. Johnson did pay his fair share of the fence costs, but it was always the Mannings who had to fix the fence. Johnson never fixed it on his own.

"Roman, good to see you're back home. How does it feel to no longer be a college football star?" The old man grinned at him.

Roman knew he wasn't trying to be rude; it was just the natural way the man spoke. But he still grated on Roman's nerves. Now that Johnsons' son was home, things were better. The old man wasn't so grumpy. Or maybe it was his health scare from a few years back? Either way, he was a new creature. "I'm very happy to be home with my family again."

"Good, good." Johnson turned his head and looked at the booth. "Whatcha doing here?"

"It's called cow cuddling. And it's quite popular."

When Johnson scrunched his face as though he had stepped in a cow patty, Roman couldn't help but laugh. "What, you've never hugged one of your cows? Or spent time grooming them?"

"Why would I?" The older man flicked his ear forward when he went to scratch his head.

"Well, for one thing, it's a calming exercise. Wounded warriors and people with emotional distress find it soothing. Plus, a lot of kids enjoy it." Roman wasn't sure why kids loved it so much, but they did. He wasn't sure, but the kids all walked away asking their parents for a cow as a pet.

"Huh, well. Is your pa around? I needed to speak with him."

Roman found his father and let the two older men discuss whatever business they had. He was more interested in ensuring his goulash was on target for the night. When he looked at his watch, Roman realized he'd missed dinner. He didn't want anything too big since he had the goulash cooking, but he would need something to get him through the rest of the day and evening.

"Can you believe it's already closing time?" Annie asked as she picked up the remaining red rings littering the ground around the duck pond. They had been so busy that neither of them had had time to clean up their booth until now.

"I know. Since when do little kids stay up to midnight?"

"It's a Saturday night, and the final weekend of the carnival. I think most parents let their kids stay up late." Roman startled the girls when he walked into their booth and bent over to pick up the rings. "Don't you normally see kids up this late?"

"Well, yeah, but never so many." Annie sighed and took a seat for a few minutes. "My feet hurt."

Sierra waved her friend down. "Don't worry, I got this." She took a bucket and continued to pick up the rings.

"Well, do you normally have this many people at your booth, period?" Roman arched a brow.

"True, true. It's been a crazy busy week. Probably one of our busiest ever." With a sigh, she blew out her breath. Annie got up and began her nightly cleanup process.

Sierra was surprised to see Roman, but glad. She and Annie didn't have any time to talk about personal matters after that boy had won his duck, until now. And with Roman present, Annie wouldn't be asking any embarrassing questions, she hoped.

"So, who's gonna join us tonight?" Sierra remembered that Roman had said he would invite a friend to eat with them and even out the numbers for a game. Although, with as tired as Sierra was right then, she wasn't sure if she had enough energy for anything other than food.

Annie's ears perked up. "Someone else is going to join us? It's not going to be just us three?" A look of anticipation crossed her features before she schooled it.

With a light chuckle, Roman said, "Yes, I invited my friend Boone. I think you met him earlier this week."

Sierra sucked her lips in before she could say something to embarrass Annie. Even though her friend deserved to be embarrassed after all of her comments this week, Sierra was better than that. "Oh, really? Isn't he that cute guy you were talking about this week, Annie?"

Well, she thought she was better than that. Guess not.

Annie's cheeks turned red and blotchy, and Sierra felt a moment of triumph before guilt got the better of her.

With a wince and a sigh, Sierra sent an apologetic look to her friend. She would have said something, but she didn't want to make matters worse.

Roman was already grinning. Sierra didn't need to add fuel to the fire.

Chapter 16

"**W**hoa, this is seriously good. And you made it in your crock pot? Really?" Sierra took another bite of the goulash that Roman had cooking all day in his trailer. She didn't think she'd had anything like this before. He'd even toasted French bread in his toaster oven. It was amazing what one could make in a trailer with just a few gadgets.

He grinned. "Yes, it's one of my favorite dishes. It always reminds me of my Grandma Holcombe. I was young when she died, but boy howdy could she cook."

They all sat in silence for a few minutes as they devoured their bowls of food.

"I can't believe how successful your booth has been this week," Boone said between bites of his goulash and French bread.

Roman hadn't expected their booth to sell out of slots like it did. They only had a couple of people so far not show up, and those who waited at their booth were happy to take any open slots, no matter how short they were. He wasn't sure, but he thought he might even have made some new contacts for selling calves to.

There was one rancher who wanted to breed Scotty with some of their cattle, but Roman wasn't sure about lending their favorite—and only—Highland bull. He had a few bull calves; maybe once they were old enough, he would offer stud services. Although, they weren't full-blooded Highland bulls. They were crossbreeds. Once this fair was over, he and John needed to sit down and figure out exactly what they were going to do moving forward. Highland cows were really hot right now, but he didn't know how long the market would last. And with the Millers next door breeding full-blooded Highlands, he might not be able to compete.

"I have a lot of ideas for expanding the business. But what we need is someone to come on who has crafting knowledge. We need to build up product for the gift shop part of our booth. It's only a couple of months until the Christmas fair, and that's always the biggest seller of crafts." Roman tilted his head. "At least, that's what my mom said. She suggested we check with the church to see if anyone wants to join us and help out."

Annie widened her eyes and looked at Sierra.

"What? Do you know someone?" Roman asked when he noticed the silent exchange between the two.

"Actually, Annie and I both like to craft. There are times when we have an entire day with nothing to do, so we spent it making things." Sierra shrugged.

"Really? What do you do with them? You have a tiny trailer; I can't imagine you have much room for storage." Boone shoved another forkful of goulash into his mouth and lowered his lids halfway in pure pleasure. "If you could do a goulash booth, you'd have lines out the door."

With a chuckle, Roman shook his head. "Nah, if we were going to do a food booth or truck, it would be something to do with burgers and steaks. But that's not what we want for our future."

Well, he didn't think he did. He had thought about selling the Highland beef at the next rodeo. Maybe he did want it? No, he wasn't a chef. If one of his brothers who loved to barbecue wanted to do that, he'd be happy for them. But he already had enough ideas of his own.

"We sell them online." Annie shrugged right before taking a small bite of the toasted French bread.

"So, you both know how to craft? What do you make?" The Mannings wanted particular products to complement their booth, but maybe if the girls had some other items that would work for a country fair, they could sell them together.

Sierra answered after she swallowed a bite of goulash. "T-shirts, wreaths, ornaments, and sometimes we even make quilts. But those are rare since they take so much time."

"Huh, do you have one of those cutting machines? Or a t-shirt press?" Now Roman was very interested in their skills. This might be just what he needed on the ranch. All sorts of ideas and plans immediately entered his brain. Like they could manage the gift shop part of the booth and work on building inventory all year long. His sisters could help when they had time, but none of them would be pressured into helping at all.

But the most important part was that both Sierra and Annie knew all about working carnivals, and working long days to sell whatever was in their booth. Granted, they were game operators, but it was still selling. They had to sell the idea that a person, or kid, could play the game and win.

"Yup, we have both." Annie grinned. "You looking to hire crafters? We don't have a lot of time being on the road in the summer, but our winter months usually give us at least one day a week to craft, sometimes two. We could make up stock for you and ship it to your ranch."

So, Sierra hadn't brought up the idea to Annie of them staying on here? Or had she, and the girl wasn't interested? It also sounded like Annie was planning on Sierra moving on with the carnival as usual. Did that mean that she had decided against staying?

Sierra turned wide eyes to Roman. "I, uh... Well, I haven't had a chance to talk to her about your offer."

"What offer?" Annie and Boone said in unison with an orchestra of clanging forks hitting plates.

Now was probably a good time to discuss the options open to the girls. And if Boone's attentions to Annie were any indication, he'd be very happy to help convince her to stay.

"So, my family and I would like to extend an invitation for both of you to stay on here, with us. We have plenty of room on our ranch, and now it looks like we even have jobs for you both." An expectant pause had Roman looking between both girls.

Boone interjected, "The ranch is a great place to live and work. My brothers and I love it. We have our own cabin on the property and have no desire to leave. You should take Roman up on this offer—you'll love it." He leaned in. "Plus, their barbecues are famous. People come to visit them just for their barbecued beef."

Roman chuckled. "My dad makes his own sauces, and we only grill up meat from our cattle. So it's all rather fresh and flavorful. Nothing like what you get in the stores or restaurants. The sliders you had the other day, was just a sample of what we can do."

"Yeah, I remember those sliders from the other morning. I don't think I've ever had such flavorful meat before." Annie pursed her lips. "But, I don't think I could leave Red and Stella. They took me in when I was abandoned and have been the best parents a girl could ever want."

Boone's eyes clouded over. "You don't want to stay?"

A wince crossed Annie's features before she schooled her face. "I do, but I don't think they're ready for me to leave them. Not yet."

Roman knew otherwise, but he also knew he couldn't yet share that information. "Why don't you talk to them and see what they say?"

Annie looked to Sierra. "What about you? Are you considering this?"

Sierra sucked in her lips and looked between Roman and Annie. "Annie, I don't want to leave you, but I also think it might be time to move on. Roman has offered to use his connections to help me find my dad. You know as well as I do that the way I've gone about it these past few years hasn't gotten me anywhere."

The conversation between the girls was turning very personal, and Roman didn't know how much Boone knew. When he looked to his friend, the confusion was evident on his face. But the young man sat there holding his peace as the girls continued.

"You're tired of the carnival life? Tired of moving around to a new city every week?" Hurt was evident in Annie's eyes, and Roman felt for the girl.

He was also sure he and Boone should leave the trailer and let the girls talk. "Boone, can you help me check on the cows? I can't remember if all of the gates were locked or not." Roman stood up to leave, and Boone scrambled behind him.

Once the door to the trailer closed, Sierra sighed. "I'm sorry, Annie. Roman asked me Thursday night to stay. I wanted to talk to you about it, but we have just been so busy. He did extend the offer to you as well. We can both stay and work here. It's a really good offer."

"And you like Roman. I get it. He's a great guy. This would give you the chance to see if there's something there, or not." Annie wrapped her arms around her midsection. "But I don't have a guy here."

"You could."

"Boone?" Annie looked around to make sure they were still alone. "He's nice and all, but I don't know if he's the one."

"If you stayed, you could find out."

Annie sat back in her seat. The table where they were having dinner was a little booth that probably converted into a bed when the table was lowered between the bench seats. "I'm not sure Red and Stella would approve."

"Annie, you're a grown woman. You can make your own choices now." Sierra reached across the table and took her friend's hand in hers. "I don't want to leave you."

"But you don't really want to stay on the road, either." Sierra nodded.

"Look, the summer season is almost over. I should finish it up with the team. Plus, if you stay here I'll need to train someone new for our booth. I can't see Red replacing us both at the same time." Annie picked up her fork and moved it around the little bit left in her bowl.

Sierra lost her appetite. Even though Roman said he had made them dessert, she wasn't in the mood now. Her decision was going to be tough. Either she left Roman behind, or she left Annie. She couldn't have both.

But she wanted them both. Annie was basically her only family. Red and Stella were more like her cooky aunt and uncle, which she loved, but leaving them wouldn't hurt like leaving Annie.

"Yeah, I get it."

"Sierra, you can stay. You know that, right?" Annie focused on her friend and gave her a small smile that didn't reach her eyes.

She scratched her forehead. "Yeah, I do. But is it the right thing for me?"

When the door opened, both girls turned to look. Roman entered, followed by Boone.

"So, did you lock everything up?" Sierra knew she should put this discussion on the back burner and wait for later. Now, it was time to enjoy what little time the four of them had left together.

After the carnival left town, the four of them would never be together again.

Chapter 17

A loud beep interrupted her pleasant dream. She had been with Roman on a ranch and her dad was visiting her. He smiled and apologized for leaving her. They finally had the relationship she had dreamed of. Both with her dad and with a good man who loved her.

"Ugh, why did I agree to this?" Sierra moaned.

A pillow ended up on her face.

"Shut that thing off," Annie moaned.

"Sorry, I promised Roman I'd go to the cowboy church with him today." She threw the pillow back at her bunkmate and rolled out of bed.

A groan escaped. "Cowboy church?" Her other roommate Lilly lifted her head over the side of the top bunk.

Evelyn also leaned over. "You gonna turn off that blasted alarm?"

"Right, sorry." Sierra pushed the off button on her alarm and grinned at the girls. "Well, since you're awake, why don't you join us?"

"Fat chance." Lilly threw her friend a scowl and lay back down, back toward the group, and put her pillow over her head.

"Even with the promise of lots of cowboys, still not happening." Evelyn pulled her sheet up over her head after laying back down.

That just left Annie.

"So, you gonna join me?" Sierra raised hopeful eyes to her best friend.

"Not on your life. I get plenty of cowboys at the booth." She lay back down and turned her back on Sierra.

With a sigh, Sierra left the little room that worked as the bunkhouse for the four of them and went to the front of the trailer where she got ready for church. Last night before leaving, she had told Roman she'd meet him at the arena entrance. She didn't want to worry about him waking her roommates. Guess she had already done that.

Without a making a sound, Sierra opened the door to her trailer and gently closed the door and locked it. Then she smiled at the sunrise peeking over the horizon. It looked to be a warm, sunny day. A perfect day for lots of families to come back to the carnival before they pulled up stakes and left.

Sierra wasn't exactly sure what she expected, but this wasn't it. Instead of sitting in the stands with a ton of other people, the arena had been changed up. There was a small podium at one end with folding chairs and long wooden benches set out in front of the stand. There wasn't a mic, no speakers set up to project the preacher's words. It was simple and small.

Roman had taken her hand in his when they walked into the arena, which she was grateful for. Out of the forty or so people there, she was only one of a handful of women.

"Are you sure it's alright for me to be here?" she whispered when no one was close enough to hear.

"Yes, don't worry. Most of the people who work the rodeo are men, so that's why there aren't many women here." He directed her to the middle of the grouping of chairs and they sat in the folding chairs. They didn't have padding, but at least there was something there to support her spine, unlike the benches in the back.

Sierra scanned the faces, not recognizing anyone. "I don't see any other carnies here. Are you sure it's alright if I join in?" She worried that it was only for the rodeo crowd, and carnies weren't invited. If it caused any issues, she'd be happy to go back to her trailer and wait for her roommates to wake up so they could go eat breakfast.

With only a few protein bars in their trailer that morning, Sierra hadn't had breakfast yet. Usually the girls went to eat breakfast with Red and Stella in their larger trailer that had a much better kitchen space, and a fridge that worked. Theirs stopped working about two years ago and no one cared to pay to get it fixed.

He turned his mocha-latte eyes on hers, and they sparkled with mirth. "Sierra, relax. Anyone is welcome to join. Even those who aren't working the rodeo or carnival can come to the cowboy church. They welcome everyone."

Before she could say anything more, an older man with graying hair, a sun-worn face, faded blue jeans, and a snap-button blue shirt stood behind the podium. "Good morning, folks. Glad you could all join us."

She liked the man. He had an aura of peace and humbleness. There wasn't anything fancy about this man. Nothing like what she had seen with the television preachers. This man was down to earth and looked like he might be a rodeo cowboy. Maybe he even worked with animals. The man had a large scar down his forearm as though he might have been grazed by a bull's horns, or quite possibly a knife had sliced down his arm.

"It's mighty nice being back in Beacon Creek, Montana," the preacher said before he bowed his head and began to pray.

Sierra bowed and paid close attention to what the cowboy preacher had to say. She'd never attended a cowboy church, and hadn't even heard the phrase until Roman mentioned it earlier in the week. The sad part was that this wasn't her first rodeo. About half of their events were tied to rodeos or round-ups. She could have attended services many times over the past three summers.

A sense that she had missed out permeated her entire being as the message continued. He spoke about God being for everyone, not just those who were perfect. Jesus even said He came to save those who were lost, not the ones who thought they were perfect.

Sierra was so far from being perfect. She did have a relationship with Jesus. When she was young she had asked God to come into her heart and forgive her of her sins, but she had put God on the shelf, so to speak, after her grandma died.

"For those how have a Bible, or an app on your phone, join me in Luke chapter 19." The preacher opened his Bible and turned to the place.

Sierra hadn't thought to bring her Bible. She had one, but who knew where it was after all of these years? When her gaze shifted to Roman, she noticed he'd pulled out his phone and had an app open with the verse showing. Cowboys were like boy scouts, always prepared.

Roman placed his phone between them so they could both follow along with the preacher. On screen, she read: *For the Son of man is come to seek and to save that which was lost. Luke 19:10 KJV.*

"Jesus wants you. He wants you no matter what you've done in your past. All he asks is that you lay burdens at his feet." The preacher went on to talk about how Jesus would forgive you, and all you had to do was ask Him.

Sierra knew she wasn't *lost* in the sense that she didn't know Jesus, but she was lost in the sense that she had no idea where she was going next. And hadn't seen Jesus in her life in quite some time. Although, that wasn't really

His fault. She was the one who stopped reading her Bible and stopped attending services.

But, Jesus still wanted her. He wanted her to come near to him. Just a few verses earlier in that same passage, Jesus went to have a meal with a tax collector—someone who was considered about as bad as a carnie.

Sure, a lot of the people who worked in carnivals weren't the best, maybe even "unsavory characters" could be used to describe some of them. But in her carnival, drinking and doing drugs would get you fired so fast that you wouldn't know what hit you. Red and Stella ran a clean operation. They even did the occasional drug test.

But the fact that Jesus wanted to dine with someone like her really hit her. Her Savior hadn't left her behind when she joined the carnival—she'd slowly left Him behind. But she didn't have to leave Him behind. She could reach out to him and live a life he would be proud of, even if she stayed with the carnival.

Although, living in a carnival did make it tough to read her Bible daily and attend services regularly. She would never be able to join a church again because she wouldn't be able to attend the same place more than two or three times a year. And that was being generous. There would be times where she couldn't go somewhere Sunday mornings, and she would constantly have to check their schedule and see if there was a good Bible teaching church in the area where she was each week.

Sierra knew herself, and she wouldn't put in the work it would take for her to do that. If only they had their own cowboy church and preacher. That would make it so much easier.

However, there was another option: Roman's offer.

Roman couldn't help himself. Sure, he followed along with the scripture verses and made sure that as much as possible he had the right ones up for Sierra to read. But he couldn't take his eyes off the pretty woman sitting next to him.

Her facial features captured his attention. One moment she would be biting her lip, then the next she'd be glowing, then her face would be a torrent of emotions. He could tell she was paying close attention to what the preacher was saying. But what did it all mean?

Was she thinking about his offer to stay? Last night, he got the impression she was going to seriously consider it. They still had until Wednesday morning. If he and his family could work their magic on her, she just might stay with them...with *him*.

When the service was over, Roman turned to Sierra. "So, what did you think?"

"I liked it. The preacher was great and everyone seems to be smiling, so they must have liked it, too." Sierra grinned as she looked out at the people milling about and talking. "Do you know any of them?"

He shook his head. "Not really. I mean"—he pointed—"that there's one of the bronc-riding cowboys." Roman pointed to a tall man with spurs on his boots and a tall cowboy hat. He was a bit showy, with sparkling trim on his light-blue-and-white checked shirt.

"Yeah." She chuckled. "I can see it."

"So"—Roman rocked back and forth on his feet—"have you given any more thought to the offer to stay here?"

She nodded. "I'm still thinking about it. Tonight after we close, I was gonna talk to Red and Stella and see what they thought about it. But I don't think Annie will be staying."

He furrowed his brows. "Why not?"

"She's just not ready to leave them yet."

"Ah, I can understand. Family is important. They're her family. I get it." And he did. Roman had no desire to move away from his family, either. He loved them, and even though playing college football was his dream, he was happy to be home again. While he was gone, he'd missed a lot and didn't want to do that again.

Even though he wanted his own ranch, he wanted to stay within an hour tops of his family. Before Johnson's son returned to help with the ranch, he had actually contemplated buying the ranch from the aging man one day. But his son had returned with the plan to run it, so that ranch was out. Besides, it was probably too big for him to afford at this point.

He would need something smaller to start. And hopefully there was a ranch nearby that he and John could buy soon.

Chapter 18

I f Roman thought the final day would be a breeze, he was sorely mistaken. So many people showed up—more than they could accommodate. The slots had all been sold out earlier in the week, but there were people who continued to stop by the booth looking for space. Not just for their kids, either. Word was out: cow cuddling was the latest craze. You didn't have to be a kid to enjoy it. And you didn't have to have a medical condition to receive a benefit.

Customers were talking online about how their outlook on life improved after just a fifteen-minute session with the cows. He had been trending all week. And it showed with the amount of people who showed up at the rodeo.

His entire family came over to help after their regular church services concluded. And most of the town came to see their booth as well.

Luther and Caleb were off in a corner talking, and Roman wondered if the old high-school buddies were just catching up, or if there was something more going on. It was the final day of the rodeo and carnival, so if the coordinators had a problem with their crowds, they wouldn't have to worry for long.

After he finished telling one family he was sorry, but there was nothing he could do to help them today, he handed them a flyer and suggested they call and make an appointment to come by the ranch next week.

Then his father called out to him and waved him over. "Roman, Luther wants to make sure you sign up for all of our events going forward." Caleb chuckled. "It seems that we've helped to bring in more traffic for the carnival than they anticipated. Even those around us who had complained on day one are now asking to always be put next to our booth. Turns out we were exceptionally good for their business."

"Hm, that makes sense. So much foot traffic here, people couldn't help but see those booths and stop in to browse. Especially when they were waiting for a turn with our cows." The idea that they had helped the fair along with the booths near them thrilled Roman. Could it be that they would get their choice of prime locations going forward?

Did they even need prime locations? With all of the hype, what they really needed was more space. And space off to the side so as not to disturb too many of their neighbors.

"We want to talk next week about how we can accommodate your cow cuddling for the Christmas fair. I assume you'll need an enclosed tent and heaters for the customers?" Luther asked.

Roman hadn't decided if he wanted to bring the cow cuddling back for the Christmas fair. At least not for sure. It would be cold and probably snowing for much of the time. The cows could handle it no problem. But did they want to be outside, even if there was a tent?

After setting up a time to meet with Luther next week, Roman texted John. *Hey, I need you to attend a meeting with me next week.*

John responded, *Why? Are you getting married?*

Irritation flickered through Roman until he felt a hand on his shoulder. "Bro, what's up?"

Sometimes, Roman truly thought he was the older of the two. How could a man so immature be married with a child and a baby on the way? He shook his head. "John, get real. We have a business meeting next week with Luther. To discuss future events."

"Just as long as one of those future events includes Sierra, I'm game." The supposedly older brother grinned. "You know, married life is the best thing ever. I should have done this sooner."

Frustration tinged with a tiny bit of the green monster flared through Roman's gut. He did want to marry, eventually. But he wasn't going to take his brother's bait. Now that Mark was happily married and living in town, John must have missed having someone around to tease and play jokes on. He'd have to remember that and watch his back. "Well, if you'd married sooner then you wouldn't have River. And something tells me married in general isn't the best thing ever. It's being married to the *right* woman."

A mischievous half-smile crossed John's features, and something in his eyes sparked. "Very true. Very true, brother." He clapped Roman's shoulder and chuckled as he walked past Roman to greet his wife. John pulled River into a hug and gave her a kiss that caused a few people in the booth to whistle and holler.

Ugh, PDA. He'd never liked it. And he doubted he ever would, even if he married the woman of his dreams.

"You know, they remind me of a couple I recently saw in a movie. They too were disgustingly happy." Sierra's soft voice filled his head.

"Sierra, how'd you get away?" Not that Roman wasn't happy to see her, he just hoped she hadn't overheard what he and John had just been discussing.

"I'm taking a late lunch and thought I'd pop over to see how your day's going." A look of uncertainty flickered in her eyes before she smiled.

"Sorry, I'm a little stressed today. We've been so busy that I haven't even had a chance to eat yet. I was hoping to have one more teriyaki pineapple chicken." He looked at his watch and then at the booth filled with his family. "Care to join me?"

She bit her lip and looked at all of the people in the cow-cuddling booth, and around it. "Are you sure you have time?"

Roman took her hand in his, and a sense of peace enveloped him. "Yeah, I do." He called out over his shoulder that he was going to lunch, and without waiting for anyone to say a word, he took off with Sierra.

As they walked away, Roman picked up one voice behind him. "Best decision ever." He knew who it was and chuckled. His brother was just itching for payback, and that thought gave him an idea.

It was after midnight before Roman made it home. The fall festival was finally over, and he could breathe a sigh of relief. Even though he had a lot of help from his entire family, he still was the one who spearheaded the event and was there from start to finish each and every day.

The house was quiet, as it should be. Everyone should be asleep by now. Caleb was the last one to leave the carnival before Roman did, more than an hour later. They had everything all closed up and the tents taken down. The only thing left was to bring out the haulers and take the cows home. They'd do that tomorrow after he slept in. He also wanted to give the cows a lazy morning before upsetting them by taking them back home in the trucks.

All of their cows were going to get the rest of the week off. The family had decided that they wouldn't take any reservations this week for cow cuddling. If anyone wanted to come back next week, or later, they would be happy to work with them. Roman's heart ached for the calves. While they did love the interaction, he was pretty sure they were tired of all of the people and noise by the end of the week. Especially the noise. And he couldn't blame them on that count; he was probably just as tired of it all as the cattle were.

Since they only had two full-week events a year, he knew the cows would recover and enjoy the work again. Cows were very social. And on the flip side, they also needed their rest. So the next full event would have a better schedule for the animals. He tried not to beat himself up over it; this was a learning curve for them all. And he would also have more calves and cows next time. Each year they'd grow their herd, and then the cows would work less and less. He and John could discuss later this week exactly what changes they could implement to make things better.

When he stopped in the entrance to the ranch house to take off his boots, a very sneaky idea came to him. To silence his mad-scientist chuckle, he put a hand over his mouth and took his boots with him to his room. It wasn't like this idea was a new one, but it was one he hadn't had in a long while.

Roman rooted around in his closet, hoping he still had the bottle. Shoot, he couldn't even remember the last time he'd used the stuff. Did itching powder go bad? He guessed he'd find out in the morning.

Too bad his answer came so early.

"Roman!" A pounding on his door before the sun rose had him rethinking his late-night prank.

"Just a second," Roman called as he exited his bed and found a robe. He opened the door to find John standing in the hallway carrying a boot in one hand and the other rubbing hard at his calf.

When a chuckle escaped him, John looked up with a red face and glared. "You did this, didn't you?"

In between chuckles, Roman asked, "Did what?"

"I thought you got rid of the itching powder when you left for college." John threw his boot at Roman, who dodged the infected thing.

He threw his hands in the air. "Whoa, I'm just finishing what you started."

"Now I've got to go and take another shower. River had hoped to sleep in today," John grumbled as he walked away, still scratching his calf.

"Ah, do you want your boot back?" Roman picked up the boot by the top edge and tossed it down the hallway. He grimaced when he noticed some powder fall out onto the carpet runner. He'd have to clean that up before Daisy got in it.

The last thing he needed, or wanted, was for the cutest little girl ever to begin itching all over. He'd never want her to be a victim of their practical jokes. While they weren't truly mean, they weren't really appropriate for a little girl, either.

There went his morning to sleep in. But all in all, it was worth it to see John scratching himself so much. Roman chuckled as he donned his rubber gloves and set about cleaning the floor. While he was at it, he went ahead and cleaned the boot, just to make sure Daisy didn't get hurt.

"Thank you for cleaning that up before Daisy came out," River said as she walked past him to the kitchen.

Currently it was only John, River, Daisy, and him who occupied rooms in that wing of the house. His parents had the master suite, but it was in the other wing. Which was probably a good thing, since the boys tended to enjoy joking around. However, now that there was a little kid and a baby on the way, Roman doubted there'd be many more jokes on his horizon.

"Sorry if we woke you up early. I guess I need to rethink some of my old pranks now that things have changed so much around here." A goofy grin crossed his face. Roman was sorry he'd woken River. She was pregnant now and he knew she needed her sleep, but he wasn't sorry he'd gotten John back.

After he had his breakfast and was ready to leave, he asked if anyone could come help him to round up the cows at the carnival.

With a raised hand, Matthew said, "Count me in."

With the help of his brother, it didn't take too long to wrangle the cattle into the hauler. "Hey Matthew, why don't you go ahead and take off? I want to head over and see if Sierra needs any help finishing. I'll be home later."

Matthew grinned. "Uh-huh. You're gonna help the pretty carnie pack up her booth? Or maybe get in some final kissing before she leaves?" He chuckled. "It's really too bad they don't have a kissing booth here." He waggled his brows up and down, then nodded to the travel trailer before heading out with his own trailer full of cattle.

"Brothers." Roman rolled his eyes and walked away. He should have known Matthew would tease him.

Thankfully, he had to drive his own truck in so he could haul the small travel trailer back with him that day. Luke had stayed the final night in the trailer since his wife, Callie, had to pull duty that night. Otherwise, he would have slept overnight in the trailer himself. But if he'd have done that, he never would have pulled that fun prank on John. He snickered as he thought about the look on John's face that morning.

Roman knew his brother would get him back, but it was worth it.

Chapter 19

"**G**ood afternoon." The welcome voice brought Sierra up off her knees.

The sun was shining in her eyes, so she put a hand up to shield her face, but she'd know that voice anywhere. "Roman, it's good to see you. What are you doing here?" She knew he had packed up his booth the night before, and as far as she knew, they didn't have plans to see each other until the next day, when she and Annie went to their ranch for a barbecue.

Today, she planned on heading out to Bozeman as soon as her booth was stowed away. She wanted to take one more look around for any signs of her dad before leaving town. Last night after talking to Annie, she realized she couldn't leave her friend in the lurch. Maybe she could come back to Bozeman after they hired and trained someone new, but Sierra wasn't going to stay. A

200

feeling of dread enveloped her. Was she making the right choice? She could always come back, couldn't she?

She hadn't spoken to Roman about her decision yet, and Sierra knew she needed to. Maybe they could talk now?

"I just put the last cow on the hauler, and Matthew is taking them home. I came by to see if you needed any help with your booth." Roman looked at what was left of her booth.

She and Annie had slept in as usual for the day after a long carnival, but they had already taken down the booth and packed everything up. All that was left was to stow their boxes in the travel trailer.

"Well, as you can see, it's almost all done. But if you want, you can help me haul the last of it to the trailer." Sierra hoped he would help. And she hoped he had time to talk before she and Annie took one last trip into Bozeman.

During the carnival, she had checked out all of the tall, blond men she could find. None of them even came close to resembling her dad. But two nights ago she had seen a familiar face, and by the time she told Annie to watch the booth, she'd lost the guy in the crowd. He was someone she'd met months ago in Wyoming who said he knew her dad. She had looked for him again, but couldn't find him. She even walked around to all of the various booths, hoping he ran one of them.

She hoped he lived in Bozeman, or nearby, and she could find him again. A sinking feeling had taken over that morning, and she wasn't sure what it meant. Maybe it was a warning about the talk she still needed to have with Roman, and maybe it was a red flag to stay away from Bozeman. She couldn't be sure, but one thing she was sure of was that she had to try the city one more time.

"Of course. Once this is completed, what are your plans for the rest of the day?" A hopeful smile crossed Roman's face.

She hated that she might be changing his joy to sadness, but she had a schedule to keep. "I'm heading into Bozeman for one more look around town. I saw a guy the other night who I recognized as an old friend of my dad's, but I lost him in the crowd. I'm hoping to find him again in the city, if I don't see my dad."

With wide eyes, Roman's mouth fell open. "Really? What did your dad's friend look like? Maybe I know him?"

A flutter tickled her chest. Was that hope? "He's kinda short. Well, short compared to you." Sierra chuckled. "Tall compared to me. I'd say he's about five feet seven inches tall, or somewhere around there. He had on a straw hat that had seen better days and his hair was a dark brown. His clothes were all rumpled and probably dirty, but that's not saying too much at a fair."

Roman laughed. "Yeah, I think most people get quite dirty by the end of the day here. And who knows, maybe he was in the rodeo. Did you check there?"

She nodded. "Yeah, I did. I walked all over this place looking for him. But I didn't see him again." Her mouth quirked up on one side. "Actually, if memory serves, he wasn't a very active kind of guy. The last time I saw him, I got a weird vibe off of him."

"Weird? How so?" Roman took two steps closer, and a fierce look covered his face.

Her hand went up. "Nothing bad. Just, well, he seemed like he was nervous when we spoke last. He kept looking around as though he was hoping no one saw us talking." Sierra shook her head. "I don't know if that makes any sense. He didn't say anything other than that he hadn't seen my dad in a long time, and—this was the really odd part—he told me I should stop looking."

"Did he say why?"

Sierra sighed. "No. And when I asked him why, he just said I was better off without him."

Roman narrowed his eyes and rubbed his jaw. "That is strange. Do you think your dad was up to no good?"

She rolled her eyes. "Yes. One thing I discovered over the years of searching was that my dad wasn't in good with the law."

"Then why do you keep looking?" Roman asked.

With a shrug, she responded, "Because he's the last of my family. Without him, I'm all alone." A pang of regret and loss zipped through her chest, and she rubbed her eyes.

"I'm sorry, Sierra. But I don't think you're all alone. You have Annie. And what about Red and Stella? They seem to really care for you." Roman's hand landed lightly on her shoulder, and he squeezed.

"I know, but it's not the same. They aren't related to me." She sighed. "Don't get me wrong—I love them, and

I know they love me." She shrugged, not wanting him to see the anguish of her heart. "It's just not the same."

Roman was quiet for a few heartbeats. Then he surprised Sierra. "How about I join you in Bozeman? I'd feel better if I helped you look some more. And if we find this guy, well, I don't want you to face him alone. Not if he gave you a bad vibe last time."

"Thanks." Sierra looked up at Roman through bleary eyes that refused to drop a tear. "Annie is going with me. We should be fine."

"Do you mind if I join you?" His request was more of a whisper, but she felt the earnestness in his request.

Sierra nodded and smiled. "I think that would be nice."

"Great, then I'll help you pack up the last of your things. Do you mind if we drop off my travel trailer at the ranch before heading out?"

"Not at all. And I'll treat you to a late lunch today, if you haven't already eaten?" Hoping to put off the bad news that she wasn't staying, Sierra decided to wait a little longer before telling him. Instead, she would butter him up and wait until he brought them back. Maybe then she'd have the nerve to tell him what she'd decided.

"Oh, really? Can we call it a date?" Laughter sparkled in his eyes.

Sierra put a finger to her chin. "Hmm, let's see. Annie will be there with us. So if you don't mind calling her a chaperone, then maybe we could call it a date." She smirked.

He pulled her toward him. "I think a chaperone would be a great idea." His lips bent lower toward hers, but before he could make contact, a noise behind her caught her attention and killed the mood.

"Um, I could stay back if you two want a little alone time." Annie grinned from ear to ear.

Sierra pulled back and put her hands in her back pockets to keep herself from touching the good-looking and tempting cowboy. "No, that won't be necessary. I think you should join us." She cleared her throat and picked up a box.

Roman chuckled and grabbed a long length of wood—one of the poles that helped to hold up the booth—and followed Sierra.

With a box in her arms, Annie followed. "Well, if I'm going along, then you two better not be all kissy-kissy. That's just gross."

Without stopping or slowing, Sierra called out, "That's only because you're jealous. I bet if you had a cowboy to kiss, you'd be doing it in front of us."

Under her breath, but loud enough for Sierra to hear, Annie said, "I do have a cowboy to kiss."

That stopped both Sierra and Roman in their tracks.

"Do tell." Sierra grinned and waggled her brows. It was time for a little payback. "Should we invite him to go with us today?"

"Or should I invite him to the barbecue tomorrow?" Roman smiled and moved on toward the trailer only a few feet away.

Annie ignored them both as pink tinged her cheeks. She dropped off her box and headed back to get more of their boxes.

"I see Annie can dish it out, but she can't take it too well, can she?" Roman smirked.

Sierra shook her head and laughed. "I think she's more embarrassed that we might know who she's talking about than the fact that there might be a guy."

"Which makes me wonder if he isn't already invited to the barbecue." Roman organized their boxes and the items that had been sitting outside the trailer while Sierra went back to grab more boxes.

It didn't take long to finish loading their trailer, drop off Roman's travel trailer at his ranch, and then head into Bozeman.

"Do you ladies have a preference for our late lunch?" They had just passed the *Entering Bozeman* sign when Roman slowed and began to turn down the city's main drag.

The highway that took them from Beacon Creek to Bozeman cut right through the middle of downtown. It wasn't the nicest part of town, but then again, Sierra figured they wouldn't find that man, or her dad, in the best parts of town.

Spying a fast food joint, Sierra pointed. "How about there? Or would you prefer something more like the Big Bear Restaurant?"

He frowned, but Roman pulled into the Burger Basket parking lot.

"If you want to go somewhere nicer, we can." Sierra didn't move to get out once Roman put his truck in park.

"No, this place is good. I really like their fries." Roman turned off his truck and looked to his two passengers, who blinked at him. "Sorry, this place just brought back a memory." He nodded over their shoulders. "Back there is where most of the homeless tend to congregate. My sister's ministry group comes out here and helps to feed and clothe those less fortunate than us."

Sierra turned around. "And you have bad memories here?"

He shook his head. "No, there's just a guy who runs the homeless here, and he's not nice. I don't see him out there right now, but stay close to me. I don't want him to harass you in any way."

Annie squeaked. "Should we go somewhere else?"

A feeling prompted Sierra to get out of the truck. "No, I think this is where we need to be." She felt her mouth quirk to the side, and she wasn't really sure what it was about this place, but there was something here that was drawing her in. It was probably just one of those chain fast-food places that she and her parents had eaten at when she was a kid. There wasn't any particular memory here in Bozeman that called to her, but there was something inside of her telling her she was right where she needed to be.

"Alright. Just keep your hands on your wallets and phones. Lots of pickpockets in this area." Roman locked the truck with his key fob and walked slightly behind the girls, turning his head around and looking at the area.

Roman didn't like this. But if this was where Sierra wanted to take them, he'd go along with it. He prayed Big Bart wouldn't come around, but his gang seemed to have a sixth sense about him and his family. They were never far behind when Elizabeth brought her family and friends here to minister to the people on the street.

Why none of the women would easily leave Bart still baffled him. And his heart went out to the women who thought they didn't deserve any better than Bart or his gang. However, for Sierra's sake he would put aside his apprehensions and try to enjoy this lunch with the girls. Sierra hadn't told him her answer to staying, and he hoped she would tell him today that she was going to stay.

If Annie was interested in Boone like he thought she might be, maybe Sierra's best friend would stay as well. Not that he thought a girl should make such a huge decision based on a guy, but yeah, he wanted the girls to stay for them as well as for a new start for themselves. Did that make him a bad guy? Someone selfish?

The three of them enjoyed their lunch, and Roman was able to introduce them to monster fries.

"I can't believe you've never heard of monster fries. That's just crazy. You two, who live with a carnival." He shook his head as he drove his fork down into the mess of cheese, salsa, and crunchy fries.

With a mouthful of the gooey goodness, Sierra put her hand in front of her lips. "I would have these every day if I could."

"I have them every time I come here." He took another giant bite and lowered his lids. He was in nirvana.

They exited the little fast-food joint smiling and talking about how successful the carnival had been for them all.

"I can't believe we're gonna get our best bonus yet." Annie looked around. "Better keep that to yourself. Red hasn't announced it yet, and he loves to be the one to share the good news."

"Will he tell us all tomorrow at the crew picnic?" Annie asked, not watching where she was walking.

"Yup, he will."

Sierra stopped when her eyes widened, and she clapped a hand over her mouth. Tears were hovering on the edges of her eyes as she stared across the parking lot.

Roman looked to see what had her so upset, and he saw Big Bart. "Great, just ignore him. He'll leave us alone if we move along. Bart hates it when we interfere." He had noticed the hardened glare the big blond man was sending their way, and he shook his head. This was the last thing he needed to deal with when he was there with only Sierra and Annie. He knew he should have taken them to a different location. There was another Burger Basket, but it was all the way across town.

Sierra shook her head. "It can't be."

Roman had been tracking Bart's movements out of the corner of his eye and noticed that he was moving closer to them with another man at his side. When he turned to get a better look, he noticed that the man next to Bart looked like the one Sierra had described. The one she'd seen at the carnival. Had Bart sent his goons to spy on Roman and his family?

He took both girls by their elbows and moved quickly to the truck. "Come on, we gotta get out of here."

Sierra pulled her arm out of his grip. "No, that's him." The tears that had threatened were now streaming down her face.

"Sierra, come on. We gotta go." Annie moved along ahead of Roman.

Roman stopped and looked between Sierra and the two men coming closer. "Sierra, they're dangerous. We gotta get going, now."

She shook her head. "Dad?"

His stomach dropped and his heart stopped. It couldn't be. No, that's not right. A man like him couldn't have fathered a wonderful young woman like Sierra. He stood there looking between them, feeling the blood drain from his face. "No."

Chapter 20

"Yes," Big Bart growled as he looked between Sierra and Roman.

"He's your dad? Big Bart?" Roman pointed to the man that had hurt so many people in the state of Montana, and was responsible for the terror that one of his goons put Leah through a couple of years back.

Not looking at Roman, she scrunched her face. "'Big Bart?' Is that why I couldn't find you all this time?"

Bart nodded and flared his nostrils as though he was about to blow a gasket. "Why are you still looking for me? I thought you'd moved on."

"Grandma died. Did you know?" The hurt that had covered her face morphed into anger, and her fists clenched at her side.

Roman could see she where she got her anger from. While her dad resembled a raging bull, she appeared to be a racehorse getting ready to burst through the winning line. She puffed her cheeks and blew in and out. When her eyes narrowed, he worried he'd have an all-out fight on his hands.

"I did." His anger softened a little before he shuttered his emotions. "I heard that you'd made some good friends who were looking after you. But why did you want to find me? We haven't spoken since you were really young."

Roman thought she was better off without her dad, and didn't realize he had made any noise until the two of them turned his way.

Bart's eyes narrowed on him. "What are you doing with my daughter?"

Roman put his hands up. "Hey man, I'm helping her to figure out her future."

"Leave him alone. At least he's been nice and offered me a place to live and a job." She crossed her arms over her chest. "He didn't drop me off with a relative I barely knew and never come back."

Bart pointed his big, beefy finger in her face. "I did that for you. You were much better off without me."

"I'd say." Roman tried to keep his thoughts to himself, but when Bart glared at him and Sierra sighed, he said, "Sorry. I'll keep my thoughts to myself." He fisted his hands at his sides and realized he wasn't being a good Christian. It was his job to set the example for how Christ would want them all to act. And he was blowing it, big time.

The man in front of them wasn't the homeless slave driver Roman knew him to be. Right now, he was Sierra's long-lost father. She may not know all of the horrible things he'd done over the years, but he was still her father. That had to mean something, didn't it?

"Why didn't you ever come back?"

Roman saw the hurt in her eyes, even as tears began filling them again. He looked to Annie, who watched in awe. He nudged her arm and motioned to Sierra. Roman wasn't dumb; Sierra needed comfort. While he wanted nothing more than to put his arms around her and tell her it was going to be alright, he doubted Bart would ignore him.

When Annie put one arm around Sierra's shoulder, Bart looked at her and then back to Sierra. "Who's your friend?"

Sierra wiped a stray tear from her eye and took a deep breath. "Dad, this is my best friend, Annie." She motioned to the young woman still holding her. Then she pointed to Roman. "And I take it you know Roman?"

Ignoring Roman, Bart smiled and put his hand out for Annie. "Annie, it's nice to meet you."

Annie reached out to shake Bart's hand and looked between the two of them. "Nice to meet you as well, Mr. Baker."

"Please, call me Bart." The smile he gave her was like nothing Roman had ever seen on this man. He looked calm, cool, and collected. Probably what Sierra's father would have looked like had he stayed with his daughter and not left her for a life on the streets as a hardened criminal.

Roman hadn't expected a warm greeting from Big Bart, but he thought at least the man would have looked at him. Instead, he kept his gaze between the two girls.

"So, you two are related. I hadn't expected that one. Not at all." Roman rubbed his chin. "But I suppose I should have when Sierra said her dad's name was Bartholomew." He wanted to add, *and her dad left her, never to return*. That sounded like Big Bart. But he was going to keep that thought to himself. While it wasn't a nice thought, he didn't need to add fuel to the fire already burning.

What he needed to do was support Sierra. Did she know about his past? Roman doubted that sweet Sierra had any idea of the crimes Bart had committed, or the possibility he was closely aligned to a mob syndicate. Was that why Bart had never come back to see his daughter?

"You look so much like your mother." Bart reached a hand out to touch her face, but he pulled it back before Roman could act.

Sierra took a step back. "What happened to you?"

"Ah, Bart?" The other man who had been with Big Bart stepped up to the group and lightly touched Bart's arm. "We gotta get outta here if you don't want her"—his gaze barely drifted to Sierra—"to be seen."

Instead of saying anything, Bart growled and turned his anger on Roman. "If I hear that you've hurt her, I'll be coming after you. I don't care what anyone has said." He turned around and walked away without a backward glance.

"But…" Sierra started, and Roman took her hand.

"Don't. Let's get out of here, now." Roman guided both girls to his truck, and they got inside.

Tears streamed down Sierra's cheeks, and she stared out the front window without seeing.

"Sierra, are you going to be alright?" Annie whispered and took her friend's hand.

Sierra gave a slight shake of her head. That was the last movement or sign that she was coherent until they got back to Beacon Creek.

"I think I should bring you both back to my place. It's safer there." Roman ran a hand down his face when he stopped at the red light.

Annie shook her head. "No, I think she needs to be with me and my family tonight. Red will keep us safe. Don't worry about us."

"I don't know. Something's not right here. Sierra, can you hear me?" Roman touched her shoulder, and she didn't even move.

"She's in shock. But we can take care of her. How about I call you later and let you know if anything changes?"

"Alright, I'll bring you back to Red's RV. But I wouldn't stay in your own trailer tonight, just to be safe. I think you two should stick with Red and Stella." He doubted Bart would do anything to his daughter, but he didn't know about the guy with him, or even what he was talking about when they left. However, Roman had a very bad feeling.

"Good idea." Annie nodded.

Roman kept running over the strange conversation with Bart as he drove home to the ranch. What Bart's goon had said wouldn't leave his head. And the fact that his goon wasn't surprised to know that Bart had a daughter. If he was the same man that had come to the carnival that night, he must have been checking in on Sierra for Bart, right? Or was he scoping out Bart's daughter for some other reason? Something nefarious?

But the man had tried to get Bart out of there before anyone would notice Sierra. Why would he do that? What did it all mean? Multiple scenarios crossed his mind before he made it home, none of them good.

He parked his truck close to the front door, something none of them did regularly. Normally they parked their vehicles on the side of the house, but today he was in a hurry. Roman didn't even take his boots off when he got inside. Instead, he headed straight for his dad.

"Pa!" he yelled out as he searched for his dad.

"In the kitchen," Caleb called out.

It wasn't quite time for dinner, so his father must have been keeping his mother company as she prepared their evening meal. It would be better to have them both there. Roman even considered calling everyone in, but by the time he walked into the kitchen, he had decided his parents would be the best ones to speak with.

"Roman, you're home early. I expected you'd stay out late tonight." Judith Manning's eyes crinkled when she smiled, and laugh lines appeared around her mouth. This woman smiled a lot, not caring about her wrinkles.

"We had a problem." Roman plunked down in a chair at the table, then got back up and started pacing the limited space in the kitchen.

His parents waited for him to calm down. And when he finally took his seat again, his mother put a cup of hot decaf coffee with cream and sugar in front of him.

"Thanks, I think I'm going to need this." Their son turned a forlorn gaze up to them before returning to fixing his coffee. "You might want to sit down for what I have to say."

"What happened?" Worry lines creased Caleb's face as he sat across the table from his son.

Judith set the pot of coffee in the middle of the table and joined her husband and son.

With a heavy sigh, Roman said, "Big Bart walked up to us while we were in the Burger Basket parking lot."

"What?" Caleb exclaimed.

Judith inhaled and put her hand to her heart. "What did he do?"

"That's the crazy part. He was angry, but didn't actually do anything." Roman took a long drink of his coffee. "Turns out Big Bart is Bartholomew Baker, Sierra's dad."

"No, that can't be right." Judith shook her head and sat back hard in her chair.

Caleb jumped up and began pacing the kitchen. "What does he want?"

"Nothing." Roman rubbed his face. "Well, I think he wants Sierra to stay away from him, and probably from us. He threatened me if I hurt Sierra, but he didn't actually say that she had to stay away from me. It was more that he needed her to stay away from him."

"So that's why she couldn't find her dad the past three years. He's off the grid and not really using his own name." Callie walked in to the kitchen and sat next to Roman. "Sorry, I heard you talking and listened in when you mentioned Big Bart."

"How's Sierra? Does she even know what her father has become?" Judith got up, took a coffee mug out of the cupboard, and set it before Callie.

He wasn't sure how Sierra felt, but Roman knew he needed to check on her. His heart went out to her. He couldn't imagine how it would feel to discover that your only living relative was a big-time criminal and tied up with the mob. "I told her a little bit about Bart. She was in shock the entire way home. I tried to get them both to come out here for tonight, but Annie insisted they go back to Red and Stella."

When Caleb finally stopped pacing, his face was red and he leaned over the back of his chair with his hands white-knuckling the top of it. "That's probably best, since they've been her family for the past three years. Do you think she's gonna want to stay here now that she knows?"

Roman snorted out a breath. "I doubt she'll want to leave the area now that she knows her dad is here. She'll probably want to talk to him more and try to help him."

"That won't work well, for her." Callie, the sheriff's deputy, would know better than any of them how a criminal would act in this situation. "I'd bet he would want to keep her safe and far away from what he does. If Bart really is in with the mob, and they find out about Sierra, they could use her against him. It would be very dangerous for her to be in Bozeman."

A thunk sounded when Roman hit his head against the table. He went back and forth between red-hot anger at Bart and compassion for Sierra's plight. How could anyone accept a father like Bart? "I know. But if anyone has figured it out yet, she's not safe in the carnival, either."

Callie pursed her lips and narrowed her eyes. "I think it might actually be safer for Sierra if she stayed here with y'all. But I wouldn't put her out in a cabin, I'd keep her here in the house." She turned her gaze to Roman. "Do you think you could handle that?"

Roman knew exactly what his sister-in-law was talking about. After discovering that John had fathered a child out of wedlock, this family no longer assumed that any of the single kids would abstain. And since Roman was the last single child in the Manning family, they were all watching him carefully. He might have been offended, but after seeing what John went through the past two years, he could understand why his family would want to make sure he kept things proper with Sierra.

He held up his hands. "No need to worry on that count. I seriously doubt Sierra will even want me to kiss her for a long while, if she even stays. This revelation just might send her packing with the carnival on Wednesday."

The welcoming sound of his phone ringing jolted Roman, and he pulled it out of his pocket. When he saw the caller ID, he smiled. "It's Sierra." He stood up and walked out of the room to have his call in private. "Hey, Sierra. Are you alright?"

"Sorry, this is Annie. I don't have your number, so I used Sierra's phone. But she's alright." Annie paused. "Well, she will be. There's been a lot of tears, but at least she's talking now and not staring off into the distance like earlier."

"That's good. It means she's processing what happened. Will you spend the night in Red's RV?" What Roman wanted was for the girls to come out to the ranch and stay with them. He knew he could protect them, and while he trusted Red and Stella, Roman wasn't sure how well they could protect the girls.

"We're gonna stay here for the night. Tomorrow is the celebration picnic before everyone leaves for different jobs. Only a small amount of us will be moving on to the next carnival."

"Okay. Call me if you need anything, or if Sierra just wants to talk. I don't care what time it is. I'll leave my phone on tonight so she can call. And will I still see you both here later tomorrow for the barbecue?"

"Yup. We're still coming out tomorrow night," Annie replied.

"Feel free to come as early as you want. And bring Red and Stella, too. We have a saying—'the more the merrier' here at the Triple J, and we truly mean it."

If all four came out, Roman would be happily surprised. And it might help to calm everyone's nerves, too. They always had plenty of food to go around, so two more mouths to feed wouldn't be an issue at all.

"Thanks, I'll let them know, but I doubt they will. It's our last night in town and there's still a lot to do in order to split up the troupe."

"I understand. Let Sierra know we're all praying for her, will you?" Roman said his goodbyes and hung up before heading back into the kitchen to update his parents and Callie.

While waiting for dinner, Roman went to his room to spend time with the one who always knew exactly what he needed. The Lord directed him to read Matthew chapter 6. As he read the words reminding him not to worry about the future, for the Lord was in control, his shoulders relaxed and he began to pray.

Then his jaw, which had been so tight his teeth hurt, loosened and his headache abated. The Lord was good. He was the only one who could help Roman give up his uncertainty and frustration over what had happened, and what might come. Roman couldn't control Big Bart or any of his goons. They were going to do whatever they were going to do. All Roman could do was pray and trust that God was in control.

Which wasn't always so easy to do.

A part of him wanted to rail against the injustices everyone had experienced at the hands of Bartholomew Baker, especially Sierra. But there were many others, like Georgia. Even though Georgia was happily married to the sheriff, she had lived for a long time in fear and uncertainty as to what would happen to her.

Thanks be to God, who took that woman out of Bart's control and brought her to the Triple J Ranch. All of the Mannings loved Georgia. She had lived with them for over a year before she married Roscoe and moved in with him. Roman knew his mother missed her friend deeply. But the new sheriff's wife did still live in town, so Judith met up with her on a regular basis. Shoot, Roscoe and Georgia came over most Sundays after church to enjoy the family barbecues they always had.

Would Sierra become part of their family as Georgia had? Would everyone look past her parentage and accept her for who she was, and not who her father was? Roman hoped his family and inner circle of friends would. But it wasn't his place to worry about that. His job was to put it all in God's hands and let Him worry about the future.

Roman's job was to be there for Sierra as much as he could. He would protect her from Bart if need be. And he was confident his family would do the same.

When John came and knocked on his door to let him know dinner was ready, Roman put away his Bible and walked out lighter than when he'd stepped into his room an hour earlier. Time spent with God always rejuvenated him and helped him to put his head on straight.

With a grin, Roman entered the kitchen and sat down to dinner with his parents, John, River, Daisy, Luke, Callie, Matthew, and Claire. And when all eyes turned to him expectantly, he knew his parents had already updated everyone.

And he was grateful.

Chapter 21

Roman had been looking forward to the dinner today. Both Sierra and Annie would be coming over after they finished the picnic with the rest of their troupe. Since she had said she would drive the carnival truck, he paced around the house, looking at the clock every few minutes.

"Come on. Why aren't they here yet?" Waiting for something he really wanted wasn't a strong suit for Roman. When he played football, he had a pre-game ritual. Most of the guys on the team had something they did. None of them were very patient, and when nerves were high, it helped to take their minds off of the upcoming game.

However, he wasn't in the locker room with his teammates. Instead, he was on a ranch with his family. They were all busy cleaning, preparing the barbecue, and taking care of the cattle. Something he probably should be doing as well. But he wanted to be at the house when Sierra arrived.

If it wasn't so late in the day, he would have gone for a ride, or maybe out to the makeshift gym they had in the original barn. Instead, he pulled out his Bible and began to read, praying that God would calm his mind and body.

Sierra hadn't told him if she was going to stay yet, and after last night, Roman doubted she would. And that uncertainty had him nervous. This was the woman he'd dreamed about for close to two years. She was supposed to be in his life, wasn't she? How could that happen if she was always on the road?

As he read and prayed, he realized that God was at work in his life. He was there for Roman. Always had been, and always would be. The peace that flowed over him was exactly what he needed. He was so into his time with God that he didn't even hear the doorbell. In fact, he didn't hear a single thing until John knocked on his door to tell him that Sierra and Annie had arrived.

Ever since yesterday when she found her father and discovered who he had become, Sierra's mind and heart were in turmoil. Part of her was glad that her dad wasn't in her life if he had chosen a life of crime. But, why did he do it? He didn't have to do it. He could have chosen his daughter instead. She knew her grandma would have let him stay with them for a while, at least until he found a new job and an apartment for them to live in. Her grandmother wasn't heartless, but she had been right to keep Sierra from finding her dad while she was growing up. Or had she? If she had been in touch with her dad all those years, would he have chosen to be such a leader of a homeless gang? That was what Roman had called him, before he knew who Big Bart was to her.

In her memories of her father, he was loving and absolutely adored her mom. When Sierra's mother died, he was devastated, but so was she. Now that she thought about it, he'd pulled away from her instead of trying to comfort her. She was a little girl; most dads would have done their best to comfort their daughter when her mother died. But not her dad.

The fact that he took her to live with her grandmother less than a year after her mom died should have told her a lot about him. Her memories of that time between were vague, but she could remember staying with neighbors a lot of the nights. Why did her father leave her alone? Now she had more questions than answers. Would he answer her? Could she find out why he'd abandoned her at such a young age? Sierra didn't know what her dad would say or do, but she wasn't going to stop seeking answers. Especially now that she knew where he was and how to find him.

For today, however, she needed to focus on the Manning family. If they still wanted her to stay with them, she would take them up on their offer, if for no other reason than to learn more about her dad.

Sierra couldn't believe her eyes when they pulled up the drive to the Triple J Ranch. She'd known it had to be a nice place, but she had no idea how nice a ranch could be. Neither she nor Annie had ever been on a ranch. Why would they?

As they parked outside the entrance to the house, an inviting sensation of warmth and welcome enveloped her. Sierra felt her lips turn up in a smile and realized it was the first smile she'd had in the past twenty-four hours. She was the sort who smiled, a lot. And of course, realizing that the house helped her to smile again only made her smile more.

The ranch-style home was large and impressive. There was a welcoming covered porch with multiple rocking chairs, a porch swing with cushions, and an afghan thrown over the back of the swing. It was exactly the sort of place that Sierra could envision herself sitting in the evenings, drinking lemonade or sweet tea. Even though she had never been here, she felt as though she was coming home. It was too large to be like anywhere she had ever lived before. Even before her mother passed away, they hadn't been rich. They'd lived in a rented apartment. Her first experience living in a house was with her grandma.

While her grandma's house was a pretty two-story Victorian, it wasn't very large and they didn't have the sort of porch that the Triple J did. So she didn't understand where this feeling of comfort and belonging was coming from.

Once she and Annie were inside, they were led to a large family room. There were multiple chairs around the room. But with all of the family members, it made sense that there would be three sofas, a loveseat, and four recliners in one giant room. It looked more like a furniture showroom than a living room. And it put a smile on her face, again, just imagining what it would be like to have grown up here and having to share the remote.

"Wow, this place is huge." Annie gawked as she looked around at the room. "I never had more than an RV. Granted, Red's RV is pretty nice with the pop-outs, but man, this place is on a whole 'nother level."

"I know." A low whistle followed Sierra's words, and they waited in the room.

It was only a minute or so before they heard a loud thunk and a yell. The two girls looked at each other with wide eyes, not sure what was going on.

"Oh, Daisy, it's alright," a woman's voice cooed from the hallway, followed by a man's asking what had happened.

Sierra looked to where she heard the voices and was about to walk toward them when Roman entered the room. "What happened?"

"Hi." Roman waved to the girls, then turned to stare in the direction Sierra was looking. "Oh, that? Daisy was riding her tricycle down the hallway, which she knows she's not supposed to do, and she ran into the wall."

"Is she alright?" A fluttering entered Sierra's chest, and she covered her heart.

A chuckle escaped Roman before he caught himself and then he cleared his throat. "Um, yeah. I think she startled herself more than anything else." He turned his ear to his little niece and listened. "No crying, so all is fine." He turned his gaze to Sierra and sighed.

Sierra looked back to Roman and felt her cheeks warm. She hoped she wasn't blushing, again. It seemed she did a lot of that in his presence lately. The one kiss they'd shared under the stars the other day entered her head, and her neck began heating as well. She had to get a grip on her emotions, and thoughts, before Roman realized what she was thinking about.

"Well"—Annie grinned and looked from Sierra to Roman—"I for one am glad she's fine. So, what's the plan?"

Roman had been staring at Sierra, and he broke the connection when he turned to Annie. Then he offered them refreshments, and they all headed out back.

"Wow, this is something out of one of those house-and-garden magazines." Sierra looked around, dazed. She hadn't thought this kind of setup was real, that it truly was only something showcased in magazines. When they walked out to the patio, there was a very large patio set that could easily seat twenty people. Behind it was one of those giant black barbecue grills she had seen on TV, the kind that was usually stationary and didn't move. They could probably grill up enough steaks at one time to feed an army.

"Is that a firepit?" Annie pointed, and Sierra turned her gaze.

Farther back, past the covered patio and grilling area, was a dirt plot that had about a dozen camp chairs and several wooden benches surrounding a large pit in the ground. In it was wood, all ready for a fire. And off to the side was a large wood pile, far enough away that the crackle from a fire wouldn't catch on the wood waiting to be burned in the pit. To the side of that was a small shed. She guessed it was where they kept more wood, or possibly other supplies. She couldn't be sure, but it had to be about a twelve-foot-by-twelve-foot enclosed shed with a regular house door that opened out.

"Yes, it is. We love to have bonfires and make s'mores for dessert after we grill up steaks." Roman's pride in his ranch was evident as he motioned for them to walk out toward the pit. "We have supplies in the shed for roasting marshmallows, or anything really. Sometimes we even put hotdogs on a large fork and roast them in the pit for a snack."

A feeling of inadequacy came over Sierra, and she wondered why in the world a family like this would welcome a carnie into their lives. She couldn't bring anything to this family that they didn't already have. Neither she, nor Annie, could really cook. Living in a trailer and traveling from carnival to carnival didn't really give them much of an opportunity to make more than soup or sandwiches. Sierra had never canned anything before, so she wasn't even sure how she could help Mrs. Manning if she stayed.

"Ma, I'd like to introduce you to Sierra and Annie." Roman motioned from a pretty older woman to them. "Sierra, Annie, this is my mom, Judith."

"Mrs. Manning, it's so nice to meet you. Thank you for inviting us for dinner tonight." Her hands were damp, and Sierra hoped her hostess couldn't see how nervous she was.

Judith put a hand out for them and smiled warmly. "Please, call me Judith. Everyone else does."

In what she hoped was a stealthy move, Sierra rubbed her clammy hand across her thigh before taking Judith's hand. "Thanks, Judith. I love your patio area. You must do a lot of grilling with a backyard like this."

Annie took their hostess's hand and looked around, admiration evident in her sparkling eyes.

"Why yes, we do. Most Sundays when the weather is nice, we like to fire up the grill and throw on steaks and chicken. In fact, that's what we have getting ready to go on the grill now." Judith turned as her husband and several other Manning men walked outside from a sliding glass door carrying trays of raw meat that looked to have been marinated in barbecue sauce.

Sierra's mouth watered as she looked at all of the prime cuts of meat parading past her nose. The tang from the sauce wafted up, and her mouth started to drool in earnest. "Wow, I bet you guys never go out to eat. Not with a setup like this."

"Oh, we do go out, but not that often." Roman led them closer to the grill. "My family loves to grill, but my mom also loves to cook. She could easily open up her own restaurant if she wanted to, and it would always be packed."

"Oh shush, Roman." Judith lightly slapped her son's shoulder. "I remember when you were in school and you'd beg me to order pizza."

"Well, duh." Roman chuckled. "The only things teens like to eat are pizza and burgers."

His statement caused everyone in earshot to laugh.

"You got that right," Matthew said. "I remember one summer when we were grilling, you refused to eat anything except for cheeseburgers. Even when we had top sirloin on the grill, you still only wanted a cheeseburger."

"Yeah, my tastebuds have changed. Now I prefer nicer cuts like filet mignon wrapped in bacon." Roman licked his lips.

John pushed his shoulder. "Dream on, bro. We've got us a grill full of top sirloin tonight."

"Don't forget, we do have a few burgers, too." River winked at Roman.

"Yeah, I'm over the whole burger phase, thank you very much."

A feeling of family and acceptance flowed through the group. It was something Sierra had wanted for a long time. Sure, she fit in with Annie, Red, and Stella, but this was different. The Mannings had a real *home*, not just a welcoming RV. It reminded her of what it was like with her grandma, and she missed her.

Chapter 22

When dinner was over, Sierra sat there with a hand covering her belly. "Umph, I don't think I could eat another bite."

"Me either," Annie agreed.

"Does that mean you don't want s'mores?" Roman teased.

The two guests looked back and forth between the firepits and each other. Then Sierra blew out a breath. "Can we wait a little bit? Let the food settle in my stomach first?"

Roman laughed. "Of course. We do usually wait. Want to go out and see the cows? I could show you two the barns and our horses."

Both girls nodded and stood up.

"Walking will do wonders for making room in my stomach for more food." Annie grinned and patted her belly.

Roman was excited to show them the barns and the animals, with the hope that both girls would stay on. He hadn't asked yet what their plans were, but he suspected they'd be leaving Beacon Creek the next day with the carnival, and the thought of Sierra leaving left a hole in his heart.

When they approached the new barn, the red walls were bright and inviting. Roman was proud of this barn. He and his brothers had built it last summer when he was home from college. It wasn't quite as large as the old barn, the one his forefathers had built, but it was still impressive. This barn was designed for cow cuddling. There was a small foyer in the front with fresh straw across the concrete ground and several wooden bench-es along the sides where people could wait for their turn to spend time with a cow. Down both sides were larger stalls, or rooms, where guests could hang out with a cow. They could either sit on a bale of hay or bring a padded bench into the space. It was large enough to comfortably fit two adults and one full-grown cow.

As Roman explained the barn and what each room was for, the girls smiled and talked about how wonderful it all was.

When he was at the back of the barn near the store-rooms, Roman mustered his courage and asked the question that had been hanging over his head all night. "So, Sierra, have you made a decision yet?"

He knew he didn't have to say exactly what he meant. She understood.

Sierra sucked her lips in and took a deep breath. "Yes. Last night and today I spoke with Annie, Red, and Stella. We all agree the best thing for me is to stay here." She turned her gaze to Roman. "If the offer still stands and you have work for me. I don't want charity. I need to work for a living."

The lightness Roman felt was overwhelming. He thought if he weren't inside the barn, he'd float away like a balloon. The grin spread from ear to ear. "Yes, of course the offer still stands. We're going to have a lot of work to do. You can help with making t-shirts and all sorts of other items for us to sell at future events."

"Good, then if you can come and get me in the morning, I've got a few things to do before everyone leaves." Sierra bit her lower lip, trying to keep her grin from spreading too large.

Roman clapped his hands. "That's fantastic. I'll be there right after breakfast." He turned to look at Annie. "What about you? Did you want to stay here as well?"

Annie frowned and shook her head. "I'm sorry, but I'm not ready to leave Red and Stella, or the carnival. I love what we do."

He nodded. "I get it. Just know that you're welcome here any time you want. Even if it's just to come and visit."

"Thanks, I really appreciate that." Annie turned to Sierra. "If you don't keep in touch, I know where to find you."

Sierra pulled Annie in for a tight hug. "Don't worry, I'll be texting you every day. You're gonna get sick of me."

"Not a chance." Annie pulled back. "And I fully expect regular pictures of your crafts and the animals."

"Do you like baby goats?" Roman thought now would be the best time to get some oohs and awws. He hadn't told them about all of their animals yet. They also had a litter of piglets he could show them.

They spent the next hour cuddling baby ranch animals and talking about what crafts the girls enjoyed making the most. None of them mentioned Bart, and Roman decided that was probably for the best. He wanted Sierra and Annie to enjoy their last night together. They would have plenty of time to talk on the phone and text all about Sierra's dad and what it all meant for her later.

"Roman!" Luke yelled out. "Time for dessert."

"Annie, are you sure you don't want to join me at the ranch?" Sierra had pulled all of her personal items out of the trailer, and Roman stood to the side of her as she said goodbye to her surrogate family.

"You know, sweetie, we'd understand if you wanted to settle down here. Beacon Creek's a mighty fine town." Stella put an arm around Annie's shoulder and side-hugged her adopted daughter.

Annie shook her head. "No, I'm not ready to leave you two yet. Besides, who would train the replacements for the duck booth?"

Red chuckled. "Annie-bell, we'll be just fine if you stay in Beacon Creek."

"I know, but I wouldn't be." Annie took Red's hand and squeezed it.

Roman could see the emotion in her face. The girl was old enough to be on her own, but with her background, he understood why she didn't want to leave the only parents who had ever wanted her. It had to be tough to be abandoned by your actual parents at a carnival and not wanted when you were so young.

"Annie, there's always a room for you at the Triple J. I hope you know that." Roman smiled at the young woman who had become a friend to him in the last week.

"Thank you. Just make sure you take good care of my Sierra. And we'll see you in December."

Roman blinked and furrowed his brows.

At his look of confusion, Annie giggled. "Didn't Sierra tell you? Red accepted the offer to come back here for the Christmas carnival this year."

He slapped his hands together. "That's fantastic! I look forward to hearing all about your fall and winter excursions in a few months."

Stella pursed her lips. "And we'll be checking in on you, Sierra. Don't think we're gonna move on and forget you. I'm always here if you want to call. Or if things don't work out, you will always have a place in the carnival."

Sierra hugged Stella, and Roman watched as a tear streaked down her face. And he wondered for the first time if he was doing the right thing. Sierra had fit with this odd family. While none of them were related by blood, they had all chosen to be a family. He knew a lot of actual families who weren't as close as those four were. Blood didn't always guarantee a family would be a family. Sometimes choosing to be one made the bonds tighter than anything else could.

Roman had always believed that blood was thicker than water, and now he had living proof right in front of him that it wasn't always the case. Should he be so happy to be breaking up this family?

"We gotta go, so let's move 'em out." Red circled his finger in the air and kissed the top of Sierra's head. Then shook Roman's hand. "Take care of our girl."

"Will do, sir." Roman held Sierra's hand when her family took off. They stood there next to his truck and watched until the carnival was no longer in sight. "Come on, let's head home. Everyone is excited for you to join us."

Sierra wrapped her arms around Roman and nodded into his shoulder.

It took Sierra two days to speak again. It wasn't because she missed her carnie family, or even that she regretted leaving them. No, it was because she was so confused about all the changes of the past few days, she couldn't get her head wrapped around it all.

Judith Manning was an angel. There was no other word to describe the woman whose patience rivaled a saint's. And if Judith could fix Sierra's crazy heart and wild thoughts, she'd probably qualify for sainthood, for that would be an absolute miracle.

Thoughts about who her father had become and who he was swirled around Sierra's mind until she was about ready to puke. Since moving in with the Mannings, she had walked into not one, not two, but four different conversations about Big Bart. None of them were good. If Sierra thought she'd have to ask her new housemates about her dad, she was sorely mistaken. All they could do, it seemed, was talk about him and the horrible things he had done.

Okay, maybe that was a bit much. They did talk about other things, like chores, and how she needed to stay inside the main house. The first night she arrived, she expected to be shown to the cabin Roman had mentioned, but when Judith put her arms around her and led her down one of the wings of the house, she was surprised to be shown to a beautiful room across the hall from the guest bathroom.

It was decorated in blue gingham with burlap accents. There was even a heart-shaped wreath decorated in jute rope, blue gingham ribbon, and white ribbon hanging on her door. It was beautiful. When she walked in, she noted the curtains matched the wreath on her door. And the stuffed chair in one corner was blue-and-white gingham with a burlap wrap on the arms. Very farmhouse look and feel. She almost smiled when she first saw the room.

Roman had been very sweet and attentive without being overbearing. In fact, Sierra was surprised that the most affection he had shown her were hugs. He hugged her several times a day, but he hadn't tried to kiss her again, even when they were alone. It wasn't that she didn't welcome his touch—it was more that she was unsure what would happen now that they knew where she'd come from.

If she let her heart go and really fell for Roman, she'd get her heart broken in so many pieces it would never be fixed. In a way, she could finally understand Humpty Dumpty. All the Mannnings couldn't put her heart back together again, especially if they were the cause of the break.

But it was time she started pulling her weight. Sitting around the house moping, mostly in her room, wasn't right. She was here to work, and it was time she asked what they wanted her to do.

"Good morning." It was her third morning on the ranch, and Sierra walked into the kitchen where Judith and her husband sat drinking coffee.

Their heads turned, and smiles spread across their faces.

"Sierra, what would you like for breakfast?" Judith stood up and motioned for her to take a seat.

"Thank you, but I think it's time I started pulling my own weight around here. Did I miss breakfast with the family?" Sierra wracked her brain for the time Judith had given her for the family breakfast, but she couldn't remember. The past two mornings she'd just had toast and coffee when she got up. But today, she thought she had made it in time.

"We normally eat together by seven-thirty." Caleb looked at his watch and then winked.

She was an hour late. No wonder she missed them all. "Sorry, I'll set my alarm so I can get up early enough to help you make breakfast, if you'll show me how." Sierra winced when she realized she only knew how to scramble eggs, toast stuff—mostly Pop-Tarts—and pour cereal. She didn't even know how to make pancakes.

"How about we start now? What do you normally eat for breakfast?" Judith asked.

Sierra practically snorted when she thought about what she normally ate. "Nothing you'd want to serve hearty men who work hard all day long on a ranch." The last two mornings with the carnival she'd had granola bars. That wouldn't last past saddling up the horses. Not that she'd know how much energy was expended doing anything on a ranch.

"Well, the family was good at cleaning off their plates so we don't have any leftovers today, but I had made an egg casserole, hashed browns, and ham steaks." Judith looked over at the pile of dishes in the sink and then back to Sierra.

"Wow, that sounds like a lot of work. I'd be fine with some cereal or a granola bar. Then I'll do the dishes." There were dishes all over the kitchen counter by the farmhouse sink, but they did have a dishwasher. Maybe it wouldn't be too bad to clean up after a ranch full of men and their wives?

When Sierra first arrived, they told her that all of the Mannings who lived on the property, even those who had their own house, had breakfast here together. Each family did their own thing for lunch and dinner, but

Caleb wanted everyone together for breakfast so they could discuss the morning work. Which explained why there were so many dishes. Maybe they really did need her help on the ranch after all?

Judith waved a hand in front of her face. "It's no problem to make you something. Do you like eggs? We still have some fresh from the chicken coop this morning. Amy said that our chickens worked overtime and she had to make two trips to get them all in here." She chuckled and headed to the fridge.

"Are you completely self-sufficient here on the ranch?" Sierra knew they raised cattle, so beef would never be an issue. She had also seen pigs and goats, but she hadn't seen any dairy cows. Or at least she didn't think she had seen any dairy cows. What did she know about cows? They all looked the same to her, but she figured she would have seen those giant milking machines the other day when Roman gave her and Annie a tour of the barns.

Judith shook her head. "No, not really. But if needed, we could be. We trade with one of our neighbors for milk, butter, cream, and a few vegetables that I don't grow. And of course I head into town once a month to do shopping for basics like rice and pasta. We have a weekly farmers' market where I get fresh fruit and vegetables that I don't already grow or trade for."

"Wow, so if the apocalypse happens you wouldn't really be in trouble, would you?" Sierra chuckled, thinking back to a few years ago when they had a major epidemic and most places closed down for long periods of time.

While that wasn't funny, it was odd that she'd ended up on a ranch that could sustain itself indefinitely if need be.

Caleb arched a brow and looked to his wife before answering. "Yes, we could. And it is by design. Those of us who have read the entire Bible and believe it to be the infallible Word of God know how it's going to end for America. And we are ready to wait it out until the Lord comes to take us home."

What a downer thought. Sierra blinked a few times and really thought about his words. She hadn't read the Bible in a while, but she did know about the book of Revelations and the end times. "But, wait—" She shut up.

"Go ahead and ask your question. I'm always available to talk Bible." Caleb poured himself another cup of coffee and took a seat.

Judith pulled out the eggs and began to make a bacon-and-cheese omelet for Sierra.

Sierra poured herself another cup of joe. "I thought that God takes his children up to heaven before the end times?"

"That's a tough question. There's a lot of debate, but one thing the Bible is clear on is that before the seven-year tribulation, God will take his elect with him to heaven. So anyone who has been saved by Jesus will go to heaven before the worst of it. But there is mention about a Western country that was once a mighty nation and is no more. Most Bible scholars believe America is that nation, and that we will somehow go through something catastrophic and will no longer be a leading nation." Caleb gulped down a large drink of his coffee and waited as Sierra processed the information.

"So you think that eventually, America destroys itself?" Sierra asked.

Caleb shrugged. "Either we do it to ourselves, which is looking to be a good possibility, or we end up in a war that we lose. No one really knows for sure. It's all conjecture as to what exactly happens, but by the time the Lord comes to take his people to heaven in the rapture, America will no longer be a great nation. If we want to survive whatever might be coming, we decided long ago to set ourselves up to keep living, and continue to share the Gospel. Plus, it's much easier for a ranching family to provide as much from the land as they possibly can. We don't get monthly payments from a regular job. We sell our cattle once a year at market—sometimes twice if we plan it right—and we have a few side projects like the cow cuddling. But that's new, and we haven't really made much of a profit on that endeavor yet. So when money gets tight, it's important to have food that we raise ourselves."

"So, it's not just about the possibility that God will come during your lifetime, it's also about sustainability of ranch life?" Sierra always thought that when God came, it would be much later. Probably wouldn't happen for another hundred years or more. She never thought she'd see the rapture. But she didn't really know much about the end times, either.

"Exactly. We look to the day when the Lord comes to take us home, but we also realize that it might not be in our lifetime. We have to take care of what God has given us, be good stewards of the land, and ensure that future generations can survive on our ranch. We operate a generational ranch, which means that we own the land and the buildings, and it is passed down to our children when we pass. A lot like the landholders from England generations ago. They worked hard to ensure they had something to pass on, even if they weren't titled."

"Ah, that makes sense. I've read a few regency books that discussed land and how they passed it on to their descendants. I never really thought about it." Since Sierra had grown up in a city, it wasn't the same. People bought and sold houses and land, or rented places. Passing down property, or even living off the land, wasn't something she had ever experienced before. This new chapter of her life was going to be very interesting.

That is, if they let her stay here.

Chapter 23

A week later, Sierra was finally ready to talk about her dad. She probably would have wanted to discuss him sooner if she weren't so thoroughly exhausted by the end of each day that she couldn't utter a word after dinner. Most nights, she took an Epsom salt bath and went to bed early.

Today, however, she felt more like herself. The days had passed so quickly, she honestly thought that living and working on a ranch would be easier than working as a carnie. Boy, was she wrong.

Never would she look down on someone who worked on a ranch or farm. The past few days she'd not only helped with breakfast and other meals, but she also helped Judith to work her kitchen garden. Although, Sierra wouldn't call it a kitchen garden—she'd call it a full-fledged garden, or field. Well, until she saw their vegetable field. Weeding and harvesting what the family needed from the *kitchen garden* was back-breaking work.

Working the duck game all day long wasn't easy, but compared to ranching, it was. Judith had told her that after a few weeks her body would adjust and her muscles would develop in the areas that she needed. Until today, she hadn't believed it. She still hurt, no doubt about that, but the pain was less than the day before. Her back felt stronger than it ever had, and she actually worked for a few hours before needing an extended break. Which was when she realized it was time to clean up and prepare lunch.

Today, she was making lunch by herself. Once the sub sandwiches had been prepared and the two different pasta salads made, she went outside and rang the bell. They also had a couple bags of chips on the table. Each rancher would fill their own plate with what they wanted and then everyone would sit down together. Except for the two women Roman had told her about.

Amy and Regina, the two homeless women who had "worked" for her father, and now lived on the ranch, had graciously avoided her. But today, Sierra knew she needed to speak to both of them who lived in one of the ranch cabins. They had been harvesting the asparagus that day and would be canning the next few days. No one had said anything to Sierra about helping with the canning, but that was one of the things she was asked to do before moving here to the ranch.

Sierra knew it was time to cowgirl up. She was now a cowgirl, after all. And it was time to deal with her father.

"Will Amy and Regina be joining us today for lunch?" Sierra thought it strange that both women didn't eat with the family and hoped it wasn't because of her.

Judith had just entered the kitchen to help her finish up the sides and discovered it was all ready. "We all thought you might like to avoid them for a while." She tilted her head and looked at Sierra instead of the table full of food. "Are you ready?"

A fluttering entered her stomach. Not like when Roman kissed her—this was more like when she was about ready to puke from being too nervous, but she knew it was time. "Yes, I am. It's time I find out more about Big Bart and deal with my demons." A snort escaped her, and she felt her cheeks warm. "Sorry. It's not really funny, but I guess..." She shrugged.

"A slip of the tongue. I get it." With a hand on her shoulder, Judith nodded. "Don't worry, no one is going to judge you based on your father. Not even Amy and Regina."

"Then why have they stayed away from me?"

"Because they thought you wouldn't want to see the reminder of what your father has become." Judith ran a hand down Sierra's arm in a comforting gesture. "But if you think you're ready, then I'll call them to join us for dinner."

"Why not lunch?" If they could join them for dinner, why not lunch? Was it just something that they did normally? Sierra wasn't sure how the process went here.

Judith chuckled. "They already ate their lunch and are just getting back to the field. But I will invite them to dinner."

"Oh, okay. Do they normally eat their meals with the family?"

Judith shook her head. "Most evenings they do join us for dinner, but they tend to do their own thing for breakfast and lunch. Unless they're helping me prepare the meals, then they join me."

That made sense. The two women lived in a small cabin and they probably wanted more autonomy, or maybe it was more about privacy. If Sierra lived in a cabin and knew how to make enough different meals, she'd probably want to cook for herself most of the time as well. As it was, she felt like an outsider at the meals. Not because anyone made her feel that way—it was probably because she was so new to the ranch. They all spoke about things that flew right over her head.

The boys tended to joke about things that made no sense to her. And the women discussed their jobs with each other. While Claire did live on the property, she had her own barn and her own horse-training business. Sierra knew nothing at all about horses. What was dressage? She'd have to look it up one of these days.

"Hey, hey, hey. This looks fantastic," John exclaimed when he came into the kitchen. "Ma said you were making us lunch on your own today. For some reason I pictured fried twinkies and cotton candy." He chuckled.

Sierra laughed so hard, she began to choke. "Sorry, but if you want fair food you'll have to go and find a carnival. I never made any of that food. I'm more of a microwave meal or packaged food kinda gal. But"—she put a finger in the air—"anyone can make a sandwich."

"Um, I beg to differ. Mine always fall apart before I can take the first bite." John grabbed a plate and started piling on the food.

Roman entered and slapped his brother on the back. "That's because you pile your sandwiches too high with the meat. You have to remember to make them shorter. Not everyone has a big mouth like yours." He grinned at his brother before picking up a plate and getting food himself.

Caleb washed his hands in the kitchen sink. "Boys, did you wash your hands first?"

"Of course we did, Pa." Roman tsk'd and winked at Sierra. "The joys of working a ranch with your dad."

Sierra grinned and stood to the side as the rest of the Mannings made their way inside. Some washed their hands outside and some in the kitchen. Matthew took a dishtowel and twirled it before snapping it at Mark, who was the last to enter.

This family joked around a lot with each other, and if she understood some of what they talked about, they were also big on playing practical jokes with each other. Sierra wondered what it would have been like to have a brother, or even a sister, while she was growing up. She did have Annie, but they were already adults when they met, so it was different.

Contentment filled Sierra as she watched the family interact. They certainly weren't quiet. It was very different from her childhood. She and her grandmother talked during their meals, which they did eat together, but since it was just the two of them, it was most definitely a somber affair compared to the Manning family meals.

Hope began to blossom, and she hoped they would keep her a while longer.

Judith tapped her shoulder. "You can go ahead and serve yourself and eat."

With her eyes on the family sitting at the table and chatting up a storm, she hadn't noticed Judith walk up to her, and she started at the touch. "Oh, yeah. Wait, what about Amy and Regina?"

"They'll be here for dinner tonight." Judith smiled at Sierra and moved to fill her own plate.

This was how a family should be, boisterous and happy. And now she would have a chance to talk to two women who knew her father better than she did. Nerves flitted around her belly and she wondered if she'd even be able to eat a thing for lunch.

After lunch, Roman walked up to Sierra. "Hey, nice lunch. Thank you." He looked intently into her eyes, and she wondered if he had been looking at her like that all week, but she was too zoned out to notice.

"Thanks, I'm glad you liked it." Sierra smiled at him, and for the first time in a week she felt the emotion cross her entire face and down into her heart. This was a good place to be.

"Um." Roman looked around and waited until his brothers left the room. "Would you like to go for a walk tonight after dinner?"

Unsure what she would be doing after dinner, Sierra bit her lip. "I was sorta hoping to talk to Amy and Regina about my dad tonight."

He looked warmly at her and took her hand. "I think that's a great idea. How about tomorrow night after dinner?"

Sierra grinned and nodded. "I'd like that."

With a light squeeze, he let go of her. "See you later."

She waved. "See ya."

So many emotions flittered through Sierra, and she thought for sure she was going to explode. It was way more than just being nervous. Here, right in front of her, were two women who had lived on the streets, and if what the Mannings had said was true, were both harassed by her dad. A man who'd once loved her a great deal.

It was difficult to accept that this new version of Bartholomew Baker was really her dad. Dinner was over, and the three of them were in the smaller sitting room with cups of coffee. Both Amy and Regina looked a bit nervous themselves, but Sierra didn't know how to allay their feelings. It took all of her restraint to stay there and wait for them to talk.

Sierra cleared her throat. "Thank you for agreeing to speak with me. I'm sure this isn't a topic you enjoy discussing." She winced when she saw the color drain from Amy's face.

Regina sat up straight and held her coffee mug in her hand. "While it's not something either of us care to talk about, we have discussed this very topic today and agree you should be able to ask us anything you want. You have a right, and a need, to know who your father has become."

Tears pricked the backs of Sierra's eyes. She told herself she wasn't going to cry. But just in case, she had brought a box of tissue and it sat to her right on the side table. "Thank you, I really appreciate you doing this." She shook her head. "When I was little, he was my Superman. He was such a loving man, and we were so close. I never understood why he left me and never came back."

Amy and Regina exchanged glances.

"Well, we don't know why he changed so much, but we do know he's become the sort of man you should stay away from." Amy's hand shook as she lifted her cup of coffee to her lips.

Regina coughed. "He has very bad friends. Well, *friends* probably isn't the right word. I've seen the fear in his eyes when certain people come to visit. I'd say he's gotten himself into something he has no way of getting out of."

"Your dad is somehow mixed up with the mob." Amy winced and looked down at her hands. "At least, I think he is."

"Almost two years ago, we saw a few guys that looked rough, and I mean really rough, come by and heard them talking to Bart. Oh, your dad likes to be called Big Bart, in case you didn't know that." Regina seemed to be the leader of the two women.

Dread filled Sierra's entire being. The mob? How in the world did a loving father and husband who had been a God-fearing man at one time end up in the mob? She took a shaky breath and reached for a tissue.

"Anyways, Big Bart's top enforcer, Rocko, was tormenting the Manning family at the time."

Sierra's gasp stopped Regina, who looked at her with wide, worried eyes.

With a wave of her hand, Sierra motioned for Regina to continue her tale. "Please, keep going. And explain to me why my dad and his, uh, *friends* would want to bother the Mannings. They seem so nice."

Amy began, "They are nice."

Regina said, "Rocko tried to kidnap Leah before she married Mark."

Sierra slumped back in her chair. "What? Did he hurt her?"

"Thank the good Lord, he didn't." Judith walked into the room with a fresh pot of coffee and topped off everyone's mugs. "I think the Lord used that as a way to get Leah and Mark together. Before that, they fought like cats and dogs. I think Mark saw her as a little sister. But after that, you couldn't keep them apart." She smiled softly. "The Lord can use any situation to His benefit. Keep that in mind as you discover more about your pa." Judith left the women to consider her words.

The room was quiet until Sierra spoke up. "I've seen Leah and Mark together. They look like they're still newlyweds with the way they're always touching each other. And Mark is constantly kissing her temple or putting his hand on her lower back. They're so sweet together."

Regina harrumphed. "Yeah, too sweet if you ask me. They recently built their own house here on the ranch and we see too much of them *being sweet*."

"You're just jealous, Regina," Amy accused her friend with a sparkle in her eye.

The two women bantered back and forth for a minute about the merits of a loving spouse. Regina, the older of the two women with long, silver hair pulled back in a hair clip, and more wrinkles than anyone her age should have, sounded as though she didn't believe in love.

But Amy, a young woman around Sierra's age, had long brown hair she pushed behind her ears. From what Sierra heard, it sounded as though she might still believe in love. And might even have someone in mind for herself.

Sierra hadn't seen them interact with anyone outside of the family, and other than Roman, they were all married. Did Amy harbor a secret crush on the man Sierra liked? She had to know where Amy and Roman stood. Sierra didn't think Roman was interested in her. He wouldn't want two women he liked living on the same property, would he? Shoot, for all she knew, all men were pigs. It wasn't like she had much experience with them. All of her knowledge came from seeing idiots at the carnivals she worked.

"So Amy, it sounds like you might have a boyfriend." A tentative smile crossed Sierra's lips, and she waited to see what Amy might say.

Instead of speaking, the quiet woman blushed and looked down at her hands in her lap. So, Amy did like someone. But did that mean a certain someone liked her in return? Not necessarily. Sierra was going to have to pay more attention to the single men Amy interacted with.

Regina waved a hand in the air. "Enough about lovey-dovey stuff. Let's get back to Big Bart." The older woman grimaced. "So, after Rocko tried to kidnap Leah, the men who pull Bart's strings stopped supporting Rocko. And, here's where it gets weird." She leaned forward and stared intently at Sierra. "We were all told to stay away from the Mannings and their friends when they came to town. But"—she put a finger in the air—"we were allowed to accept their brown bags." The older woman sat back and looked triumphantly at the two younger girls.

"And what happened?" Sierra didn't know what it all meant, and Regina had left her hanging. She hated it when people did the whole pregnant pause thing, hoping to get a rise out of their audience. It was so annoying. Why couldn't they just finish their story in one go?

Regina held the attention of the two women a bit longer.

Sierra looked to Amy. "What happened?"

The younger woman shook her head. "I wasn't part of the group until about a year ago."

A chuckle escaped Regina. "Bart couldn't do a thing to the Mannings. They have powerful friends. The type of friends that the man above Bart didn't want to mess with. So they took all of their support from Rocko, who's serving some serious time in prison, by the way. And whenever one of us left Bart's group, he would rail at those who were still there, but he never laid a finger on anyone in the Manning group. In fact, at first he stayed at least a block away whenever they came to visit us."

"Whoa, really? Is that why you decided to leave?" Ignoring the tissue in her hand, Sierra sat forward, intent on hearing more.

"Bart thought that intimidating us, and in some cases beating us, would keep us under his thumb." Regina scoffed. "But it didn't work. More of us began to leave with the Mannings when they showed up. There's only two of us here now, but another six women have been helped and given a home and a job somewhere else. A place that Bart knows nothing about." She crossed her arms over her chest in triumph.

This was interesting. Sierra knew that these two women weren't the only ones who had come through here, but she didn't realize there were other places the women were going. How many people had left Bart? The more important question was, how many were still under his thumb?

"Does this mean there aren't very many homeless people left in Bart's crew?" She hoped it did, but feared he just replaced them like batteries. There must have been some sort of Buy Mart he could go to and pick up a large pack of homeless people who would fear him and do his bidding without complaint.

This was not the man she once knew.

A tear streamed down Amy's cheek. "No, Bart has connections all over the place. When one person leaves, at least two more take their place. He always has new people becoming his slaves."

That comment hit Sierra to the core. What sort of work did her dad force people into? "I hate to ask, but what did you both do for him?"

A very unladylike snort resonated from Regina. "Bart has his hands in a lot of crime, but his biggest form of revenue is thievery and begging. Most of us did that." She turned sad eyes on Amy. "A few he tried to turn into prostitutes."

"No, he didn't." Sierra gasped and looked to Amy. She was a pretty girl, and looked younger than her twenty-one years. She could have easily passed for a teenager.

Amy shook her head vehemently. "As soon as he tried to force me to, ah... Well, I saw Elizabeth Manning and ran to her for help."

"Oh, thank the good Lord." Sierra put a hand to her heart.

"But that doesn't mean some of the women don't do it. Some do. Some even like it." A shiver ran through Regina, and she took a long drink of her coffee.

"Okay, I think I know enough about Bart." He was not Sierra's dad. She wouldn't even refer to him anymore as though he was. This man was evil to the core. "Thank you, and I'm so sorry you had to go through this. But grateful the Mannings helped you to freedom." She bit her lip. "Are they good to work for?"

Bright smiles covered both women's faces.

Amy nodded.

Regina said, "Oh, yes. I don't know if I ever want to leave. They've said I can stay here as long as I want." She looked to Amy. "Neither of us have family to go home to, so we might as well stay somewhere that puts a nice roof over our heads, warm food in our bellies, and where the people treat us right."

"Wow, this sounds like heaven." Sierra chuckled. She knew she liked the people and the place, but she didn't realize it was such a haven for these women. They worked hard from what she gathered, but if it was such a nice place to be, who wouldn't want to pull their weight?

That night Sierra prayed like she hadn't in years. She also cried. Tears were shed for the loss of her father, the man she had once known. He no longer existed. Instead, a monster lived in his skin. Was this what happened to people who completely turned their back on God? Or was this an unusual situation? Crime was growing all over the country, she knew. But was it like how Caleb described it? The end times?

Chapter 24

The next few days flew by. Sierra got into the swing of things, and even learned how to can asparagus and corn—something she had never thought to do. If she ever wanted vegetables, she could go to a booth at the carnival, or head to a diner. Veggies weren't really a big part of her diet. At least not since joining the carnival. Sure, she loved the grilled corn on a cob. That she ate all the time, but other than fried pickles there weren't a lot of other options.

Thursday night, she asked to speak to Caleb after dinner. "Caleb, I think I need to talk to my dad. But I don't think it's really safe to do. Do you have any suggestions?"

The patriarch of the Manning family sat back in his chair sipping decaf coffee. "May I ask why you want to speak to Bart?"

For a moment, Sierra pursed her lips and considered her reasons. "I think I need to say goodbye. And I have a few questions. I need to know why he chose this life over me."

As the emotions creeped across her face, Caleb watched Sierra. "I can take you Saturday morning, after the chores are done."

Hope filled her chest, and she took in a deep breath. "Really? You'd be alright taking me?"

He nodded. "I think that since I have the least experience with Bart, I'd be the better one. He doesn't hate me already like he does all of my children." An ironic kind of chuckle escaped. "I can't believe I just said that. But my kids have taken a lot of people away from Bart and helped them to get back on their feet, or make it home to their families. Something I'm very proud of."

"As you should be." Sierra winced. "Just as I should be ashamed and appalled at who my dad has become."

Caleb reached across the table and took one of Sierra's hands in his. "Sweetie, don't beat yourself up for his choices. And trust me when I say this, they were *his* choices, not yours. You can't take responsibility for the things Bartholomew Baker has done." He shook his head when Sierra began to protest. "Listen to me, he was an adult when he left you with your grandma. Which, as it turns out, was the best decision for you. Somewhere deep down, he loved you enough to give you a safe home. Remember that part of him."

"I don't see how he could have ever loved me if he chose to leave me and turn to a life of crime. He didn't have to do that. He could have stayed with my grandma.

She wouldn't have turned him out if he looked for work."
Sierra pulled her hand back from Caleb.

He heaved a heavy sigh. "We may not know why he
did what he did."

Sierra interrupted. "That's why I want to see him. I
need to know why he left me all those years ago and
never came back. He never even sent a letter or a card."

"I know. But after this Saturday, I hope you choose to
stay clear of him. He's not a good man. And being near
him could be very dangerous, especially if the rumors
about him being a part of the mob are true."

Her nose twitched and stung with the threat of new
tears. "Do you really think it's possible he's involved with
the mob?"

Caleb nodded. "Sadly, I do. He's protected from the
police somehow. The Bozeman sheriff hasn't been able
to get a judge to issue an arrest warrant for the man, and
any time someone might be willing to testify or even
sign an affidavit against him, that person changes their
mind or disappears." He took in a deep breath. "He's
connected somehow."

"But so are you, aren't you?" Sierra tilted her head and
wondered who the Manning family knew that kept them
safe.

A wry smile crossed his lips. "My family has been here
for a while. We do know a lot of powerful people, as
do friends of ours. Not to mention the fact that one of
the women we helped to escape Bart is now married to
our own local sheriff. My guess is that whoever is pulling

Bart's strings knows he can't control us, or our friends. So Bart has been ordered to stay away from us."

"Do you think that order will change?"

"I think anything can change at any time. My kids are very careful to stick together in groups when they head to Bozeman. Even when they go there to shop. We pray and rely on God to protect us, not man."

When Roman entered the kitchen a half hour later, Sierra was ready for their nightly walk. For the past few nights, the two of them had been taking walks after dinner together.

This was Sierra's favorite time of the day. Even though she lived in the same house as Roman, she didn't see him nearly as often as she thought she would. They took all of their meals together, but those were the only times she saw him. That was until they began walking at night.

Roman's hand was warm when he took hers. The coolness of fall was here, and the summer heat had left them feeling the brisk nights. Sierra enjoyed this time of year. She wished they had more deciduous trees in the area that changed colors, but the few trees that did turn yellow were nice. Most of the local trees were evergreens and didn't lose their leaves during the fall months.

"I'm glad we can take this time each night, just the two of us." The warmth from his hand holding hers also came through in Roman's voice.

She felt a zing all the way through her toes and pulled herself just a little bit closer to him. "So am I. This is really nice." Sierra looked out at the land and the cows dotting the area near them. She knew that Roman liked to keep the cow-cuddling stock close by, and they seemed to like hanging out near the barn. They would open the doors and let the cows inside during the day, if they chose, but for the most part the animals liked the outdoors. Even on blustery days.

However, tonight was perfect. There was a slight breeze, and it was above fifty degrees still. She knew the temperature would be changing very soon, and the nights were going to be extremely cold. Even though she wasn't from this area, Sierra knew they wouldn't be able to keep walking at night for much longer. "What will we do when it gets too cold for our evening walks?"

Roman squeezed her hand. "We can sit inside and play board games, or card games. I'm open to either."

"What about sitting in front of a fire sipping hot cocoa or tea?" While she was on the road, she used to dream of lazy winter nights like what she had seen in the sweet and clean romance movies she would occasionally watch with Annie and Stella.

"Mmm, that sounds marvelous." Roman leaned over and kissed the top of her head.

Sierra liked it when he did small things like hold her hand, kiss her head, or put his hand on her lower back. Actually, that was one of her favorite touches. He wouldn't push her around, but he did guide her gently around a puddle or cow pie.

The first time he did it on their nightly walk, she wasn't looking where she was going. Instead, she was looking up at the wondrous night sky. To be honest, she was remembering their first kiss and hoping he would kiss her again. When he put his hand on her lower back and steered her in a different direction, she was confused at first. Then she noticed the black spot on the ground. It was dark and she hadn't noticed it. At least not until she looked.

A grin covered her face as she remembered that moment. He had pulled her closer, but he didn't kiss her. In fact, he didn't kiss her at all that night. So far, he had only kissed her head, cheek, and forehead. If he didn't touch her lips with his soon, she would have to pull him in and plant a sweet kiss on his lips. She almost did it last night, but chickened out. Maybe she could do it tonight?

They were headed toward Claire's barn, which was off to the side and not easily seen from the house. Each night they seemed to head in a different direction. And Sierra loved it. She enjoyed seeing the ranch at different times of the day, and watching the animals. Tonight, she'd get to see the horses Claire was training.

So far Sierra hadn't been inside of Claire's barn, and she was looking forward to it. Matthew and Claire had built their ranch home on the other side of the barn, about seven or eight hundred yards away from the outer edges of the corrals. It was close, but not too close to hear the horses unless they were in distress.

Claire had invited Sierra over to afternoon tea earlier that day, which was how she knew this. Sierra liked Claire. The woman was a strong, business-minded lady who didn't brook no sass from anyone. She hoped the two of them would become friends. Claire was older than any of the other sisters-in-law, but that was to be expected since she had married the oldest Manning brother. She was also expecting a baby.

It seemed all of Roman's brothers and sisters either had a baby or were expecting. Those cousins were going to all grow up together and be as close as siblings. Would they appreciate the fact that they would all be so close?

How would everyone work the ranch once the kids were older? Matthew, the oldest, would most likely take over when his mom and dad passed away. Sierra couldn't imagine them ever leaving the ranch to move to Florida like so many elderly tended to do. Caleb would most likely work the land until his dying breath. And Judith would never sit still. She'd continue to cook, clean, and garden until the end.

What would Roman do? Before she had a chance to ask him, he stopped them along the side of the barn and grinned at her.

"What?" The tension that had been there since she'd first met him almost two years ago was strong. Sierra was very much attracted to this cowboy, and she thought he might be interested in her, but the fact that he hadn't kissed her again did have her wondering. But now, the way he looked at her—with hunger in his eyes—told her he was about to kiss her.

"How do you like living on the ranch? Are you adjusting to this new pace?" He turned her so her back was against the wall of the red barn and he leaned in close to her. Almost like he was trying to keep her body heat in their tiny circle while he shared his own with her.

She looked at his lips, curving up in a sexy smile. Then she licked her lips and looked up into his eyes. "Yes, I think I'm finding my pace. It's different, but..." She didn't get to finish her thoughts because his warm lips were on hers.

When he moved his lips against hers, she knew this was the place to be. Everything in her screamed to kiss him back, and she did. Her arms wrapped around his neck of their own accord. All thoughts fled from her brain and she just acted on instinct.

She felt her body curve into his, and when he deepened their kiss, her entire body exploded with the fireworks going off in her head. No one had ever kissed her like this, and she never wanted anyone else to again.

When Roman finally pulled back, breathing heavily, he put his forehead to hers. "I knew it would be even better than our last kiss, but I had no idea it would be this wonderful."

Sierra had to take a moment as her heart slowly began to get back in rhythm. "I'd been waiting for you to do that ever since we started our nightly walks."

His deep chuckle sent shivers down her spine. "I've wanted to kiss you again ever since that first night on the bridge, but with everything going on, I wasn't sure if you were ready."

A contented sigh escaped her, and Roman pulled her close for a tight hug. "Can we end every night like this?" she asked.

This time, he groaned. "I'd love to, but we have to take it slow."

Sierra nodded against his chest. "Yes, we do."

They stood there together for a little while, and once she started to shiver, Roman pulled back. "Are you cold? I'm sorry, we should have dressed a little bit warmer. The temperature is supposed to take a nosedive tonight. Let's head back for a hot cup of cocoa."

The next night they went out for another walk, and butterflies screamed through Sierra's stomach as she thought about kissing Roman again. If they kept kissing like that, she might have a difficult time keeping to the rules Judith had set in place.

While their bedrooms weren't next to each other, they did sleep in the same wing of the house. And with all three barns on the property, and the cabins, there were plenty of places they could hide away in for a romantic tryst. While she'd never ever done anything like that before, she found herself daydreaming about the cowboy and his kisses and wondering what it would be like with him. Then she'd get mad at herself for thinking things she ought not to.

It was no wonder Judith had warned her not to spend too much time alone with Roman. Their connection was strong. And his kisses made her weak in the knees. She'd seen movies and read books that talked about this sort of feeling and never understood it. At least not until now. When she heard about girls getting pregnant in high school she'd scoffed at them. How hard could it be to keep your libido in check? If she ever saw Misty, she'd have to apologize for the mean things she thought about the poor girl.

If Sierra had met Roman in high school, she might have done things she knew were wrong, too. Now, even though she was an adult and was supposed to be more in control of herself, she worried she might succumb to the temptation.

This time, they walked toward the cabins. The Mannings had built four small cabins, each with a tiny kitchen and bathroom. They all slept four people comfortably. They could have taken out the single beds and put in bunkbeds and made room for eight if they needed to, but so far they had yet to fill the cabins as they were.

Amy and Regina lived in the cabin closest to the main ranch house. Then the three orphan boys who had lived there for a few years now had the cabin farthest from the house, to give the girls more privacy.

Sierra had met the three Smith boys. Carter worked next door at the Johnson ranch, so she only saw him coming and going on occasion. Flynn worked in town at the general store. But Boone worked on the Manning ranch, and she saw him a lot. He was a nice guy. Would they see any of them tonight on their walk? She hoped not, but she also hoped they did. She and Roman needed a chaperone.

As usual, Roman held her hand. "I hear you and my dad are going into Bozeman tomorrow to see, uh." He scratched the stubble on his chin. "Bart?"

Since Sierra had learned about Big Bart a few days ago, she had stopped referring to him as her dad. Actually, she hadn't mentioned him much. "Yeah. I've got some questions, and your dad offered to take me since he doesn't have much history with Bart."

"I see. I'd be happy to take you." Roman stopped them next to one of the empty cabins. The light from the porch was on. All the cabins had porch lights that came on automatically when the sun set and stayed on for five hours.

"Thank you, but I think your dad will be just fine." The fact that Roman wanted to go wasn't a comfort. When they'd met up with Big Bart last time, Roman and Bart didn't seem to get along well. The last thing she wanted was another confrontation. She didn't need the added stress, and she believed Caleb would be a good middleman.

He stepped back from her. "You don't want me to go?"

She shook her head. "I think the tensions will be high enough. The last time we were there, my, uh— I mean, Bart didn't seem to care much for you."

He threw his hands in the air. "Really? You're worried about whether I can get along with your dad?"

"Roman, why is this a big deal?" Sierra tilted her head and narrowed her eyes at the cowboy, who was acting like a spoiled child.

"I'm your boyfriend. You should be taking me with you to meet up with a dangerous man, not my dad."

"Um." Confusion sped through her, and then irritability. And if she were honest, a bit of anger simmered under her surface. "Since when did we have a title?"

"But, ah..." Roman spluttered and took his hat off before running a hand through his hair. "We've kissed a few times, and you're living at my ranch. All the dates. I thought it went without saying, actually."

"Men. Since when did you get the right to decide who I can and can't take with me to see someone else? If he weren't my father, would you want to see him again?" She put her hands on her hips and glared at him.

"Of course I would. He's a dangerous man..."

She interrupted his words. "So, your dad can't take care of me? And oh, I don't know, I can't take care of myself? Are you saying you're the only one who can protect me from my *dad*?"

"Yes!" Roman stepped closer and glared down at her. "Bart is dangerous and evil. It won't matter to his guys that you're his daughter. In fact, it might even make things worse for you. And maybe even him. If he shows even the slightest bit of care for you, it could go very badly for all of you."

She threw her hands in the air and began to walk back to the main house. Then she stopped and turned around. "I don't believe what I'm hearing. Bartholomew Baker would never hurt me, or let anyone else hurt me. And I don't need you"—she pointed a finger at him—"to protect me from anyone else. I can do that all on my own." She turned around and huffed as she speed-walked back to the house and her room.

Roman stood there, flabbergasted as the woman yelled at him and basically ran away. What was she doing? She was acting like a child. More like a spoiled, rotten child who had to have her way. She should have been happy that he'd thought they were a couple. Why didn't she feel the same way?

He startled when he heard a voice. "Hey man, that was harsh."

When Roman turned, right behind him stood Boone Smith. "I know, right? She wasn't being very understanding at all."

Boone snorted. "No man, I mean you were harsh. Put yourself in her shoes. She just found her dad after how long, something like fifteen years? Then she finds out he's a real piece of work." He shook his head and ran a hand over his face. "If I found a parent now after all this time, and discovered they were in a gang or the mob, I'd be freaked out."

"That's exactly why I should go with her. She needs me," Roman complained.

Boone chuckled. "Yeah, right. She needs you like she needs the IRS all up in her stuff. Give her a break, man. And let her tell you what she wants or needs from you right now. Your dad is probably one of the toughest men around. He can protect her."

"Yeah"—Roman nodded—"I know he is. But she needs more than just protection right now."

"Yeah, she needs you to listen to her. And do what she asks of you. Did you ever think she might be ashamed of her dad and not want you around him?"

Roman hung his head and breathed out. "No, I didn't think of that."

"Of course not—you've got the perfect family." Boone leaned against the side of the empty cabin. "As someone who had a truly messed-up family, I can tell you she needs space right now. And she's most likely ashamed of where she came from. Especially after seeing all this." He motioned around the property. "It's a lot to live up to."

"Thanks, man." Roman clapped Boone's shoulder. "How did you get to be so wise?"

"You mean, such a wise-acre?" Boone chuckled and walked off. "Give her time and space. She'll come to you when she's ready."

Chapter 25

The ride to Bozeman was quiet. It also took forever, or at least that's how it felt. But Sierra knew it was less than thirty minutes. Caleb was quiet, giving her the headspace she needed to deal with what was to come.

Not only did she have to deal with who her *dad* had turned out to be, she also had to deal with Roman. He wasn't the caring, understanding man she'd thought he was. Instead, he was stubborn and sexist. Who in this day and age had to have a man protect her? *Pft. What a tool he is.*

As they passed the neighboring ranch fields, Sierra felt tears prick the backs of her eyes. And how dare he just assume they were a couple without talking to her first? Granted, she didn't have a lot of experience in this arena, but surely it was still kosher to *talk* about being a couple before declaring it. Actually, *demanding* it. Maybe it wasn't going to work out after all. She had a lot to deal with right now, and Roman wasn't at the top of her list of issues. That probably meant something important. But, it was something she'd deal with later.

The stores lining the city limits came into view, and she sat up straighter. It was time to focus on the situation at hand, even if it was going to be tough. She owed it herself, and her mother's memory, to find out what went wrong. Could she have done anything different? Could her grandmother?

Sierra knew her grandmother wasn't too fond of Bartholomew. But he was her dad. Grandma wouldn't have kept him from her; it had to be her dad who stayed away. But why? That was the biggest question. Why did he abandon her in her time of need? Wasn't she worth loving?

"We're here." Caleb pulled into the Burger Basket parking lot.

Sierra looked around and frowned. "Why here?"

After Caleb turned off the engine, he pointed out her window. "See those streets over there?"

She nodded.

"That's basically the area Big Bart controls. He keeps most of his homeless in those six blocks so his guys can easily guard them."

"Are they his prisoners?" Horror filled her entire being as she realized what everyone had been saying about her dad. He was more than their leader—he was their prison warden.

"In a way." Caleb sighed. "While they do live on the street and are technically free to leave, he has them under his thumb."

"How?"

"He uses fear, intimidation, and even violence to make the poor people who live on the streets kowtow to him. Over the years, he's developed some sort of network that pulls homeless or those down on their luck from other cities across the county and brings them here with hopes of a new life, and even a job. When they get here, they're stuck."

"How do you know all this?" Sierra bit her lower lip, having difficulty with this depiction of her father.

"My children have been working with the homeless in Bozeman for a few years now. And thankfully, we've helped quite a few of the women get away from this life. We even built those cabins to give them a safe place to live while we assisted them in getting home to family, if they had any. Or with finding a new job somewhere far away from here. There are a few good organizations that help women get off the street. My oldest daughter Elizabeth has worked with them, along with one of the local churches here in Bozeman, to get the women into a better situation."

"These women you've helped, they told you what my—I mean, what Big Bart did to them?" It was difficult to stop referring to him as her dad, but she'd drive herself mad if she didn't think of him as Big Bart instead of as Dad.

He nodded and turned in his seat to look at Sierra straight on. "You've met Amy and Regina. I'm sure they've told you some of their story. But what about Georgia? She's now married to our local sheriff. She was with us for over a year before she married Roscoe. But her story was a bit different. More difficult."

"No, she hasn't told me her story. I did meet her at the barbecue you hosted after the carnival finished. I knew she had been homeless, but to talk to her, I wouldn't have thought so." Sierra remembered hearing she had once worked for a lawyer's office in California and got burned. That was a far cry from being homeless and a prisoner of the streets in Bozeman, Montana.

"Well, you might want to talk to her when you're ready." A look of foreboding entered Caleb's eyes. "I don't want to disparage your pa, but he's not the man you knew as a kid. If he'll tell you about himself, will you be able to handle this?"

Emotion clogged Sierra's throat, and she had to clear it a few times before she could speak again. "Yes, I have to know what happened." She looked at her hands sitting in her lap and began to pick at a hangnail on her left thumb.

"Will it help you to move forward in life? Or will the truth about him hold you back?"

She took a moment and thought about his question. "Doesn't the Bible say the truth will set you free?"

He chuckled. "The Lord was talking about salvation."

"Ah." She shrugged. "I think I do need to know what happened so I can let it, or him, go and move forward."

Caleb put the truck key in his pocket and opened his door. "Alright, I'm with you. Whatever you need, let me know."

"You mean that? You aren't going to go all caveman on me and tell me what I need?" It was a dig at Roman, and she knew it, but Sierra couldn't help it. She was still frustrated with him over the things he'd said the night before.

"I take it you're referring to the argument you had with my youngest son?" He arched a brow. "Yes, I know all about it. And for the record, he acted wrong. But you should give him some slack. He cares about you. We raised our sons to care for women and to always protect them."

"I can't think about him right now. Maybe later. Right now, I need to focus on Big Bart and what in the world created the monster he turned out to be." She got out of the truck and waited for Caleb to join her.

Together, they walked side by side to the man in question, who stood across the street with his arms over his chest and a scowl across his face.

"Mr. Baker." Caleb put a hand out for the blond man. "I'm Caleb Manning."

"I know who you are." Big Bart ignored the offered hand and glared at the cowboy standing in front of him. "What do you want?"

Caleb turned to Sierra and nodded.

"Dad, I have some questions," she started, but stopped when the man growled.

"I'm not your dad. I'm no one's dad."

When they'd first walked up to the tall blond who was a harder and older version of the man who'd once loved her, she was frightened. But now, anger drilled through her veins and she narrowed her eyes. "You're right, the man standing in front of me isn't my dad. But you know what happened to him." She pointed a finger at his chest. "I want to know why you were created."

Bart scoffed. "You want to know? Listen here, little girl, I don't owe you anything. Including an explanation. If you know what's best for you, you'll get back in that truck and head on out of town and never come back." He pointed to where Caleb's truck sat. "In fact, you would do well to leave the state and never look back."

She slapped his chest. "No. You're going to tell me why you dropped me off and never came back. You owe me at least that much."

It was obvious he was angry. If this were a cartoon, steam would be streaming out of his ears and his face would be ruby red. As it was, red did tinge most of his face. "You were nothing but a drain! I never wanted you when you were little, and I certainly don't want you now." He scoffed. "Unless you want to work for me." He looked her up and down. "But I doubt I could get much for you. You're too scrawny."

Without even realizing it, her hand came up and slapped his face so hard, it turned to the side.

Bart put a hand on his jaw and massaged it. "Get out of here, before I have one of my guys teach you a lesson."

"Come on, Sierra. I think we should go." Caleb put a hand on her arm. But before they turned around, he said in a low voice, "No father should ever treat his daughter like this. But I will pray for you to change your ways."

Bart turned around and walked away without a backward glance.

Sierra let Caleb put an arm around her shoulders and guide her back to the truck. The entire way home, she sobbed into her hands.

Chapter 26

For the next two days, Sierra didn't leave her room. Judith brought her meals and a pitcher of water or a coffee carafe, but she didn't eat or drink much. Then, on the third day, the sheriff came to visit.

"Sweetie, I'm sorry to bother you, but Sheriff Roscoe is here and he needs to speak with you. It's important." Judith's voice came through the door loud and clear.

Still wearing the same clothes she'd had on when she went to Bozeman on Saturday, Sierra opened the door. Her eyes were so blurry from the constant tears that she didn't even notice all the people in the hall outside her door. "Can't this wait?"

The sheriff stood there with his Stetson in his hands. "I'm sorry, Miss Baker, but this is official business and it can't wait." He cleared his throat. "Is Bartholomew Baker your pa?"

Sierra nodded and wiped the tears from her eyes to look more closely at the man standing in front of her. Behind him, Caleb, Roman, and River stood with a sadness permeating the hallway. Judith put her arm around Sierra's shoulder.

"When did you last see him?" the sheriff asked.

"A few days ago, on Saturday." She nodded to Caleb. "I went to Bozeman with Caleb and, well"—she looked down—"I got into an argument with him and we left."

"Have you seen or spoken to him since?"

She shook her head.

"What condition was he in when you left him?" The sheriff twirled his hat in his hands and looked down the hall.

Sierra knew there wasn't anyone back there. It was the end, where Roman and John's rooms were located. She pulled her shoulders back and looked at the sheriff, even though he didn't return her gaze. "He was mad, but fine."

"He wasn't fighting with anyone when you left?"

Now she was confused. "What? Why? What's going on, Sheriff?"

"I regret to inform you that your father was in a mighty awful fight. He's in the hospital, barely hanging on. It appears that several men roughed him up somethin' fierce. But worse still is the fact that whoever was supporting him has removed their support, and the state police have come in. The entire homeless operation has been busted up, and some of the men and women in Bart's gang have been arrested. Others, well..." The sheriff pursed his lips and looked around at all of the wide eyes staring at him. "If you have room for some of the women, I'd greatly appreciate your help. They're out on the street all alone now."

Judith's intake of breath caught Sierra's attention.

"What? What's that mean?" Since Sierra didn't know much about the homeless, she didn't understand the significance of any of this. But what she really wanted to know was what happened to her dad. "Who beat up my dad? Can I see him?"

"Of course. He's at Bozeman General. He's got a guard on his room, so you'll need to bring your ID to prove who you are. No one other than family will be permitted to see him."

All of a sudden, wracking sobs took over Sierra's body. It didn't matter that she had been crying for most of the past two days—the tears started anew and didn't stop. She heard more questions and talking taking place around her, but none of it seemed to make sense. Judith led her back into her room and held her tight as she cried.

Her dad might die, and the last thing they'd done was argue. Who would attack him like that? And why would they do it? If he was protected by a mob boss, what could have happened to bring about something like this?

"Sweetie, why don't you take a hot shower and I'll get you some clean clothes set out. Once you're ready, Caleb and I will take you to see your dad." Judith stood up and helped Sierra get to the bathroom.

"K." Sierra hiccuped as she walked to the bathroom across the hall from her room.

An hour later, she was in the kitchen with the family. "Thank you, I really appreciate your help. Can we go now?"

"Why don't you sit down and I'll make you a sandwich. You've hardly eaten anything for the past two days, and it's going to be important to keep up your strength." Judith pulled out the chair Sierra normally sat in.

Roman took the seat next to hers. He put an arm around her shoulder as she waited for the food. "I'm so sorry. I'm sorry for the fight the other night, and I'm sorrier than you can imagine for what's happened to your pa."

"Why? You didn't hurt him, did you?"

He shook his head. "No, I didn't. But I'm sorry you have to go through this." He put his other hand on hers. "I'm here for you. I'm not making any demands, or telling you what to do. I'm here as your friend. And I'll help you in any way you want."

Sierra nodded. "Will you come to the hospital with me?"

"Of course I will. Whatever you want." Roman leaned in for a sideways hug.

His warmth seeped into her skin, and she was glad for his comfort. "Do you think he'll make it?"

"I don't know. He's in God's hands now. But I'll be happy to pray with you, if you like?"

"Please."

Roman prayed for Bart's healing and for the man's salvation. He also prayed that Sierra and her father would be able to reconcile.

Not an hour later, the four of them were at the hospital and Sierra was pulling out her wallet to show the police officer guarding Bartholomew Baker's room her driver's license. Roman also showed his license, and the guard let him in with Sierra. Caleb and Judith had to wait in the hallway.

With a shaky breath and fresh tears, Sierra covered her mouth when she saw her father in the hospital bed. He looked to have a broken leg, arm, and there was a bandage over his head. Black-and-blue shadows covered just about every inch of his skin. "How could he have survived?"

Roman put an arm around her shoulders and followed her lead as she walked to the side of his bed.

"Dad?" The tiny squeak that left her lips wasn't more than a whisper, but it was loud enough for him to hear.

Bart opened the only eye that wasn't swollen shut. It wouldn't open all the way, but a red orb stared back at her. "Sierra?"

Tears fell over her lashes as she nodded. "Yeah, it's me, Dad. Who did this to you?"

Bart licked his lips. "Water?"

Roman took the cup with a plastic straw and held it to his lips. After he took a couple of sips, Roman pulled it back.

"Thanks." Bart took a shaky breath and closed his one eye. "I'm in a lot of trouble. And so are you. You'll need to hide now."

"Why? What happened?" She sat in the chair next to his bed, and Roman stood behind her shoulder.

"Better if you don't know," his raspy voice whispered.

The door opened, and Sierra turned her head.

"I'd like to know more about what happened as well." A tall man with a dark-blue suit and bright-blue tie walked in the room. A large police badge hung from a lanyard around his neck. "I'm Detective Reynolds, and I'm the one who'll be conducting the investigation into what happened to your dad."

She turned in her seat but didn't stand up. "Okay. Do you know who did this?"

"We have an idea based on traffic cam footage, but I need to know more." The detective walked to the other side of the bed, and Bart's wary gaze followed him. "Can you tell me why you were beat up and left for dead?"

Sierra whimpered and put a hand over her mouth.

Roman leaned down to her. "Do you want to wait outside while they talk?"

She shook her head. "No, I need to hear this."

The detective asked a few more questions, but Bart refused to answer or said he didn't know. A sour look covered the detective's face, and he put his notepad back in his inside coat pocket. "Mr. Baker, if you don't help me, I can't help you or your daughter."

"If I spill, she dies." Bart turned sorrowful eyes on his daughter. "I'm so sorry, baby. This is all my fault."

"You're darn right it is. Now tell me what happened." Sierra stood up and put fisted hands on her hips. "If you did something to put you in this situation, you need to spill. Help the police put these people in jail."

He shook his head slightly, then winced and stopped. "No, I meant that it's all my fault I got here to begin with."

She sat back down. "Go on."

Bart started back at the beginning, when they were still a family. "When we found out your momma was sick, I had poor insurance. The regular cancer treatments weren't working, and our insurance company wouldn't cover your momma for the new experimental treatment."

Sierra knew that most insurance companies didn't cover new procedures. And those types of cancer treatments could be very expensive. Some families mortgaged their homes to get the money they needed. And since they didn't own a house, there was nothing to mortgage. No collateral to use with a bank loan.

"I shouldn't have been so proud. Instead of going to your grandma, I went to a loan shark. I thought for sure I could keep up with the payments, but when your mother died, I lost my job and couldn't pay anymore. I had nothing. Nothing except for myself. They took me and were going to kill me, but they had an opening for a job and I said I'd work for free until everything was paid back." Bart stopped and had to take a few breaths in order to speak again.

"That's when you dropped me off at grandma's?" Sierra asked.

"Yeah. She knew I was in trouble and even offered to help, but I was too proud."

"So you abandoned me for your pride?" Sadness had turned to anger once more as Sierra remembered when her dad dropped her off with her grandma. He had told her it would only be for a little while, but he'd never written or come back for a visit.

"I was stupid. I should have taken the help your grandma offered. The loan shark only wanted his money back. But—" Bart coughed a couple of times.

Roman brought him the cup of water with a straw, and he took several long sips.

"But, they had me use my construction knowledge to help them break into a few businesses and steal. I got caught after only a month on the job and went upstate for a year. When I got out, the loan shark said I still owed him a lot of money, and the interest had compounded over the year and now the amount I owed him doubled."

Sierra put a hand over her face. "So you never made enough to pay him back."

"Exactly."

"And let me guess. That loan shark was a mob boss?" Sierra asked.

"He was the mob boss's youngest son. I basically became his slave. Over the years, I proved my worth to him and he sent me out here to run his new operation." Bart's eye closed and he sighed.

The detective had stood on Bart's blind side and stayed quiet. He gave Bart a moment to collect himself before grilling him with more questions. "Was the loan shark Mickie 'The Shiv' Solomon?"

Still keeping his eye closed, Bart answered, "Yes."

"Would you be willing to testify against him in a court of law if we protected you and your daughter?" The excited gleam in the detective's eye worried Sierra.

Bart turned his head and opened his eye. "No. You can't protect me from the Solomon crime family. They have people everywhere."

"Not in the Marshals Service, they don't." A grin spread from ear to ear on the detective's face.

"Would my little girl go into the witness protection program with me?" Bart asked.

"I'm not giving up my life. You should do it, and join the program, but I'm not moving away never to speak to the few friends I have." A shudder spread through her body. She could never lose touch with Annie, Red, or Stella. And now that she was with the Manning family, she couldn't leave them, either.

"Miss Baker, if you don't go with your father, your life will be in danger. Plus, you'll never see your dad again." The cop scribbled something on his notepad.

With a deep sigh, she looked at her father. "It looks as though my life was already in danger all these years. What's the difference?"

"I would like to know you. If I'm leaving this life behind, I'd like the chance to make amends and get to know you." A tear dripped from Bart's one decent eye.

This was what she wanted, wasn't it? To get to know her father? Spend time with him and have a family? Then why did it all feel so wrong? Sierra looked between the detective and her dad. "You should tell him what you know."

It was as though a knife went through his heart. Roman had to take a step back. She was choosing her dad over him and this new life he and his family had offered her. But could he blame her? Bart was her dad. The man she'd been looking for the past fifteen years. While Roman knew exactly what sort of man he was, she had only seen a glimpse of his life of crime. And if Bart was going to be given a fresh start, could he be the man Sierra needed? Could he stand in the way of her getting to know her father, the only family member she had left in the world?

Now was the time to put himself in her shoes. If their roles were reversed, what would he do? Boone was right—Roman was a grade-A jerk. Until this very moment, he hadn't considered what it would be like to have no family and then to finally find the only remaining family member he had left. Family was important. He knew what he had to do. It was going to be tough, but he had his family and God to help him get through this.

He stood there behind Sierra as her support, but kept his mouth shut. He'd talk to her later that night when they were home and alone. If she was ready to speak with him, that was.

"Alright, I'll get the Marshals Service to come down and make sure you're safe." The detective wrote a few more things on his notepad. Then he turned to Sierra. "How do I reach you? We'll need to arrange for a protection detail."

"I'm staying with friends." Sierra looked over her shoulder at Roman. "They'll keep me safe for now."

Roman nodded his agreement. If the cop wanted to know what they could do for Sierra, he'd tell them. But the less anyone else knew, the better. Roscoe would help, as would a few of their friends. Plus, the entire Manning family knew how to deal with criminals.

Then Sierra gave her cell number to the officer.

"I'll be in touch, Miss Baker, when we have a team to protect you. In the meantime, I'll keep this information quiet." The hint that there might be a mole in the police department didn't escape Roman's notice.

"We'll protect Sierra," Roman said. "It's not the first time we've had to deal with criminal elements." He tried oh so hard, but his gaze landed on Big Bart.

The injured man looked away from Roman before closing his eye.

Chapter 27

The ride home was subdued; Roman was stuck in his own head. He couldn't get her words out of his mind—the ones that ended their budding romance. She was going to join her father in WITSEC.

Bart's participation was the smart thing to do. The mob family needed to be taken down, or at least the one part of the family that Bart was involved with. Sierra's dad had only talked about Mickie "The Shiv" Solomon. Since he had gone out on his own, would the rest of the Solomon crime family come after Bart, or anyone else, once Mickie was in prison? Roman had no way to know how that family would react.

From the mob movies he'd watched, it seemed like they would. Or at the very least, those in Mickie's syndicate who weren't caught would come after anyone left on Bart's team, including any family members. Wasn't that what they did—kill family to get back at someone they couldn't touch? Sierra was in a tough situation, and he was finally beginning to understand it.

The right thing to do was for Bart to testify against Mickie. Which would put Sierra in danger. The Shiv had already tried to kill Bart once, and the man was lucky to be alive and expected to make a full recovery. Roman was being selfish, again, to want Sierra to stay on the ranch with him. By the time they made it home, he knew she was doing the right thing.

Roman Manning was going to support Sierra Baker as she did the right thing. It was what he would want should the roles ever be reversed. But he didn't have to like it.

"Can we talk?" Sierra asked the moment they were outside of Caleb's truck.

He nodded. "Where do you want to go?"

"How about on the porch?" She pointed to the rattan chairs sitting off to the side.

"I'll bring out some coffee for you both." Judith took Caleb's hand and led him inside the house.

Roman led Sierra to the chairs and scanned the area in front of them before sitting down. Being in the front of the house might not be the safest place, but if no one knew what was coming yet, then Sierra might be safe for one more night.

He was going to protect her as long as she was on their land. And he knew his entire family would do the same. Sierra wasn't the first person to come their way who needed their help, and he was sure she wouldn't be the last.

"First," Roman began, "I want to apologize for my behavior the other night. It was wrong of me to assume anything about us, and it was even worse for me to tell you what to do." He grimaced and turned his head to look her in the eyes. "Can you forgive me?"

Her smile didn't reach her eyes. "Yes, of course I can. You know, it's strange how being in a situation such as this puts things into perspective. Two days ago, I thought you were horrible and rude. Today, I realized you were trying to show you cared for me. Even though it wasn't the right way, you did care for me. So I want to thank you. And ask your forgiveness for how I acted."

"You did nothing wrong. Sierra, you're a strong, independent woman and you stood up for yourself. Don't apologize for doing that."

"Thanks, but I could have handled it better." Sierra looked down at her hands and then turned around when she heard the door open.

Judith walked out on the porch with a tray of coffee. "Matthew knew we were almost home, and he had a full pot waiting for us when we walked in. He also put out some of my chocolate chip scones."

"Thanks, Ma. That sounds wonderful." Roman took the cup and plate offered to him by his mother and fixed his coffee the way he liked it—two sugars and one cream.

Sierra picked up a cup and added two creams and two Splendas. "Thank you, Judith. Your scones are delicious."

The two of them drank their coffee and ate their scones in silence.

Halfway through his treat, Roman put his cup and plate down. "You're doing the right thing. I may not like it, but I'm going to support you any way I can."

"You don't like what?" She furrowed her brow.

"You joining WITSEC with your father." He held up his hand when Sierra began to protest. "Hold on, I'm being selfish and I know it. The only reason I don't like it is because I don't want you to go. I wanted you to stay here, with me. But I know it's much more important to get Mickie and his crew of criminals off the street."

"What makes you think I'm leaving?" She tilted her head.

Roman blinked a few times and ran over the conversation in his head. "You told the detective and your father that you thought he should testify and join the program. That means you have to go into protection as well, doesn't it?"

Her eyes softened and she put down her cup and plate. "Roman, I said *he* should do it. I never said I'd be joining him. In fact, I told the detective that you and your family could protect me. You can do that, right? I mean..." Sierra began to pick at her thumbnail, a sure sign of nervousness.

Roman had noticed her doing that a few times since they'd met again this year. Most of her nails were short and ragged, but he assumed that was because of the game she operated. But was it because she picked at her nails so much? Those were the sorts of things he wanted time to discover. He wanted to know everything there was about her.

"Roman, if it's too dangerous for you and your family to help me, I'll leave. I don't want any of you to get hurt because of me or my dad." She took a deep breath and looked longingly over the ranch in front of them.

He sat forward in his seat. "We can and will protect you. If you want to stay here, then we want you here, too."

"Really?" Hope filled her eyes as she sat forward.

Roman took her hands in his. "Yes." He drew in a shuddering breath. "It might be dangerous, and you probably shouldn't go out anywhere alone. Not that you can't take care of yourself, but it's much easier to defeat an enemy if you have a partner."

Her cheeks turned a pretty shade of pink, and she looked down at their joined hands. "Does that mean you want to be my partner?"

He grinned from ear to ear. "Yes ma'am, it does. I know I assumed before, but now I'm asking. Will you be my girlfriend?"

Sierra looked up at him through her long lashes. "Yes. I want you to be my boyfriend."

He stood and pulled her up and to him. Slowly, so as to give her time to pull away, he inched closer and closer to her lips. It only made sense to seal their decision with a kiss, right?

The second before his lips could touch hers, the front door slammed open. "Roman, Sierra, something's happened. Come inside." Caleb's terse voice broke the mood, and the couple turned in confusion to see his pursed lips and hard eyes looking at them.

Sierra couldn't imagine what would have upset Caleb so much. She may not have known him well, but she did know him to be a levelheaded man. One who didn't overreact to anything. A sinking feeling came over her, and she grabbed Roman's hand before they went inside and followed his dad to the living room.

They both sat together on the couch and watched in horror as a reporter stood in front of the Bozeman hospital telling what amounted to a horror story.

A female reporter wearing a black jacket and jeans with long, wavy brown hair looked seriously into the camera. "Officials haven't said much, but from what we've gathered from witnesses, a group of thugs entered the hospital with guns and began shooting. At least three police officers and fifteen patients or visitors have been shot. At this point, we don't know if anyone has died from the gunshot wounds. The story is still developing, but someone mentioned the possibility of it being gang violence. The shooters headed up to the second floor and went to an area with a patient who was actively being guarded by a police officer." The reporter moved off as another police officer pushed her away from the hospital and refused to answer any questions. The cop put up a line of yellow police tape running from the front entrance of the hospital to the exit.

"Jessica, can you tell us who that patient is?" the male in-studio reporter asked as the view changed to two anchors. A small inset of the onsite reporter moved to the top right of the screen.

"Sorry, officials have refused to release his name."

"Can you tell us anything more about the shooters? Have they been apprehended?" the female anchor in the studio asked.

"Most of them are dead, from what I've heard so far. Again, we can't get anyone to tell us anything yet. The only thing the police have said is that they are still investigating, but they will let us know shortly. The sheriff said that the state police were sending in investigators and they would hold a press conference later today."

Before Jessica, the onsite reporter, could say more, a police officer pulled down the tape and let a caravan of white trucks and vans through to the hospital.

Jessica put her fingers to her earpiece and nodded. Then she turned back to the camera. "The state troopers have arrived, and they brought a forensics team with them. As soon as we get more information, we will let you know."

The man in the studio was now framed in the picture, and he looked directly into the camera. "Thank you, Jessica. Stay safe and let me know the moment you hear about the shooters."

The female in-studio anchor was now shown on the screen. "If anyone has any information about this shooting, please call our hotline listed on your screen."

Caleb turned the volume off and turned to everyone in the room.

Matthew walked in with several shotguns in his arms. "It's time we arm up. We'll need to keep shifts and have everyone who's living in the cabins move into the main house. I also think all of us with houses on the property should either move in here, or into town." He turned to look at his dad. "What do you think, Pa?"

"You're right. Everyone who knows how to use a weapon needs to keep one on them at all times." Caleb looked to Sierra. "Do you know how to use a gun?"

Sierra shook her head. "The closest thing I've ever used is the water guns at the carnival. I haven't even played the shooting gallery game with the BB gun."

"Alright. Roman, stay close to her. And if there's a chance, you should teach her how to shoot a shotgun, at the very least." Caleb ordered each of his sons who were present to gather their families and take them into town. The fewer on the ranch, the better.

Before anyone could leave to do as ordered, the house phone rang and Judith answered it. She nodded and said a few yeses, then put her hand over the mouthpiece. "Caleb, it's Roscoe."

Caleb walked to his wife's side and took the phone. Before he put it to his ear, he told Judith to grab a gun. "Yes, Roscoe. What's the situation?"

Everything going on had Sierra frozen to the spot. She couldn't believe how fast it was all happening. Was her dad still alive? She turned to Roman. "My dad, is there a way to find out about him? Do you think...?" She couldn't finish her question. The idea that her dad might not have survived just didn't compute for her. Not after everything she'd been through, and all he'd done. He had to survive. They needed a chance to get to know each other again.

Roman put his arms around Sierra's shoulders and held her tight. "I'm so sorry. I don't know. Maybe that's what the sheriff's calling about?"

While everyone around them moved and began closing the blinds and arming themselves with what appeared to be a massive armory, Sierra stood still in Roman's strong embrace. He only let go of her long enough to strap a weapon holster around his waist and put a handgun in it. She wasn't any good with guns, but she knew it wasn't the kind the cowboys used in the old-west movies. Roman's looked to have a magazine clip, but she couldn't say for sure.

This family was surprisingly tough. What could have happened to make them own so many guns? Even Judith took a shotgun and a box of shells with her when she left the room.

After what felt like forever, Caleb hung up, and everyone stopped what they were doing and looked to the leader of the Manning family.

Caleb took a deep breath and let it out slowly. "That was the sheriff. He's been on the phone with the state police. It looks as though Mickie and his crew targeted the hospital. Thankfully, none of the patients or police have died, but several are in emergency surgery. We should all be praying for everyone to heal."

"What about my dad?" Sierra called out, not wanting to wait for him to finish his story.

"He's fine. Thankfully he had been taken to the X-ray department for an MRI when they attacked. And they didn't find him." Caleb sat down before going on. "There was a large shootout. Because of Bart's possible testimony, several agents from the U.S. Marshals Service were upstairs waiting for him to come back. When they heard the shooting, they were prepared for Mickie and his gang."

Sierra squeaked. "Did the cops get them?"

Caleb nodded. "Most of the mobsters died or are probably not going to make it. Mickie was one of those who died in the shootout."

A collective gasp filled the room.

Matthew spoke up first. "Will his mob family be coming to town to seek vengeance?"

Sad eyes looked around the room at his family. "I don't know. The sheriff has requested extra help to guard our family. He's asked for anyone who has been deputized in the past to join the posse."

Sierra sank back on the couch and looked at the ground as tears spilled down her cheeks. "I'm so sorry I brought this trouble to your doorstep. I shouldn't be here. I bet if I leave, Mickie's family won't bother with you."

"Sierra, we've been a thorn in Mickie's side for years. I'm sure his family knows all about us. If they're going to seek retribution, they'd come here even if you weren't here. We're the ones who took in all the women who were part of Bart's gang that wanted to get their lives back. We still have more than half of them on property." Caleb walked over to where Sierra sat and put a comforting arm on her shoulder.

"My dad's right. You being here won't change a thing, other than the fact that we can protect you." Roman sat down on Sierra's other side and took one of her hands in his. "Trust God, and us, to help protect you, Sierra."

She turned tear-stained cheeks on Roman. "It's all in God's hands now, isn't it?"

Roman nodded. "Yes. God has given us all certain skills, and we are to use them, but we must trust God to protect us now. He can choose to use any of us to get us through this situation, or He can choose to end it another way. All we can do is pray and keep an eye out."

"How can you be so calm? We could all die today." A shaky breath escaped her mouth and she almost cried again.

"Because I know where I'm going when I die." Roman cleared his throat. "You believe the Bible is true, right?"

She nodded.

"Well, it says that we all have a time to live and a time to die. We can't decide when God calls us home. Even the Apostle Paul said that to die was to gain. He was happy to live or to die. Because when we die we are in God's presence, if we have a saving relationship with Him." Roman looked her in the eyes. "Are you saved?"

"Yes, I was saved as a teenager." Sierra looked down. "But I know that the past few years I haven't lived for

Him. I got out of the habit of praying and reading my Bible."

"I've seen you pray lately, and read the Bible," Roman said.

Sierra nodded. "Yeah, since you came into my life again, I've been praying and reading. And I do know that God is in control, but it's scary. I don't want to die yet. I'm so young and have so much I still want to do."

"Nothing says you're going to die now. It's dangerous, yes, but that doesn't mean now is your time." Judith pushed Caleb out of the way and to Sierra's other side. "Trust that God will take care of you no matter what, and it won't be so scary. He'll give you peace to get through this, no matter how it ends."

Sierra winced. "I want to believe that's true. I really do. But after watching what Mickie and his team just did at the hospital..." She shivered. "I don't know what to expect now."

"Remember, most of his team died with him. And those who make it will be in custody." Roman pulled her attention back to him. "We may not have to deal with anyone coming after us. Mickie's family might decide enough is enough and leave it alone. They haven't been too supportive of Bart and his team in the past, so maybe there's a reason why Mickie came out here from wherever the family resides."

"I didn't think about that." Sierra worried at her lower lip and looked around at all of the faces in the room. They all looked like fierce warriors with their guns. She didn't doubt that they would all fight to protect this family until the end. But did that include her? Did she deserve to be included in this family?

One thing was certain: she needed to pray.

"Roman, will you pray with me?" The tears had been wiped away, and she sat up straight. She was going to be strong.

"Always." He took both of her hands, and together they prayed while the rest of the family left the room to handle the arrangements for protecting everyone.

Chapter 28

For the next two days, everyone prayed. All of the pregnant wives and children went into town and stayed with Logan and Elizabeth in their house. But the Manning men stayed at the ranch to help run things as well as to help protect everyone there. Even the three Smith boys who lived on the ranch stayed and helped to protect everyone. The only one to stay at the ranch and not pull protection duty was Sierra.

"Don't you think I've practiced shooting enough now? I can help protect the family and the ranch." Sierra put her hands on her hips and glared at Roman.

He stood his ground. "Sierra, two days of target practice doesn't make you an expert marksman. We've all grown up with guns."

"Not the Smith boys." She knew she had him there. Boys who grew up in the foster care system weren't exposed to guns.

"They've lived here for a few years now, and we trained them on gun safety and target practice once they made the decision to stay. They've earned their status. I'm not trying to be mean or controlling. Ask my dad—he'll tell you the same thing. You need more practice. We're happy to help you learn, and once my dad feels that you're ready, then I'll be the first one to accept you as a protector of the family." Roman put his hands on her shoulders and looked softly into her eyes. He'd learned his lesson about trusting that she could take care of herself. Sierra had been a natural at shooting a gun, but two days still wasn't enough time for anyone to be proficient.

"But, I want to help. I am part of this problem, aren't I?" Instead of throwing a fit, she was going to be mature, and smart. And she was going to prove herself to this family.

He enveloped her in a warm hug. "You're not part of any problem. And you are helping, by listening to what my father says and doing your part."

"Pft." She rolled her eyes. "Fine, I'll play nice. But I want to do more than cook and clean."

Roman chuckled. "You are doing more than cooking and cleaning. You're learning how to fire various weapons and clean them. This won't be the last time we have to deal with a criminal element. My guess is the next time robbers or cattle rustlers come to town, you'll be ready to help. So what you're doing is very important. And don't discount the power of your prayers."

That helped to put her mind back in the right place. "True, I am doing a lot of praying. And going through a lot of ammunition. Are you sure you have enough?" She had probably gone through a case of ammo in the past two days. If they had a long shootout, she prayed they wouldn't run out.

A cute smirk crossed Roman's features before he schooled it. She found him more and more handsome every day. He pulled her in for a hug. "Sierra, we have enough. Don't worry, the sheriff can always give us more ammo if we need it."

She leaned her head on his shoulder. For the first time in two days, they were all alone in the living room. Even when they were out on the shooting range, they had company. Sierra doubted anyone was acting as an official chaperone, but it had felt like it at times. Now it was just the two of them, and she wasn't going to waste this time.

Her arms wrapped around his waist, and she turned her face up to him. "How long do you think we'll be all alone?"

Smoldering eyes met hers right before his lips crashed onto hers. She would never tire of his kisses. Every time he kissed her, she fell deeper and deeper for him. Before him, she didn't realize that knees could actually go weak when kissed by the right man. She was the one who deepened the kiss this time. So far, she had let him lead the few times they kissed, but today she felt a sense of urgency. A deep desire to be closer to him, and she couldn't wait.

He had tried kissing her a few times over the past two days, but they were never alone long enough for his lips to do more than graze her cheek. Until now. And he must have felt the same sense of need, as he crushed his mouth to hers and held her tight.

By the time he pulled back to get a breath, she was ready to come up for air as well. However, she didn't like it when he put more distance between them. She wanted him to kiss her again.

Then she heard it.

A noise outside that had her eyes opening wide.

"What's going on?" Sierra turned around and looked at the entrance to the room they were in.

At the entryway, she saw Judith and Caleb both running past, carrying their guns.

"Stay here. I'll go see what's going on." Roman took off after she sat in a corner chair.

Once more, she began to nibble on her nails. While she heard loud voices coming from outside, she couldn't understand what they were saying. She didn't know if they were friend or foe. For all she knew, it could be the local deputies coming to warn them that the Solomon crime syndicate was on their way to kill them all.

As much as she wanted to be out there next to Roman, helping to defend what she had come to love, she knew better. Sierra would stay where she was until someone told her it was safe. But that didn't mean she would sit there calmly.

"It's over!" Roman screamed as he ran into the room all smiles and laughing. "It's really over."

She jumped up. "What do you mean?"

Sheriff Roscoe walked into the room behind Roman, with the rest of the Manning family following suit. "The Solomon crime syndicate leader, Marco, has publicly denounced the crimes Mickie committed in Montana. He said he loved his son, but sadly, the young man had gotten himself into trouble that had nothing to do with the family businesses."

"What?" Sierra fell down onto one of the couches in the room. "What does this mean? Sorry, but I don't know anything about mob families."

"It means that Marco Solomon has decided that in order to protect his living family and their businesses, he has decided that he won't seek retribution for his son's death. We are all safe." Caleb's happy voice boomed throughout the room and filled Sierra's ears.

Was this from God? Did He orchestrate this ending? There was no other reason it could have had such a good ending. Her father was going to make a full recovery, and they were all safe now. None of the patients or cops shot the other day were in danger anymore, and they were all going to make a full recovery. And the men who were responsible for breaking up what little family she had left were dead or heading to jail.

"So, you're sure Mickie's family isn't going to come after us?" She had to double-check; this was too good to be true.

The sheriff nodded. "Yes. The FBI and all sorts of other cops from various alphabet agencies have been keeping a close eye on the Solomon crime family and their businesses. My guess is that Marco realized this was too hot. With so many of Mickie's crew dead, he could save face and not cause a war."

Caleb added, "Most crime syndicates these days also have legitimate businesses. They can't afford to bring too much attention to their families anymore. This way Marco can grieve the loss of his son while claiming no knowledge of what Mickie was up to. The feds will keep an eye on them, and maybe even open up an investigation, but since we're so far away from the family's main holdings in Illinois, we shouldn't have to worry about them."

"Well"—the sheriff put up a hand—"I'd still stay vigilant for a while. Just to be on the safe side. But I think it's fine to bring your families home and go back to life as normal. Just don't ignore anything that looks or feels *off*."

"Don't worry, we won't." Roman hugged Sierra and kissed her cheek.

Joy bubbled up from her soul, and she looked around the room at the men and women who had quickly become her family. Her protectors. Her world.

While she never would have wished to have a group of mobsters rush into a hospital and attack, she also knew that this was the best outcome possible. When a person trusted in God, miracles could—and would—happen. "Is this really happening? I'm not dreaming?"

Roman shook his head. "No, you aren't dreaming. We're together and safe."

She laughed. "So, when do I start the crafting you hired me to do?"

Judith walked over and beamed at them both. "I'm so proud of you both. You've handled this all so well."

"Thank you, Judith. I can't thank you enough for opening your home and hearts to me. Is it too soon to ask about my father?" Now that he wasn't going to be needed to testify, what were the police going to do with him?

Roscoe walked over and took off his hat. "Well, that hasn't been decided yet. But my guess is he'll be tried and convicted of his crimes once he's healed. I'm sorry to say, but your father is going to serve time."

It stung, but it wasn't a surprise. "That's only fair." Sierra turned to Roman. "But would you be upset with me if I wanted to see him? Keep in touch with him?"

"Come on, let's leave them alone." Caleb ushered his family out of the room and left Roman and Sierra to talk.

Roman sat next to her on the couch and took her hand in his. Sierra felt the warmth from his touch, and her heart leapt at the emotions roiling through her. On the one hand, here she was loved by the Manning family. If she knew anything at all, it was that Judith and Caleb loved and accepted her as one of their own.

Shoot, all of the Mannings had shown her nothing but kindness and love since she'd moved in. And during this tense situation, not a single one of them had been cross with her. She'd never even overheard anyone talking negatively about her.

The only question now was how did Roman feel? For she knew exactly how she felt about him. She wasn't sure when it happened, but she was in love with the cowboy. Even when he was being bossy and overprotective, she still loved him.

Roman lifted her hands to his lips and kissed them. "Sierra, I'm here for you. If you want to go and see your dad, I'll gladly go with you. And if you don't want me to go with you, I'll stay back and pray for you." He squeezed her hands. "But please, let me go with you. If you want a relationship with your dad, I want one with him as well."

Her eyes widened, and the shock of his words zinged through her body. "But he's caused so many problems for your family. How could you want to spend any time with him?"

"Because I love you, Sierra. He's your father. And even if he wasn't your father, I would still forgive him. God is very clear that we are to forgive those who trespass against us. None of us is perfect. How can we expect God to forgive us if we can't forgive others?" One lone tear formed at the corner of Roman's eye.

"Oh, Roman." Tears loosed and flowed down Sierra's face without control. And she didn't care. "I love you, too." She leaned in and hugged him.

Roman pulled her closer and held her tight. He kissed the top of her head. "As long as we strive to follow God's word, we'll know joy and contentment. And we'll be together."

"That's what I want. I want to serve God with you. And I'd love it if you came with me to see my father."

"I'll ask the sheriff when we can go back." Roman released her and stood up. "Come on, let's go see what everyone else is up to. I'd bet they're already planning on a celebration barbecue for tomorrow night."

His deep, throaty chuckle sent tingles of delight through her entire being.

Even though her father was a criminal, she'd forgiven him. He left her to protect her. She never would have survived if her father had kept her with him while living his life of crime. She had a wonderful childhood that was filled with love from her grandma and lots of friends. She grew up knowing that her mother loved her. And now she realized that her dad did love her. He did what he could to protect her.

It broke her heart that he'd let his pride get in the way of finding a better solution for her mom, which didn't work out in the end, anyway. Maybe, just maybe, Bartholomew Baker would turn his life around and find God.

Who knew? Stranger things had happened when people learned to forgive and let God live in their hearts.

Epilogue

Christmas

"Annie! It's so wonderful to see you again." Sierra exclaimed as she ran to her best friend. The carnival had just come to town and they were in the process of setting up when Roman drove Sierra in to find her friend.

"Sierra!" Annie squeaked out and ran to her bestie.

"Ladies, it's not like you don't see each other every day." Roman shook his head. Since the day Annie left, the two women had Facetimed each other and as far as he knew, they hadn't missed a single day.

The women embraced and when Sierra pulled back, she gave Roman a sour look over her shoulder. "It's not the same thing as being together in person and you know it."

He put his hands up. "Fine, fine, who am I to get in between two screaming women." A chuckle escaped his lips before he turned and left the women to their gabbing.

"Oh, before I forget, I have a trailer full of crafts for you. I hope you have room to sell them all." Annie pulled Sierra to her trailer and left her booth unfinished.

"Whoa, we can finish your booth first, then get your crafts and take them to the Triple J booth. And trust me, if this Christmas is anything like the fall festival, they'll all sell out." Sierra rubbed her hands together. "But, I can't wait to see everything you've made. Once we got the canning all done and out of the way, that's pretty much all I've done."

Annie giggled. "That's not all you've done." She waggled her brows.

"Hmm," Sierra pursed her lips. "I have done a lot of target practice and learned how to bury bodies."

"Fine, fine. I see how it's gonna be." When a familiar young man walked past them, Annie stopped in her tracks. "Is that who I think it is?"

Sierra looked at the cowboy and waved. "Yup, and I think he's gotten even more handsome since the last time you saw him." She nudged her friend's shoulder. "Go on, say Hi. I'll catch you later. I'm gonna go help Roman finish settin' up our booth." She giggled as she walked away.

Over the past couple of months, Annie had asked about Boone Smith. And Boone had asked Sierra about Annie. Maybe, just maybe Annie would change her mind and decide to stay with them at the Triple J Ranch. Then she'd have more family close by. It would be nice if Red and Stella would get a place nearby for when they weren't working, but she'd as them once Annie was living here.

At least her dad was close by.

Now that her dad had been officially arrested, he was kept in a jail not too far away from Beacon Creek while he awaited his trial. They all knew Big Bart would do time. Probably a lot of time, but since Sierra had forgiven her father for abandoning her when she needed him, a load of bricks had been lifted from her shoulders and she had peace about her father's future. Maybe while he was in jail, he'd get into reading the Bible and attending church services.

The thing that had really surprised her was that Bartholomew Baker enjoyed his visits from Roman and Caleb. Sometimes, they even went without her. She knew they were witnessing to him and the one thing Sierra prayed for daily without stop was that her father would give his life over to God. A reality that didn't seem too far off after her last visit with him.

Everything had changed so quickly for Sierra. After spending most of her life wondering about her father, she was finally getting to know him again. And her life had done a total one-eighty once she left the carnival.

Life on the ranch was so much more than she ever expected. Judith had set up one of the extra rooms in the house for Sierra to use as a crafting room. She had put it to good use, too. The room was full and Roman had packed up a trailer full of different items that they were going to sell at the Christmas fair. They'd even started an online store and sold enough each week to pay her salary. She didn't make a lot of cash, but her room and board were covered and that alone was worth quite a bit of money. Especially on a ranch like the Triple J.

The next day was the official opening of the Christmas fair and everyone was excited. Daisy, cute as a bug, in her little Miss Santa Claus dress with white tights and red boots, had come straight from school to the fairgrounds.

"Sierra, Sierra!" The little girl yelled as she ran to their booth. "I'm ready to work. And I brought customers." She waved her hand like Vanna White showing a completed puzzle, one hand on her waist while the other pointed to a long line of school kids and their parents.

This time, they had a craft booth set up in a tent next to the cow cuddling stalls. It looked more like a circus tent then a craft fair booth, but after the success from the fall fair, everyone agreed they needed a larger space.

Sierra's eyes bulged as she looked at what must have been twenty people lining up to get a spot with the cows this week. The Christmas fair started on December fifteenth and lasted right up through December twenty-second. They would have one day to take everything down and then rest before all of the craziness of Christmas cooking began on the ranch. "Wow, I don't know if we have enough cow cuddling spaces left for today." She picked up the sign-up sheet and looked at what was left for the day. They planned to sell the slots in advance again, since it worked so well last time.

Amanda, one of the homeless girls who had been too afraid to leave Bart before his arrest, and now lived on the ranch and helped Sierra with the crafting, walked up. "Sierra, let me take care of the sign-ups. I think you might want to man the register." She gave a sheepish look at the fancy electronic tablet that worked as their point-of-sale device for cash and credit.

Sierra put a calming hand on Amanda's shoulder. "You can do anything you set your mind to. Don't let fear cripple you."

With eyes shining from unshed tears, Amanda nodded and went back to the cash register. "I will get my fears under control."

Since she had come to live at the ranch, Sierra had taken Amanda under her wings. At first, she thought it was about trying to make amends for the way her father treated the women, but then she realized that she really did like Amanda. The young woman was only two years her junior. They got along well, and somehow Amanda had mad crafting skills.

The one thing that still bothered Sierra about Amanda was her lack of confidence. It was something they were working on together and Sierra knew that her new friend would get there.

The day went exactly as how Roman had said it would, they had a ton of people lined up outside their booth to not only sign-up for cow cuddling, but also to get a look at their crafts. Sierra was social media savvy and had been posting about the various items they would be selling for the past four weeks. People who had been paying attention, were now excited to see everything that the Triple J was doing. And they all wanted a cow cuddling t-shirt. Even those who couldn't get a spot when they wanted it, still bought the t-shirts.

They also sold a lot of Christmas wreaths, ornaments, and signs. In fact, all of the different items they had created over the past month sold well. But what did the best, were the items that tied the Triple J to the craft. She'd have to remember that for future crafting projects.

Halfway through the week, Annie came over for dinner at the trailer. They had goulash again, and Boone joined them as well. For this week, Roman had offered to stay every night in the trailer and keep an eye out on their booth and the cows.

"Does this remind you of something?" Sierra looked between Annie and Boone.

Boone gazed lovingly at Annie who blushed prettily.

"This is just like the final night of the fall festival. The four of us having dinner in the trailer and playing board games." Annie looked down at her bowl of goulash with the melting cheese and crushed Frito's on top.

"Yup, but tonight, we're gonna play Settlers of Catan." Sierra beamed and put her fisted hands on her hips.

Annie's mouth opened and her head popped up. "You bought one?"

"Yup, I found one at the Target in Bozeman of all places."

"Wow, we looked everywhere after ours was destroyed." Annie had taught Sierra how to play when she first joined them in the carnival. When their game board was destroyed by a freak windstorm, they had looked everywhere for one but couldn't find it.

"Maybe Montana is a great place to live, after all." Annie looked at Boone and smiled.

"It's a fantastic place to live," Boone agreed.

"Okay, so is anyone gonna tell me about this game?" Roman sat down at the table next to Sierra with his bowl.

After he prayed for their meal, they all dug in and Sierra and Annie took turns telling the boys all about the game and how to play it. Sierra's favorite part of the game was the fact that the board changed each time they played it. So, a player's strategy had to change on the fly as well.

In the end, Sierra beat everyone else, hands down. And by the end of the night, when Boone was getting ready to drive him and Sierra back to the ranch, Annie pulled Sierra aside.

"Do you think the offer to move into the ranch still stands?" Annie bit her lower lip waiting for Sierra's reply.

A slow grin crossed Sierra's face. "Why, Annie, do you want to move here to be with me? Or does a certain cute cowboy have anything to do with it?"

Pink tinged Annie's cheeks and she glanced over to the truck where Boone and Roman stood chatting. "Yeah, I think so."

"You think so, what? That you want to be here for me?" Sierra pointed to her chest. "Or for the cowboy?" She pointed to Boone and smirked.

"Can't it be for both?" Annie's shoulders moved up to her ears and back down again.

"Yes." Sierra called out over her shoulder before joining Boone at the truck.

Annie threw her hands in the air, not happy with Sierra's cryptic response.

But she had nothing to worry about, by the end of the week, Annie was offered a cabin to share with Sierra. And Sierra was actually glad to be moving out of the house and into a cabin with her best friend in the whole world. She still came to the main house for crafting and helping with the meals, but now that she wasn't sleeping so close to Roman, she breathed easier.

Things between Roman and Sierra had gotten serious, quickly. So much so, that was why Roman had volunteered to sleep in the trailer the entire week of the Christmas festival. They needed space. Not to figure things out, but to slow things down. Neither wanted to do anything they'd regret later, and both agreed to wait for marriage before doing anything more than kissing. But it was much easier said than done when you shared a house with someone you had fallen in love with.

Christmas morning, Annie jumped on Sierra's bed, early. Way too early for Sierra's liking. Sure, the men got up before a decent hour to feed the cattle and all the barn animals, but that didn't mean that Sierra needed to be up before the rooster crowed.

"Annie, what are you doing?" A grumpy Sierra moaned.

"It's Christmas morning! Get up so we can get you all pretty." Annie jumped on the side of Annie's twin bed.

Sierra turned her back to her friend and pulled the covers over her head. "Go away."

"Sierra," Annie whined. "He's going to ask you to marry him today. I just know it. And you can't have bed head or be in your Christmas jammies. You have to get up and make yourself pretty."

Sierra cracked an eye and looked at the clock on her bedside table. "It's not even six o'clock yet. We aren't meeting for breakfast until eight. I don't need two hours to get ready."

"Yes, you do if you want to be gorgeous for the pictures that you know everyone will want to take of you and your ring."

With a huge sigh, Sierra sat up. "Annie, he's not going to propose to me today. Today isn't about us, it's about God and family."

"And you're his family now. What better time to propose?" Annie jumped up and pulled Sierra's covers back. "Come on, get out of bed, now!"

Before Sierra got out of bed, she stared at Annie. "Wait, did he tell you he was going to propose to me today?"

"No, but I overheard him and John talking about jewelry. Roman wanted to give you jewelry for Christmas. What does that tell you?" Annie's feet moved impatiently in place as she motioned her hands for Sierra to get up.

"I bet he got me the earrings he saw me admiring last week at the fair. One of the booths had these gorgeous snowflake earrings that would go perfectly with the necklace my grandmother got me for our last Christmas together." Sadness overtook Sierra for a moment. She knew her grandma would love Roman and his crazy family. She would have loved to be here for Christmas. Sierra wished her grandma was there, but she knew the loving motherly figure was always with her in her heart and memories. And one day, in heaven, they could talk about all of the wonderful things she did on Earth with Roman and his family.

Grandma Ruth would approve of Roman. It helped that her dad had already given his blessing for them to be together. Since recovering from his attack and going to jail, Bartholomew Baker had returned, and Big Bart was the one who died that day on the street after the beating that left his body near death. While Sierra wished her dad could be with them on this Christmas, she knew sins had consequences. And he would have to serve his time in jail, even if he had repented and changed. When he got out, Sierra knew that her dad would never go back to a life of crime.

She just hoped that the Mannings would accept him in their lives if he chose to live nearby. From what she knew of them, she didn't doubt that they'd be there to pick him up and help him to find a new life the second he was released from prison. One where he could serve the people instead of hurt them.

Annie sat down on her bed, deflated. "You don't think he's going to propose?"

With a shake of her head, Sierra laid back down. "No, it's too soon."

After a few moments of silence, Annie stood back up. "Good, that means you and I can continue to be roomies for a bit longer. But, you should still get up and look your best."

"Fine, fine. I doubt I'll get back to sleep anyway. Maybe the kids will be up and we can watch them open their stockings before breakfast. I heard that Santa planned to visit them at the main ranch house last night and leave their presents and stockings there." Sierra loved how the family honored God, but still found a way to enjoy Santa and the myth surrounding the jolly man.

"You know, Judith told me that if I didn't believe in Santa, I wouldn't get presents." Annie made her bed and waited for Sierra to move.

Sierra chuckled. "She told me the same thing." She got out of bed. "So, will you have a present from Santa today?"

Annie grinned. "Of course. I've been a very good girl this year." A frown suddenly crossed her face. "But wait, I've only been here a couple of days. Will Santa know that I'm here and not with Red and Stella?"

"Of course, silly." Sierra made her bed and the two girls got ready for the day.

They did, in fact, make it in time to see the little manning kids get their stockings before the men came in from feeding the animals. Normally, Judith made a big breakfast, but today they were going to have a smaller fare for breakfast. She had made dozens of cinnamon rolls and when Sierra and Annie walked into the house, the scent of cinnamon permeated the air.

With a deep breath, Sierra moaned. "I love home-made cinnamon rolls. I wish candles could do the scent justice. If they did, I'd burn them every morning." She tilted her head. "And maybe even all day long."

Annie grinned. "Coffee?"

When the time came to open gifts, a strange feeling hit Sierra. What if Annie had been right? What if Roman didn't buy her the earrings like she thought, but instead had a ring for her? Was she ready? Yes, she loved Roman. If he asked, she'd accept and then ask for a long engagement. That would give her time to prepare herself. But not too long.

Roman handed her a small box wrapped in glittery red paper with a silver bow. Sierra's hands shook when she accepted it. Her mouth went dry and perspiration lined her brow. This was it, he was going to propose in front of everyone. Sierra was so glad that she listened to Annie and got ready early instead of wearing her Christmas jammies like everyone else.

But, when Roman took the seat next to her, and didn't get down on one knee, she furrowed her brow.

"Open it." Roman's excitement was contagious, and Sierra pulled the bow off.

A feeling of excitement, and relief, passed through her when she opened the box and saw the glittering earring she had wanted. "Oh, they're so beautiful. Thank you, Roman. It's exactly what I wanted." She leaned in and kissed his cheek.

And she was very happy that it wasn't a ring. Sierra loved Roman and knew he was the one, but she wasn't quite ready to make that leap.

In time, when they were both ready, he did propose. And he got down on one knee on the foot bridge where they had their first kiss. This time, when he gave her a tiny jewelry box, she was more than prepared to say "yes" and not the least bit worried.

"Roman, it's perfect." The box in Sierra's hand held a platinum band with a one carat princess cut diamond. It was exactly what she would have chosen if she went with him. Which only meant one thing, Annie helped him pick it out and she kept it a secret from her.

Annie was horrible at keeping secrets, so Sierra had no idea this was coming.

It was a good secret, too.

Sierra and Roman were about to start the greatest adventure of their lives, together.

Author's Notes

I hope you loved reading the Triple J Ranch series as much as I enjoyed writing it. This has been such a wonderful year of publishing, and these characters have become a part of my heart. While this series has come to its end, I'm not done with the Manning family or with Beacon Creek. Join my newsletter and find out when the next series will come. It will have more cow cuddling and possibly a new ranch co-owned by Roman and John, and their wives.

Next up for my writing is a standalone rom-com. I can't wait to share this with you. And if you're reading this after June 2021, then it's already available. Check my website for all of my available books: jennahendricks.com

I'd love to thank my friends and sprinting partners, Audrey and Amie for all of their help with keeping me on track for my release dates with this series! I couldn't have done this without you sprinting and cheering me on! May God bless you both abundantly!

And I'd also like to give a special shout out to my editor, Shavonne. She's been with me on this series from the very beginning. Any time I was stuck on a plot point, she helped me. When I was late with my final draft, she worked with me to find a new date that she could edit my book. She's been fantastic! Thank you Shavonne! So glad we met in Edinburgh back in 2019.

And to you, dear readers, thank you so much for taking this journey with me. The Cowboy's Game makes book 6 in the Triple J Ranch series. I've never written a series this long before. Stick with me, and you'll see some fun stories as well as stories full of heart and God.

During the journey to write this series, I've learned that my writing is my own mission field. Sure, most of the readers of my books will already be Christians, but some won't be saved. And of those who already know God, some will need the lessons that come in the form of clean & wholesome romance books. I hope you'll think to share my books with your unsaved friends, or friends who need encouragement, a laugh, or just a good read. Sometimes, a good book can take us away from our problems, and when we've finished the book, the answer to our issues will come to mind. I hope my books can help in that way for you.

When writing book 5, Cowboy Blessings, I began crafting to help calm my mind and relax my body. I was having trouble sleeping because I couldn't get all sorts of ideas to stop bombarding my mind when I went to bed at night. So, I started making different things. I discovered that making themed wreaths was a lot of fun. Then I began using my Cricut machine my parents got me for Christmas and a whole new world of ideas came to me. LOL

So, I've started to sell book themed merchandise, as well as crafts that I wrote about in this book. I don't have a current site to sell my crafts, but I do offer a Crafty Author Book Box each quarter. This includes a variety of books, stickers, bookish items, and a craft made my yours truly. Sometimes I'll even plan ahead and write a special craft into my book that will also be in the book box, or available for those who subscribe to my newsletter to order. I will also have t-shirts, mugs, tote bags, etc themed for the Triple J Ranch, as well as other book series. Join my newsletter to see what I've been making lately. I've begun pottery as well as sublimation, so check out my fun book-themed projects! And if I can ever get my website updated with a sales page, I'll start selling my crafts on my own website.

After my standalone rom-com, I'll be focused on writing and publishing several Christmas themed books! After I finished the Big Sky Christmas series I began a sort of follow-on series to the Big Sky Christmas series of books. It's not necessary to have read any of the Big Sky Christmas books, but if you did, then you'll recognize the town and some of the side characters. The new series is about US Military veterans and how they find peace after coming home. The Crooked Arrow Ranch is a place for veterans from all branches of service, but

I did start out with Army since I'm an Army Veteran myself.

Keep reading for a sneak peek of this series.

Oh, don't forget to keep reading to get Grandma Holcombe's goulash recipe! It was Roman's favorite dish!

Grandma Holcombe was my real life grandma. She was the best! Sadly, she passed away before I began writing. But I know she would have been my biggest fan. She loved to read. As she got older, that was what she did the most. And she's the one I got the crafting bug from. She used to craft all year long and then go to Christmas craft fairs with her creations. I still have items that she made me as a kid, and into adulthood. I also have access to her fantastic cookbook! I'll have more recipes from her as time goes on. And recipes that I've concocted along the way, as well. Eventually, I'll do a cookbook with everything included from my books.

Newsletter Sign-up

B y signing up for my newsletter, you will get a free copy of the prequel to the Triple J Ranch series, Finding Love in Montana. As well as another free book from J.L. Hendricks.

If you want to make sure you hear about the latest and greatest, sign up for my newsletter at: . I will only send out a few e-mails a month. I'll do cover reveals, snippets of new books, and giveaways or promos in the newsletter, some of which will only be available to newsletter subscribers. You'll also get a heads-up when I'm running sales on my books!

JennaHendricks.com/newsletter/

JENNA HENDRICKS
Finding Love
In
Montana
A Triple J Ranch Prequel

Contact Me

For those of you who love social media, here are the various ways to follow or contact me:

Newsletter:https://jennahendricks.com/newsletter/
BookBub: https://www.bookbub.com/authors/jenna
-hendricks
TikTok: https://www.tiktok.com/@jennacleanauthor
Instagram: https://www.instagram.com/j.l.hendricks/
Twitter: https://twitter.com/TinkFan25
Facebook: https://www.facebook.com/JLHendricks
Author
Website: https://jennahendricks.com/

Grandma Holcombe's Goulash Recipe

Roman's favorite dish.

2 lbs ground beef

3 cans diced tomatoes

3 cans tomato sauce

1 C shredded cheese

1T garlic

1T taco seasoning

3t Italian seasoning

1 t chili powder

1t spicy ranch seasoning (powdered) (If you don't have
any, you can use extra taco seasoning mix)

1t ranch dressing mix

1t pepper

½ t salt

3 bay leaves

16 oz package of uncooked elbow macaroni

I crock pot liner

Brown the ground beef in a skillet over the stove.

Insert a crock pot liner into your crock pot to help with an easier clean up. (This isn't necessary, just a clean-up hack.)

Once beef is browned, drain the grease and put it in the crock pot followed by all ingredients, except the macaroni and cheese. When adding the cans of diced tomatoes, include the juices.

Mix it all up and put on high for at least 2.5 hrs. longer if you want. Or you can cook it on low for 5 hours.

Thirty minutes before serving, ensure crock pot is turned to low. Add the uncooked elbow macaroni to pot. Stir and cook for 30 minutes, or until noodles are soft.

Once the macaroni is soft, it's ready to serve.

Dish up into bowls and top with cheese to taste.

For an added dash of crunch and flavor, you can crush up a handful or two of Frito's chips and top your bowl.

Sneak Peek

A Broken Heart Mended

Crooked Arrow Ranch was designed to be a safe haven for the wounded when they return from war.

Sam Marley should know, he'd been there for almost two years, and he was finally beginning to feel warm and safe.

But when the pretty new dog trainer shows up expecting a service dog to be the answer to his problems, more than the love of a good woman will be needed to heal his wounds. This Army Ranger is going to have to learn how to lean on God in order to move forward. But with only one good arm, will he find the strength to trust?

Nelly Wilson decided to move her business to Frenchtown, Montana. All she wanted to do was help wounded veterans heal. But what she found might just have her turning tail and running.

As Nelly and Sam work together to clean up the "dump" that her ranch is, they get closer and closer.

Who in their right minds would kill a black bear and leave its carcass inside a ranch?

But when her ex shows up offering to support her new business if she'd only come home, will she choose him over a wounded vet?

Can a curmudgeonly Army veteran with only one arm let himself be loved? Will the pretty dog trainer get past his gruff exterior? Can they both work together to get past their fears and discover a happily-ever-after?

A Broken Heart Mended is the first in a series of clean & wholesome cowboy romances starring wounded veterans who learn to trust in God and the power of true love.

Looking for the eBook version of this one? Try: http s://books2read.com/u/3nEwe9

The paperback is sold everywhere. If you can't find it in your favorite store or libary, ask an employee to order it for you. Or you can contact me to get an autographed copy. You can connect with me via my Contact Me page above.

A Broken Heart Mended

Nelly Wilson parked her Chevy truck outside the Frenchtown Roasting Company and sighed when she took in the scents of coffee and sweetness. She'd just driven twelve hours that day, after three other long days of driving from Georgia to get there in time to have the weekend to settle in, and she was exhausted and hungry. A black coffee and cinnamon roll were exactly what she needed and deserved.

When she exited her truck, the four dogs in the back began to bark and whimper.

"Nein, halt." Nelly reached into the dog crate closest to her. The dogs had done so well with their travel, but even they were getting tired of the drive. "Braver hund." She rubbed between Rogue's ears, and he settled down again. She couldn't ignore the rest of her pack. So she moved around the truck bed and scratched or rubbed each dog and spoke to them in their German commands, calling them good dogs—"Braver hund."

Even though she did speak to them in English a lot, she also tried to reinforce their German command training. She'd already successfully placed six different dogs with patients who were doing very well with their service dogs. And these four were on their way to being even better than the rest.

"I promise, once I have my coffee and bun, I'll take you all for a walk before we find our new home." She grinned at her dogs, knowing that while they didn't fully understand what she was saying, they did know she'd take exceptional care of them.

She could only pray that the coffee shop was still open. It was just past six at night, and in small towns the coffee shops usually closed after lunch. When she walked up to the door and noticed the sign still read *open*, she breathed a sigh of relief. "Thank you, Lord."

But when she turned the door handle, it wouldn't budge.

Nelly pounded on the door and looked through the window. "Oh, come on. I need the caffeine and sugar."

A barista was behind the counter, and from Nelly's angle it looked like she was counting her till. Nelly looked for a sign stating their hours. It was Friday night and the sign said they were open until nine, so why was the door locked and the cashier counting out?

"Please, I just need a black coffee and I'll take any pastry you have. I can pay in cash," Nelly yelled through the window when the barista looked up at her.

The woman bit her upper lip and looked around. Then she put the cash drawer back in the till and walked to the front door. When she unlocked and opened the door, Nelly smiled and profusely thanked the girl.

"I'll leave a good tip, I swear. I just need coffee and sugar. I'll take whatever you have. Even if the coffee is only warm, I'll be happy with it. I promise." Nelly held up her hand as though she was being sworn in at a hearing.

"I don't know. I was supposed to close early tonight. The head barista is getting married tomorrow and I'm supposed to join them for the rehearsal dinner tonight." The barista looked back over her shoulder at the pastry counter. "All I have left is one cinnamon roll. The coffee is still hot, but I've already cleaned the espresso machines, so I can't make anything fancy."

Nelly waved her hands and grinned. "That's perfect. I'm not into froufrou coffee. I like mine strong and black." An image of her ex passed through her mind, and she tried so hard to block it out. He used to always tease her that the only reason she liked her coffee strong and black was because that was how she liked her men. She didn't always date black men. In fact, she never really paid much attention to the color of a person's skin. When she really thought about it, she'd probably dated men from a variety of races. All she cared about was what was on the inside, and if they loved the Lord. She only dated Christians.

Skin color didn't make the man, it was the heart that made the difference between a good man and a scally-wag.

"And a cinnamon roll is my favorite. Can you heat it up?" Nelly looked hopeful as the barista opened the door and let her inside.

Instead of eating in the shop, she respected the girl's need to get going. The tag on her shirt read Anise. And Nelly didn't want to keep Anise from joining her boss at the rehearsal dinner.

"Thank you, Anise! I'll be back for more coffee and treats this weekend. Have fun tonight." As she left, Nelly was sure to put a generous tip in the jar. And when she got back in her truck, that was when she noticed the handwritten sign stating the shop was closing early for the rehearsal of Dana and Jerod.

A twinge of regret entered Nelly's heart. She would have already married Mick if she'd not decided to completely change her life. It didn't do to dwell on the past, and she knew it. It was time to look forward.

Nelly's forward momentum took her to her new home as she left her past where it belonged.

"Alright, kiddos. We're home," Nelly announced when she pulled up in front of her new ranch-style home that also sported a large barn in the back. From the pictures she had seen, it would be perfect for the dogs to kennel in.

The outside wasn't exactly what she expected. Sure, there was a wraparound porch, but it needed to be scraped and several coats of paint would make it look new again. One of the windows had been broken and boarded up. "Hm, well. Maybe the inside is better than the outside?" She looked down at her dogs and shrugged.

But when she opened the front door of the house, her mouth dropped open and she almost cried.

The dogs did it for her. It was their whines and whimpers that brought Nelly out of the momentary stupor that had claimed her mind.

"How in the world? This is nothing like the photos the Realtor showed me." The smell hit her before her foot crossed the threshold.

Even Rogue, who was fantastic at making his own disgusting smells, whined and backed out of the house, almost hitting Nelly's leg.

"Why, that good for nothing...weasel! How could he show me pictures that had to be years old?" Knowing it was her fault for not coming to see it in person, but not actually wanting to admit it, she backed out of the pig sty and covered her mouth.

"No, that's not right. Calling this place a pig sty is an assault on all pigs. Something, or several somethings, must have died here." She sat down hard on the porch steps and yelped when a board below her cracked. "Now what?"

Nelly jumped up and walked away from the house. A real fear of the place crashing down around her filled her heart.

Buffy, a chocolate retriever and her only female dog, rubbed up against her leg in support. Instinctively, Nelly reached down to pet the wonderful dog who was lending her support and warmth. Not that it was cold outside, just a figurative warmth that was missing from this place.

On her other side, Spike, a male golden retriever, scootched closer to her. "You guys, and gal, are the best. Thank you. Braver hund." She patted their heads.

A distant bark caught her attention and she looked around. "Buffy, Spike, Angel. Okay, Rogue is that you?" Nelly took off around the house to see if she could find the source of the barking. All three of the other dogs were at her heels, tongues lolling with the excitement.

The sight was not what she expected. Yes, Rogue was standing there, almost pointing like a pointer who'd spotted a duck. But instead of a dead duck on the ground waiting for her to pick up and put in the pack for supper, she found something much more to her liking, and the dogs—if their wagging tails were any indicator—appreciated it as well.

A large red barn with white trim looked to be in almost pristine shape. Quite a dichotomy from the view of the ranch house. The keychain the Realtor sent her had several keys on it, and she hoped one of them was to the barn. If the outside was any indication, then at least the dogs would have a safe, dry place to sleep that night. And maybe, just maybe, if the good Lord was looking out for her, she'd have a safe place to rest her head for the night as well.

"Well, the doors won't open themselves." Nelly looked down to her four dogs sitting on their haunches just waiting for her to do something. She put her hand out, palm down and commanded, "Bleib." She tried to keep her commands in German as much as possible, even when they weren't technically working. It was simpler for the dogs and would keep them from misunderstanding.

Nelly took the keys she still held in her left hand and proceeded to open the barn door. With a sharp intake of breath, she about had a heart attack. "Whoa. Not what I was expecting. Not at all."

Rogue growled behind her, and she listened to his warning. While she didn't feel a threat, she did sense something weird going on in the barn. Without turning her head, she motioned for them to follow. "Heir."

In almost unison, with Rogue taking the lead, all four took up positions on her flank.

"Hello? Is anyone in here?" Even though she felt the place was deserted, Nelly wanted to give anyone a chance to come forward. If they surprised the dogs, they might not like what happened.

While all four dogs were trained very well, they were also extremely protective of Nelly. They would feel her trepidation and most likely they'd feel the same way. Especially if a man came from nowhere.

Slowly, she took a few steps and looked around in awe.

If the house had been taken over by animals, this place was surely saved from anything, or anyone. In fact, it looked like someone had been keeping it up quite nicely for some time. The interior was sparkling clean, for a barn. Fresh straw lay on the ground, and each horse stall had a door on it that provided a bit of privacy for the animal.

There were no animals present, other than her dogs. That much she was sure of. Her dogs would have at least whined if another animal was present that they hadn't been introduced to. Nelly watched her dogs. They sniffed the air but didn't seem the least bit upset. Other than the growl that emanated from Rogue when she opened the door, they didn't seem to be the least bit worried.

"Rogue, Lauf." Nelly pointed forward, indicating the direction she wanted the dog to check. The other three dogs stood there waiting for their directions, and when she pointed where each one was to go, they went quietly and without any issue.

Nelly couldn't have been prouder if they were her own kids. All four searched their areas without a peep. When they were done, they came back and dutifully sat on their haunches next to her.

"Well, I guess that means we're safe." She took a few more steps inside and peered into the horse stalls closest to the barn door. While the sun was in the process of setting outside, there was very little light inside.

Even though it was early June, this was Montana and the sun set close to nine at night, which meant she needed to hurry up and find the light switch. Before she left Atlanta, Nelly had arranged for the power to be turned on at the property. It wasn't big, just enough space for her dogs to train. But she would need power and water to get started.

Nelly noticed a large propane tank on the side of the barn. She made a mental note to check it tomorrow to make sure she had enough fuel to power whatever ran off propane. Probably a gas stove, water heater, house heater, and maybe even some lights.

It didn't take long to find the switch; it was located to the right of the barn door. With the flip switched up, she could see even more of the immaculate barn. If she didn't know any better, she'd think an entire cleaning crew had come through the day before and spruced the place up for her.

As she began a slow inspection of the place, she noticed a set of stairs in the back. When she crested the top of the stairs, she praised God for providing. On the other side of the locked door was a bed. It was only a twin bed, but the mattress looked to be in good shape. She had a box of linens she could make work, at least long enough to figure out what she was going to do for sleeping arrangements while she fixed the house.

There was no way on God's green earth she was going to sleep in that cesspool of garbage and animal carcasses. "How is it possible this place is so pristine while the house should be bulldozed?" Nelly shook her head.

She unloaded her truck into the barn and got the dogs settled for the night before she went upstairs with a hot cup of peppermint tea. In her search, she also located a breakroom of sorts that had an electric tea kettle and running water in the sink.

Her last thought before drifting off into a dreamless night of sleep was how good God was.

Does this sound like fun? If you enjoy reading about people who live and love in quirky small towns in Montana, then this book is for you! And it can be enjoyed year-round. So, check out today! You'll be glad you did. It's full of fun things like service dogs, unconventional couples, veterans who find a way to heal and enjoy life again, plus a lot of community! And for those who enjoy cowboys, this will be right up your alley.

Her Montana Christmas Cowboy

Chloe Manning's first Christmas in Frenchtown was heartbreaking. Will Santa give her her heart's desire during her second?

Brandon Beck left behind a woman for the benefit of his family ranch last Christmas. Now that he's back after a year, why can't he get her out of his heart and mind?

When Santa plays matchmaker, will Chloe and Brandon fall under his Christmas Magic? Or will past hurts keep them apart?

Don't miss out on the first Christmas story of the heart-warming Christmas Cowboy romance series, Big Sky Christmas. Where the romance is clean, and Christmas takes center stage!

Her Montana Christmas Cowboy https://books2read.com/u/m2Zx0r

www.ingramcontent.com/pod-product-compliance
Lightning Source LLC
Chambersburg PA
CBHW011127190726

48289CB00012B/2931